Under the Distant Sky

OTHER BOOKS BY AL LACY

Angel of Mercy series:
 A Promise for Breanna (Book One)
 Faithful Heart (Book Two)
 Captive Set Free (Book Three)
 A Dream Fulfilled (Book Four)
 Suffer the Little Children (April 1997)

Journeys of the Stranger series:
 Legacy (Book One)
 Silent Abduction (Book Two)
 Blizzard (Book Three)
 Tears of the Sun (Book Four)
 Circle of Fire (Book Five)
 Quiet Thunder (Book Six)

Battles of Destiny (Civil War series):
 Beloved Enemy (Battle of First Bull Run)
 A Heart Divided (Battle of Mobile Bay)
 A Promise Unbroken (Battle of Rich Mountain)
 Shadowed Memories (Battle of Shiloh)
 Joy From Ashes (Battle of Fredericksburg)
 Season of Valor (Battle of Gettysburg)
 Wings of the Wind (Battle of Antietam)

UNDER THE DISTANT SKY

BOOK ONE

AL AND JOANNA LACY

MULTNOMAH BOOKS

UNDER THE DISTANT SKY
© 1997 by Lew A. and JoAnna Lacy
published by Multnomah Books
a part of the Questar publishing family

Edited by Rodney L. Morris and Deena Davis
Cover design by Left Coast Design
Cover illustration by Douglas Klauba

International Standard Book Number: 1-57673-033-6
Printed in the United States of America.

For information:

Questar Publishers, Inc., Post Office Box 1720, Sisters, Oregon 97759

LIBRARY OF CONGRESS CATALOGING-IN -PUBLICATION DATA
Lacy, Al.
 Under the distant sky/Al and JoAnna Lacy.
   p. cm. -- (Hannah of Fort Bridger; bk. 1)
  ISBN 1-57673-033-6 (alk. paper)
   1. Frontier and pioneer life--Wyoming--Fort Bridger--Fiction.
2. Fort Bridger (Wyo.)--History--Fiction. I. Lacy, JoAnna.
II. Title. III. Series: Lacy, Al. Hannah of Fort Bridger; bk. 1.
PS3562.A256U53 1997   96-40158
813'.54--dc21   CIP

97 98 99 00 01 02 03 04 05 06 — 10 9 8 7 6 5 4 3 2 1

This book is lovingly dedicated to my precious sister, "Honey,"
who is like a mother to me…my friend…

and in memory of my sweet little sister, "Hauna,"
who is now in the presence of the angels.

I love you both with all my heart.
"Jody"

A Word from Al Lacy

It is with great pleasure that I introduce my precious wife JoAnna to those readers who have followed the Battles of Destiny, Journeys of the Stranger, and Angel of Mercy series. As I've written the books in these series, she has given valuable input on story ideas, and she has helped me with descriptions of feminine things and with the way women think and react under certain circumstances.

What a joy now to have her coauthoring our new Hannah of Fort Bridger series.

PROLOGUE

In 1802, U.S. President Thomas Jefferson had his eye on the great expanse of land west of the Mississippi River, known as the Louisiana Territory. His desire was to purchase the Territory from Spain, which had purchased it earlier from France. When the disturbing news came that Spain had secretly retroceded the Territory to aggressive Napoleonic France, Jefferson dispatched Robert Livingston and James Monroe as diplomats to offer the Frenchmen $2 million for New Orleans and West Florida.

The French, to whom the Louisiana Territory was of diminishing importance, offered to sell the entire Territory to the surprised diplomats for $15 million. The treaty of cession was dated April 30, 1803, and the U.S. flag was raised over New Orleans on December 20, that same year.

The Louisiana Purchase, extending from the Mississippi River to the Rocky Mountains and from the Gulf of Mexico to British North America, more than doubled the land area of the United States.

On the far edge of this unexplored Louisiana Territory was a vast section dubbed "Oregon Territory." This section included the present states of Washington, Idaho, Montana, Wyoming, Utah, and Oregon.

In May 1804, President Thomas Jefferson dispatched a group of explorers, led by Meriwether Lewis and William Clark to find a land route to the Pacific Ocean, strengthen U.S. government claims to the Oregon Territory, and gather information on the country and its Indian inhabitants.

The group started up the Missouri River from St. Louis in May 1804. In 1805, Sacajaweah, a Shoshone Indian woman, led them across the Rocky Mountains. She guided them to the Clearwater, Snake, and Columbia Rivers, and they wintered on the Pacific Coast.

When Lewis and Clark arrived back in St. Louis in September of 1806, their glowing reports sparked tremendous interest in the vast new land to the west.

Word spread into the eastern states that there was fertile soil, better climate, and acreage for the taking in Oregon. "Oregon," according to Lewis and Clark's crude maps, meant the Willamette Valley between the western coastal range and the Cascade Mountains.

Hardly had Lewis and Clark made their report to President Jefferson when explorers, fur trappers, hunters, and other audacious men packed up and headed west, braving the hardships of the wilds in search of adventure. Among them over the next few years were such men as Jedediah Smith, David Jackson, Kit Carson, William Sublette, and Jim Bridger. Others followed them by the hundreds.

In the early 1830s, missionaries headed west, some to try to civilize the Indians, and others to preach to them the gospel of Jesus Christ.

In 1838 the Army Corps of Topographical Engineers was formed by order of President Martin Van Buren. The Corps was a body of military explorers made up of surveyors and mapmakers—thirty-six intellectual elite of the military led by John C. Fremont. Congress had allotted Fremont—who became known as The Pathfinder—some $30,000 to survey and map the Oregon Trail. It took them until 1842 to finish the job.

When the maps were published, there was more enthusiasm than ever among the people in the east to move west. Thus, 1843 became known as the year of the "Great Migration." Eight hundred seventy-five in two hundred wagons—now including women and children—headed west.

In that same year, adventurer Jim Bridger established a fur-trading and supply post at the 1,026-mile point from Independence, Missouri, the main "jumping off" place onto the now mapped-out Oregon Trail. For some unknown reason, Bridger called the trading post "Fort Bridger," though there were no military personnel established there.

The 1843 migration gave birth to the "wagon trains" that followed in the years to come. Many of the Indian tribes were angered by the white man's continual encroachment on their land, the killing of their buffalo and other big game. The wagon trains were often attacked, as well as the homes of the emigrants who left the trains to take up residence on land they fell in love with along the way. The government found itself obligated to protect the wagon trains and the settlers. Thus, forts began to be erected along the Oregon Trail so the U.S. army troops could stand as threats to the hostile Indians. Though the presence of the army often hindered the Indian attacks, the forts were spread too far apart to stop them.

The California gold rush, in 1849, demanded that a trail be cut straight west to northern California. Thus, the California Trail was established. Some sixty-six miles northwest of Fort Bridger, the new trail was blazed due westward at a point called the "Parting of the Ways." Those going to Oregon would continue northwest toward the Snake River and head for Oregon City. The California-bound wagons would head west toward the Sierra Nevada Mountains, and beyond them, Sacramento.

In 1857, the trading post that bore Jim Bridger's name burned to the ground. In 1858, the U.S. Army took over the site and actually built a fort there, calling it Fort Bridger. A few years afterward, a settlement was established next to the fort, and by the late 1860s was on the verge of becoming a town. In view of this, the people of the settlement decided their town would go by the same name as the military post—Fort Bridger.

As stated above, Independence, Missouri, was the main "jumping off" place to the Oregon Trail. Some wagon trains, however, crossed the Missouri River at St. Joseph, then joined the established trail a few miles west of the river.

From Independence, the Oregon Trail followed the Santa Fe Trail (established in 1822) some forty miles, then veered north to cross the Kaw River (now known as the Kansas River). It continued west across the windswept prairies to the Platte River, then followed along the Platte to the fork. It then wound along the North Platte to Fort Laramie. From there the trail moved deeper into Wyoming Territory to Fort Caspar.

Still following the North Platte out of Fort Caspar, the trail led in a southwesterly direction until it reached the Sweetwater River. It followed the Sweetwater past Devil's Gate in dangerous rattlesnake country to the main range of the Rockies and across the Continental Divide at South Pass. The route turned southward across the Green River, then dipped down to Fort Bridger.

Travel on the Oregon Trail, and whether to stop and settle along the way or follow it to its eventual end in California or Oregon was not for the faint of heart. Death stalked the trail in the form of Indians, disease, severe weather, and sometimes thirst and starvation. Though relatively few were killed by Indians, massacres were highly publicized and instilled fear in the hearts of those who followed the trail westward.

Travelers were warned of the graves that lay beside the trail, and the terrible dust, knee-deep mud, flooding streams, buffalo stampedes, mosquitoes, and snakes. Still they set their sights toward the western sky and pressed forward to realize their dreams of a new life on the American frontier.

They were a hardy and determined people, the likes of which, on the whole, are unmatched today.

UNDER THE DISTANT SKY

CHAPTER ONE

T he wagons! It's the wagons!" Five-year-old Patty Ruth Cooper squealed with delight and ran toward the open door of her father's store.

"Patty Ruth! Don't go into the street!" Hannah Cooper's voice floated from the back of the store just as the little girl, her auburn pigtails bouncing, skipped outside and jumped off the boardwalk into the soft dust.

She held tightly to her best friend, a stuffed bear named Ulysses, as she tried to get a closer look at the wagons and their occupants. She was caught up in the excitement and didn't see the man on horseback riding alongside the wagon train. His attention was on a wagon farther up the line, and he was equally oblivious to the child's presence.

Raymond Wilson, who owned the saddle shop next door to Cooper's General Store, saw that Patty Ruth was about to be run over. He bolted across the boardwalk and scooped her up in his arms, narrowly dodging the horse and rider. Patty Ruth saw the horse thunder by and gasped. She wrapped her arms around Wilson's neck, her heart pounding.

Wilson was still holding Patty Ruth when the man skidded his horse to a stop and wheeled about to ask anxiously, "Is she all right, sir?"

"Yes," Wilson said. "Just a little frightened. It was a close call."

"Yes...I'm really sorry. I wasn't aware that she was there until I saw you whisk her out of my path. I—"

"Patty Ruth!" A breathless Hannah Cooper dashed across the boardwalk and reached for her little girl. "Is she all right, Ray? What happened?"

"She's fine, Hannah. She ran out of the store, shouting something about the wagons, and jumped into the street right in the path of this gentleman, who was moving at a good clip beside the wagons."

"I'm sorry, ma'am," the rider said, touching the brim of his hat. "I was trying to catch up with a wagon at the front of the line. I shouldn't have been riding so fast. I just didn't see her."

Hannah looked at Patty Ruth and then at the man. "She shouldn't have been in the street, sir. I've told her not to step off the boardwalk unless she's with an adult or her older brother or sister."

"Well, the main thing, ma'am, is that she's not hurt, thanks to this quick-thinking gentleman."

Wilson stepped close to the man's horse and extended his hand. "Name's Ray Wilson, friend. I own the saddle shop here."

"Bob Ross, sir," the rider said, as they shook hands. He turned his gaze back to Hannah and said, "I heard you call her Patty Ruth, ma'am." He reached his hand into his pocket. "Is it all right if I give Patty Ruth some money to buy some candy?"

"That's very nice of you, Mr. Ross," Hannah said with a smile, "but since her parents own the store, she can have all the candy we allow her."

Bob Ross looked up at the sign beneath the false front on the store. "So you would be Mrs. Cooper? Well, I'm glad to meet you, ma'am. Would there be anything else I could do for Patty Ruth to make up for her scare?"

"It wasn't your fault, Mr. Ross. Anyway, she'll be fine now."

"All right, then, ma'am. I'll be on my way. 'Bye, Patty Ruth."

"'Bye," Patty Ruth said in a weak voice.

When Ross was gone, Hannah Cooper turned to Ray Wilson and said, "There are no words to express my gratitude, Ray." Then she looked toward the sky and spoke in a low tone, "And thank you, Lord, for having Ray here at the right time to rescue my baby girl."

"Mama," Patty Ruth said, watching the wagons go by, "are we gonna buy a covered wagon and go west like you and Papa talked about?"

Hannah avoided Ray's inquisitive gaze as she said, "Well, honey, I'm not sure. Papa and I have talked about it some, but that's as far as it's gone. There are a lot of things to think about when a family leaves their home and moves west."

As Hannah eased her daughter to the ground, she noticed that Patty Ruth wasn't holding the bear. "Honey, where's Ulysses?"

Patty Ruth glanced around in a panic. "Where's Ulysses? Oh, Ulysses?" she wailed.

Ray Wilson's eyes flicked to the spot where he had rescued the little redheaded girl. He stepped off the boardwalk, picked up the bear, and dusted it off as more wagons and riders passed by. "Here you go, sweetheart. I hope Ulysses isn't hurt."

Patty Ruth took the bear, checked his black shoe-button eyes, turned him over twice, and said, "He's not hurt, Mr. Wilson. Thank you."

"You're welcome." He patted her head as he said, "That little bear seems to be pretty special to you. I don't think I ever see you without him."

"I take him everywhere 'cept to church. Mama makes him stay home when we go to church."

"Is that because he can't sing the hymns?"

"He can sing 'em! Mama just can't hear him, so she makes him stay home."

"Ulysses is Patty Ruth's best friend and most prized possession, Ray," Hannah said. "Her Grandma Cooper made him.

She's no longer with us."

"Oh, I see. That does make him special then, doesn't it?"

Hannah looked down at her daughter, who was holding the bear close. "Patty Ruth..."

"Yes, Mama?"

"What do you say to Mr. Wilson for saving you from being trampled?"

The little redhead smiled and said, "Thank you for saving me from bein' tramped, Mr. Wilson."

"Trampled, honey," Hannah said.

Patty Ruth raised her free arm toward Wilson, indicating that he was about to get a hug.

He bent down and let her wrap an arm around his neck. "You're a mighty sweet little girl, Patty Ruth. Say, did you give Ulysses his name?"

"Well-l-l...Papa helped me a little bit."

"Uh-huh. And is he named after President Grant?"

Patty Ruth nodded. "President Ulysses S. Grant used to be a soldier in the Cibil War. My papa was a captain in the army. He fighted for President Ulysses S. Grant when he was a gen'ral."

"I know, honey, and your father was a real hero, too. He—"

At that moment, Solomon Cooper appeared at the door of the store and stepped onto the boardwalk. "What's going on out here?" he asked, putting his arm around Hannah.

Solomon was a slender, clean-shaven man, standing an inch over six feet. His thick, reddish-brown hair was like Patty Ruth's. He walked with a limp—a souvenir from the Civil War at the battle at Shiloh.

Hannah tilted back her head to look into her husband's eyes as she said, "Ray just saved our baby girl from being trampled by a horse."

Hannah briefly explained the near tragedy, and Solomon breathed a prayer as he took his little daughter into his arms and thanked Ray Wilson for his quick thinking.

Just then, several customers entered the general store, and the Coopers excused themselves.

As Ray Wilson turned to enter his saddle shop, he met the gaze of a man who had witnessed the brave act.

The man nodded and smiled. "I was right here and saw it all," he said, lifting his hat. "Mighty fine thing you did. You could've been trampled, yourself, you know."

"I'd risk life and limb for that little girl anytime," Ray said. "They don't come any better than Patty Ruth Cooper."

CHAPTER TWO

The Cooper family lived on a small farm half a mile north of Independence. The schoolhouse was situated on the north edge of town, making it a relatively short walk for the three older Cooper children.

The three-room schoolhouse allowed a division of grade levels that separated the Cooper children—first through third grades in one room, taught by Miss Stone; fourth through sixth in another, taught by Miss Powers; and seventh through twelfth in another, taught by Mr. Barrick.

Mary Beth loved her teacher, Miss Henrietta Powers, who was a Christian and always started the day with prayer. Mary Beth's goal in life was to be a teacher, and she wanted to be exactly like Miss Powers. She paid close attention to Miss Powers's gestures, how she walked, sat at her desk, wrote on the blackboard. She was especially intent on the way Miss Powers spoke. Sometimes, when she was alone, she practiced trying to sound like Miss Powers.

At the end of lunch period, while the teachers stood on the porch, a wagon rattled into the schoolyard. The teachers recognized elderly farmer, Jess Pemberton at the reins. He spoke to Misses Stone and Powers first, then to Barrick. "You folks hear about Patty Ruth Cooper?"

The trio exchanged glances, then Barrick replied, "Guess

none of us have, Mr. Pemberton. I hope something bad hasn't happened to her."

"Almost did. 'Bout an hour and a half ago, she just about got trampled by a gallopin' horse. I just thought I'd come by and tell it like it happened so's if the other Cooper kids heard about it before goin' home, they'd have the facts. You know how secondhand information can get twisted.

"Well, I just didn't want Chris, n' Mary Beth, n' B. J. to hear somethin' that would make 'em think their little sister had been hurt. I saw the whole thing, and she's fine."

Hannah Cooper and her youngest daughter left town in the family wagon at about two o'clock. Hannah seldom worked at the store, but this morning she had filled in for their full-time worker, Randy Chase, who had gone on family business to Kansas City. He was the oldest son of their pastor.

When they pulled into the Cooper yard, Biggie, the family dog, bounded off the porch, tail wagging a friendly welcome. Biggie—short for "Big Enough"—was a small black-and-white short-haired terrier, and the special object of affection in the Cooper household. He ran alongside the wagon as Hannah drove toward the barn and corral.

The big bay gelding in the corral with the white blaze face and four white stockings was Papa's horse, Nipper. Patty Ruth had ridden Nipper lots of times while Papa held the reins and walked in front of him.

The smaller gelding was a strawberry roan named Buster. He was Chris's horse. Patty Ruth had never ridden Buster because Chris said he and Buster understood each other, and if someone else rode him, it could mix Buster up.

Patty Ruth knew Chris considered himself to be an expert horseman, and she smiled to herself as she looked at Buster.

Chris wasn't really an expert; he just acted smart in the saddle to impress Lula Mae Springer, who lived on a farm two miles down the road. Chris was always riding over there on Saturdays to see Lula Mae, and sometimes on weekdays if there was time between chores and supper.

Both Nipper and Buster nickered as Hannah and daughter alighted from the wagon. Biggie got himself petted by his favorite redheaded five-year-old, then dashed to Hannah for attention as she unhitched the horses from the doubletree. She took time to pat Biggie's head and rub his sides while Patty Ruth opened the corral gate.

Patty Ruth went upstairs and sat on the window box in her and Mary Beth's room. She fixed her eyes intently on the road and watched for her brothers and sister to appear. She wanted to hear Mama tell them how close they had come to losing their sweet little sister that morning.

There they were, right on time, at 3:30.

Patty Ruth heard Mama tell Biggie that the kids were coming up the road, then the front screen door squeak open and close. Biggie came into view, barking happily, as he charged through the yard and hurried to meet the other Cooper children.

Patty Ruth ducked back from the window and tiptoed down the hall to the edge of the stairs. "Listen, Ulysses," she whispered to her stuffed bear, "they're gonna be glad nothin' bad happened to me."

Patty Ruth was surprised when she heard her siblings ask Mama about her near miss by the big horse. Somehow they had learned before leaving school that Patty Ruth was almost killed.

All three asked questions, but Mary Beth's voice was the loudest. Then Patty Ruth heard her mother say something she couldn't make out.

Whatever it was lost its importance, for she heard Mary

Beth running toward the staircase, saying, "I'm going up to see her!"

Patty Ruth darted back to the bedroom and quickly hopped on her bed just as Mary Beth appeared at the open door. Patty Ruth gave her sister a solemn look but didn't speak.

Mary Beth, the only blonde in the family, had dimples and a beautiful smile like her mother. As she moved toward Patty Ruth's bed, she smiled. "Hi, honey. We heard at school what happened this morning...and Mama explained it to us just now."

Patty Ruth gave her a pitiful look, but still said nothing.

Mary Beth sat on the edge of the bed and laid a hand on Patty Ruth's shoulder. "I'm sure glad you didn't get hurt. I know it must have frightened you. Are...are you okay?"

Patty Ruth sighed, placed the back of her hand to her forehead, and said as she had practiced, "Oh, I'm all right, Mary Beth, but you almos' didn' have a little sister no more. That big ol' horse jis' about killed me."

Mary Beth knew her little sister well and could see she was all right. She glanced down for a moment to cover her laughter and said, "Well, sweetie, we can thank the Lord that Mr. Wilson was there to keep you from getting killed."

Patty Ruth sent a wounded glance toward the door. "Where's Christopher and B. J.? Don't they care that I almos' died?"

"We're right here, little sister," came Christopher's voice at the door.

B. J. took a step ahead of Chris and moved up close beside the bed. "Mama told us Ulysses almost got killed, too, Patty Ruth," he said, eyeing the stuffed bear pressed close to his little sister's heart. "Is he okay?"

"Yes," Patty Ruth said with a sigh, making the most of the attention she and her bear were getting. "Mr. Wilson had to grab me pretty fast, 'cause that big ol' horse was gonna tramp me. An' I dropped Ulysses. He fell pretty hard, but he just got dusty."

"Trample, honey," Mary Beth said.

"Mm-hmm. That's what that big ol' horse almos' did to me."

"Well, I'm just mighty glad you and Ulysses are all right, Patty Ruth," Chris said. "I sure wouldn't want anything to happen to either one of you."

Patty Ruth managed a weak smile. "Thank you."

B. J. grinned. "Patty Ruth, if you had been killed today, I would've taken care of Ulysses for you...for the rest of his life. He could even sleep in my bed with me."

Patty Ruth sat up and frowned. "No you wouldn', B. J.! If'n...if'n I had died, I would've tooken Ulysses to heaven with me. Me an' Ulysses would sit on Jesus' lap together."

Hannah Cooper had come to the bedroom door in time to hear this last remark. Now she leaned against the door frame with her arms folded and set her chocolate-brown eyes on Patty Ruth. "So you're going to sit on Jesus' lap when you get to heaven, are you?"

Patty Ruth slid off the bed, clutching her bear, and said, "Mm-hmm. If'n I go to heaven when I'm a little girl, I will. Jesus loves little girls an' likes to hold 'em on His lap."

"I can't argue with that," Hannah said. "Well, boys, you've got chores to do. And girls, we need to get down to the kitchen and start supper. Papa will be home in another hour, and he's unloading goods off a freight wagon this afternoon, so he'll be hungry as a bear."

Patty Ruth smiled as she looked into the shiny shoe-button eyes of her best friend. "Hear that, Ulysses? Papa's gonna be as hungry as *you* are!"

"I'm gonna hurry and get my part of the chores done so I can ride Buster for a while," Chris said. "I need to work on my horsemanship."

Patty Ruth looked at her big brother impishly. "I know why you want to learn to ride better, Chris...so's you can show off in front of Lula Mae. That's where you're gonna ride, isn't it? To Lula Mae's house?"

Chris tightened his lips and looked toward the ceiling. "Oh-h-h! You may have had a close call this morning, baby sister, but you're still the same Patty Ruth!"

Everybody laughed, and Chris hurried down the hall to change his clothes.

B. J. couldn't resist teasing his little sister, who was so possessive about her stuffed bear. "Patty Ruth, you couldn't really have taken Ulysses to heaven with you if you'd been killed today. Stuffed bears don't go to heaven. But I would've put him up on the barn roof and laid him on his back so's he could look up and wish he was in heaven with you."

Patty Ruth's eyes flashed fire. "No you wouldn't, B. J.! An' stuffed bears do go to heaven! Don't they, Mama?"

"No, they don't, do they, Mama?" B. J. said in mock seriousness.

To B. J., Hannah said, "Brett Jonathan, you get your clothes changed and do your chores. Do you want your father to come home before you have them done?"

"No, ma'am." B. J. headed for the door, then stopped to look back over his shoulder. Patty Ruth said, "Stuffed bears do too go to heaven, B. J.!"

B. J. opened his mouth to reply but changed his mind when he saw the look in his mother's eyes.

When B. J. was gone, Patty Ruth said, "Sometimes brothers are so dumb. Anybody who's smart knows Ulysses is goin' to heaven."

"Let's drop the subject, Patty Ruth," Hannah said. "Come on girls, we need to get supper started."

As they headed for the stairs, Patty Ruth asked, "Can we go to the Square and see all the wagons tomorrow, Mama?"

"Yes, we can do that."

"Are you an' Papa gonna talk some more about movin' out west?"

Hannah was silent for a few seconds, then said, "Probably. It's a big step, though, honey. Nothing to rush into."

"I think it would be neat to move out west, an' so does Ulysses. Don't you think it would be neat, Mary Beth?"

"I might," Mary Beth said, "but it wouldn't be easy to leave Grandma and Grandpa and all of our friends here in Independence."

Patty Ruth jumped the last two steps and landed on the floor with a thud. Her mother frowned, and the little redhead remembered that Mama had said ladies didn't do that. To escape a sharp reminder, she said in a rush, "That would be hard. 'Specially leavin' Grandma and Grandpa. But they could go with us."

"Your grandfather plainly stated that he wasn't ever leaving this town, honey. And when his mind's made up about something, nobody's going to change it."

"I know how we could make him change his mind about movin' west," Patty Ruth said.

Hannah moved to the big cookstove. "How's that?"

"Well, if we took Grandma with us, he'd come pretty soon 'cause he wouldn't have Grandma to cook for him!"

"Wouldn't work," Hannah said with a chuckle. "Grandma won't hardly leave him to go shopping. She certainly wouldn't leave him to go west with us."

Mary Beth nodded, then looked soberly at her mother and said, "I guess moving west is something that takes a lot of thought."

"Yes, and a lot of prayer." Hannah picked up firewood and dropped it into the firebox of the stove. "Be a terrible mistake to sell the store and the farm and move west if it wasn't God's will. Jonah ran ahead of God and got himself swallowed by a whale."

Mary Beth smiled. "And Peter followed afar off behind Jesus and got himself in deep trouble for not staying close."

"Mm-hmm. That's why I said it takes a lot of prayer. Neither your father nor I want to get out of God's will."

Patty Ruth looked up at her mother with searching eyes. "So if the Lord wants us to move west, then we'd better do it, huh, Mama?"

"That's right, sweetie. He will show us His will. If it's to stay, we'll stay. If it's to go, we'll go."

"Well, it'll be all right, whichever it is, 'cause whether we go or whether we stay, my best friend will be with me."

Patty Ruth looked down at Ulysses and gave him a juicy kiss on the nose.

CHAPTER THREE

The grandfather clock in the hall struck nine as Solomon Cooper descended the stairs and entered the parlor. Hannah sat by lantern light, patching a pair of B. J.'s Levi's. The soft lighting cast a warm glow over her bent head.

At the sound of Solomon's step, Hannah looked up with admiring eyes and said, "You know what?"

"What?"

"Whenever I look at you, it makes my heart smile."

"Oh, it does, eh? And where did you first hear that?"

"From you."

"Uh-huh."

"Well, if your heart smiles when you look at me, it's all right for mine to do the same, isn't it?"

"It sure is, darlin'. And I'm so glad it does."

Hannah crinkled her nose at him. "Everybody settled down up there?"

"Yes, finally. The little one insists on giving her biggest brother a hard time about riding to Lula Mae Springer's house. Chris takes all he can stomach, then lashes back. I told him to just let it go in one ear and out the other, but he's not always willing to do that."

Hannah nodded. "And I've told Patty Ruth not to tease him about Lula Mae. But she couldn't resist it today."

"So is that what all the fuss was about?"

"Yes. But I cured it, at least for a while."

"You made them kiss each other?"

"Mm-hmm." Hannah chuckled. "What is it with brothers and sisters, anyway? I've never been able to figure out what's so awful about having to kiss your brother…or the other way around."

"Maybe that's because you were an only child, and never had a brother."

"I suppose. But you never had a sister, so you probably don't understand the brother-sister feud any better than I do. I know you and Daniel fought, because I've heard you two laugh about it."

Solomon paused a moment, then leaned down and placed his hands on the arms of her chair "You know what?"

"What?"

"I didn't have a sister to have to kiss when we fought, but if Pa was here tonight and told me I had to kiss the most beautiful woman in the world if I started a fuss with her, I'd start the fuss just so I could kiss her."

Hannah smiled and met his tender gaze with one of her own. "How about since Pa's not here, we skip the fuss and just kiss?"

"I was hoping you'd say that."

They kissed tenderly, then Solomon turned up the flame of the lantern by his chair and picked up the novel he had been reading the night before—*Great Expectations*.

All was silent in the house as Solomon read and Hannah sewed. When the grandfather clock struck the half-hour, Solomon chuckled.

Hannah looked up. "I didn't know you were reading a comedy."

"Oh, I'm not. It's just that this is so different from anything else Dickens has written. I see Dickens himself in the hero, Pip.

It's as if he's letting us look into his own mind while we explore Pip's mind, as he cries out against the brutal hardships he suffered as a young boy."

"I suppose that's what novelists often do," Hannah said. "Show us themselves in their characters. And when the novelist is as good as Charles Dickens, he can actually help his readers by sharing his own trials and defeats."

Solomon's eyes took on a faraway look. "Maybe some novelist ought to ride one of those wagon trains west. You know…give the positive and the negative sides of traveling to the American frontier."

Hannah was used to her husband's way of, sooner or later, turning the conversation to the subject of moving west. She smiled without comment, then looked at the work in her hands and sighed. "That youngest son of yours is twice as hard as Chris ever was on his clothes. It's a rip here and a tear there. If that boy makes it to adulthood, it'll be a miracle."

Solomon laughed. "Well, honey, B. J.'s just a chip off the old block. I was exactly the same way."

She giggled. "And you still haven't outgrown it. You—"

"Ah-ah-ah! Just sew up the boy's pants, and leave me out of it!"

Hannah rolled her eyes and went back to her work.

Solomon was engrossed in his book once again when Hannah said, "Sweetheart…"

"Hmmm?"

"Did we have a good day at the store? I mean with the wagon train people today?"

"Sure did. If the season goes as well as it's starting out, it's going to be a good one. The first day the wagons started rolling in last year wasn't nearly as good as today has been. It kept Randy and me hopping like jackrabbits this afternoon. We never did get that freight wagon completely unloaded. In fact, today's receipts were so good, I had to wire Chicago for more supplies."

"The Lord has been so good to us, darling," Hannah said. "The store has done better this year than ever. And now, the wagon train season is here. Isn't it wonderful that we've been able to do so much for the church in the past few months?"

"Well, as Pastor Chase so often says, 'You can't out give God.'"

"Amen. And we've never had as much money in the bank as we do right now. God has been so good to us!"

Solomon grinned. "I sure am glad you feel that way, sweetheart. I...ah...I extended credit to the Wolversons and the Beattys again today."

Hannah's rosy cheeks brightened and her smile deepened the dimples on either side of her mouth. "Wonderful! I prayed while driving home that you'd go easy on them."

"Looks like your prayers were answered. The Wolversons came in, offering to pay what little they could on their bill. The Beattys showed up a little later to do the same."

Hannah's thoughts went to the Glenn Beatty family. They were members of the same church as the Coopers. When the Beatty house had burned down three months ago, Hannah and Solomon had taken the family into their home until a new house could be built.

Glenn and the men of the church, as well as other men in the community, were rebuilding the house. Progress was slow, since the bulk of the work had to be done on Saturdays. Hannah had worked Saturdays at the store so that Solomon could help the rest of the men. The Beattys had moved into the house two weeks ago, even though there was still work to do on closets, cabinets, doors and window frames, and finishing touches on the roof.

The Beattys had lost everything in the fire, including valued family heirlooms, and Helen had taken the loss hard. She feared they would never recover from the financial loss and be able to care for their children properly.

As Hannah spent time with Helen, trying to help her find peace of mind in the midst of it all, she had shown Helen Scriptures such as Isaiah 26:3—"Thou wilt keep him in perfect peace, whose mind is stayed on thee: because he trusteth in thee." Hannah had laid claim to this verse many times in her own life.

"Honey..." Hannah said.

Solomon raised his eyes and eased the book onto his lap. "Hmm?"

"I was just thinking about the Beattys, and how wonderfully the Lord provided their household needs through the people of the church and the town."

"Yes. They were praising the Lord about that in the store today, in front of all those wagon train people. There were several among the wagon train who are Christians. We just about had a revival break out. The Beattys were telling people how the furniture they were given was better than the stuff that burned, how folks in this town had pitched in and restored all the necessary things they had lost in the fire."

Tears shone in Hannah's eyes. "Isn't that wonderful?"

"Sure is! And Helen was telling the whole bunch about how you taught her to lay hold on the truth of Isaiah 26:3 by fastening her mind on Jesus for peace of mind in the midst of trials."

Hannah wiped at her eyes with the back of a hand. "Bless her heart. I was just thinking of something I had never thought of before, in connection with that perfect peace the Lord promises..."

"Well, let's hear it."

"Do you know why the peace He gives is perfect and comes from fixing our mind on Jesus?"

"Mm-hmm. Because Jesus said in John 14:27 that the peace He gives us is *His* peace. 'My peace I give unto you', He said. It's perfect because He is perfect. That same peace is what believers can have if they will stay their minds on Him."

Hannah's eyes grew wide, and a look of mock disgust came over her face. "Solomon Edward Cooper! You smart aleck! Why is it you're always ahead of me? I thought I was going to teach you something."

"The husband is supposed to stay ahead of his wife in learning spiritual truths. I'm...ah...just trying to be the husband I'm supposed to be."

Hannah laughed. "Well, Mr. Know-it-all, answer me this. According to the Bible, what was Herodias's daughter's name? You know, the one who danced before Herod at his birthday party?"

Solomon snorted playfully. "Anybody knows that."

"Okay. What does the Bible say her name was?"

"Salome."

"Well, I'm about through here, and it's getting close to bedtime. Since your Bible is upstairs in our bedroom, why don't you go on up and find that verse."

"All right, I'll just do that. You want me to put out these lanterns before I go?"

"No, thank you. I'll take care of them as soon as I'm finished. Besides, you'll need some time to look for Salome. See you in a few minutes."

Solomon gave her a jaunty grin and headed for the stairs.

Hannah allowed herself a smug little smile.

Nearly fifteen minutes had passed when Hannah entered the bedroom to find Solomon furiously turning from one passage to another.

Hannah flashed him a smile and said, "Okay, Mr. Theologian, read it to me."

Solomon was stumped. "If I was a betting man, I'd have

put my last dollar on this one," he said. "The only Salome in the Bible is the one who accompanied Mary Magdalene, followed Jesus, and showed up at the Lord's tomb on the morning of His resurrection."

He stood up and pulled Hannah into his embrace. "I love you, Miss Smarty," he said, giving her a kiss before releasing her.

Hannah sat down in front of the dresser mirror while Solomon began pulling off his boots. Out of the corner of his eye he saw her remove the pins from her hair. His heart leaped when the luxuriant dark-brown tresses cascaded down her graceful shoulders, and he couldn't keep his eyes off of her. He took a deep breath and said in a low tone, "I sure am glad I married you."

Hannah looked at his reflection in the mirror and smiled. "I've got a little secret to tell you, darling."

"Oh?"

"You didn't marry me, I married you."

"Which means?"

"You can't ever go away from me. I own you."

"What man in his right mind would leave you? Not this man, that's for sure."

While Hannah watched her husband in the mirror with a contented smile on her lips, Solomon looked at her reflection and said, "Honey, you should've been at the store this afternoon when those people from the wagon trains came in. I mean to tell you, just to see the excitement on their faces and hear them talk of fulfilling their dreams out west thrilled me to the bone."

Solomon felt Hannah tense at his words. Though they had discussed it many times, and the desire was powerful within him, he would not push her to pack up everything they owned and move to the Wild West. But he had secretly prayed that the Lord would do a work in Hannah's heart and plant the desire in her to join the westward move to the American frontier.

His heart thumped a little harder as Hannah laid down the brush and pivoted on the stool. "Darling," she said, "I know Horace Greeley's famed editorial in the *New York Tribune* has lit a fire in many a man to go west...and it sounds very exciting, but I'm concerned about how we would make a living."

"Well, honey, we—"

"We know people who made the trip all the way to Oregon or California and came back, finding life too hard out there."

"Hannah, darlin', I know it wouldn't be easy, but ever since the government put through the Homestead Act in '62, lots of people are making a good living on their farm land."

"A good living?"

"Yes. And the homesteaders aren't all going to the west coast to do it. There's plenty of land for the taking anywhere west of the Missouri River from the Canadian border to the border of Mexico. If a man uses his head, he can grow a lot of crops and graze a lot of cattle on a hundred and sixty acres."

"And this is for anybody who wants it?"

"Well, they have to be American citizens, or have applied for citizenship. Whoever accepts the land is required to build a house, barn, and necessary outbuildings immediately after the government has officially assigned them the particular piece of land."

"And it costs them absolutely nothing?"

"Not if they stay on the land for five years. It belongs to the government until that time period elapses, then it's deeded to the homesteader. However, if the homesteader wants to own the land before the five-year period is up, he can buy it for $1.25 an acre after he's been on it for six months. Pretty good deal, either way, wouldn't you say?"

Hannah was quiet for a moment. "Yes, I have to say that it's a good deal, but there's so much involved in making such a move. We would have to leave most of our personal things behind—our furniture, the piano...my parents."

"Honey, I have a feeling that if we really decided to go, your parents would break down and go with us. As for the furniture and the piano—"

"I know. Part of the adventure is building your own furniture. And as soon as we're established on the frontier, you'll buy me a new piano."

"Right."

"But I love that old piano. It belonged to my great-grandmother."

"Tell you what. We'll buy two wagons and two teams of oxen, and take the piano and as much of the furniture as possible in one of the wagons."

Hannah shook her head. "No, that would be foolish. If...if the Lord shows us we are to go, there'll just have to be some sacrifices."

Hannah moved close to her husband and said, "Sol, you are the kindest, most wonderful man God ever made. I have watched this 'go-west' fever grow in you. I love you with all my heart, and I wouldn't do anything to hinder your dream. I just want to be dead sure it's the Lord's will."

"I do, too, sweetheart," he said, hugging her close. "We'll keep on praying about it until the Lord gives us a yes or a no."

After a moment, Hannah said, "Just how far is it from Independence to Oregon City?"

"They tell me that in round figures it's two thousand miles. For the California-bound wagons, it's nineteen hundred miles to Sacramento. There are a few places along the way where travelers can stock up on food and supplies. Fort Bridger, Wyoming, is the halfway point, and from what I'm told, there's a trading post there."

"A trading post at an army fort?"

"Well, there's a town springing up around the fort. They call the town Fort Bridger, too."

Hannah nodded and looked thoughtful. "If I've heard right, it takes a good six months to make it to Oregon City, Sol."

"Yes, something like that. Some of the wagon masters have told me their goal is to average between twelve and fourteen miles a day when they're on flat land. It drops to about six or seven miles a day in the mountains. Most of the trains make it to Oregon City in about five and a half months. Two weeks shorter to Sacramento."

Hannah shook her head. "Whew! Makes me tired just thinking about it."

Solomon chuckled. "Tough little gal like you could handle it, all right."

"But how about my parents if we did talk them into going with us? Could they stand the trip? I mean, they're nearly seventy years old."

"Older folks are doing it all the time, Hannah. There were several of them in the store today. They were like a bunch of little kids, all excited about their new venture."

Solomon and Hannah got into bed and doused the lanterns. Moonlight filled the room as Solomon continued to tell Hannah about people from the wagon trains, and the things they said.

Hannah listened, then brought up questions about the hardships of the trail—storms, flooding rivers, people getting sick with no doctor to look after them…Indians.

Solomon countered, explaining that since the wagon trains started moving west twenty-seven years ago, there was only a small percentage of people who didn't make it.

When the grandfather clock downstairs struck twelve, Hannah said, "It's time to go to sleep, Sol."

"All right, sweetheart. Let's pray."

Solomon took Hannah's hand in his and asked the Lord to guide them in making the right decision about a move west.

When they kissed goodnight, Solomon was asleep in a

minute or two, but Hannah lay awake for a long time. One thing her husband wasn't facing—Hannah's father. Ben and Esther would never move away from Independence.

Patty Ruth Cooper stirred awake and blinked at the silvery moonlight shining through the windows. She didn't know what had awakened her until she noticed the covers thrown back on the unoccupied bed next to her and saw her sister carefully closing the bedroom door.

Mary Beth tiptoed toward her bed as Patty Ruth sat up and rubbed her eyes. "Where you been, Mary Beth? What time is it?"

"Shhh! It's just past midnight," Mary Beth whispered. "An hour ago, when the clock downstairs struck eleven, I wasn't yet asleep, and then I heard Mama and Papa talking, first from downstairs, then when they came up to their room. I went down the hall and stood outside their door. They kept talking about it till just a few minutes ago when they decided it was time to pray and go to sleep."

"Talkin' about it? You mean, movin' west?"

"Yes!"

"So what did they say?"

"Lots of things. Most of what I heard was about people from the wagon trains who were in the store today. Papa told Mama about a man named Drake, who is taking his family all the way to Oregon. Papa told Mama that Mr. Drake described Oregon as a paradise. It has lots of mountains and valleys, rich soil, and lots of rivers and creeks."

Patty Ruth cocked her head to one side and crinkled her nose. "Rich soil? I thought only people could get rich. How does dirt have money?"

Mary Beth had to suppress the giggle struggling to come out, and she shook all over.

"What's so funny?"

"Patty Ruth, rich soil means it grows crops and fruit trees real good."

"Oh."

"Anyway, Papa said Mr. Drake told him cattle grow good out there, too. They're always real fat. Papa was really impressed."

"Sounds like Papa's ready to go."

"I think so. But Mama brought up the dangers. Storms, rivers flooding, people getting sick, and the Indians killing wagon train people and taking their scalps."

Patty Ruth's face paled in the moonlight. "In'ians takin' their what?"

"Their scalps."

"That's awful!" Patty Ruth said with a gasp. Then she cocked her head again and said, "Mary Beth..."

"Mm-hmm?"

"What's a scalp?"

"Your *hair*, honey."

"What do they want people's hair for?"

"It's their way of showing they've conquered their enemy when they take his scalp."

"Oh. That's dumb."

"When they were talking about the Indian danger, Mama reminded Papa that last year they read in the paper about a massacre in Kansas. The Pawnees killed and scalped a family who was traveling west all by themselves. They had five wagons. I guess there were grandmas and grandpas, and aunts and uncles and cousins...all in the same family. About thirty of them."

"Why do the In'ians do that? Don't they like us?"

"Well...tell you what. We can talk about this later. It's time for you to get back to sleep." Mary Beth yawned. "And it's time for me to get to sleep, too."

CHAPTER FOUR

The next morning at breakfast, Patty Ruth was slipping morsels of pancake under the table to a grateful Biggie.

"Patty Ruth…"

"Yes, Papa?"

"Are you feeding Biggie under the table?"

"No, sir."

"What's your hand doing under the table?"

"I was jis' restin' it."

"Let's see it."

Her chubby little hand came into view covered with syrup and dog saliva.

"Looks to me like somebody's been licking your hand."

"Oh, jis' me." Patty Ruth proceeded to lick her fingers, syrup, dog saliva, and all.

Solomon's frown deepened. "Patty Ruth, you lied to me, didn't you?"

Patty Ruth's face lost color as she said, "Well, not exactly, Papa. I wasn't feedin' Biggie when you asked. He already had the pancake in his mouth."

"Patty Ruth, you knew what I meant, didn't you?"

"Y-yes, sir."

"You know Papa loves you, Patty Ruth. Right?"

Hannah bit her lip and tried not to look at the tears in

Patty Ruth's eyes. The other children sat in silence, knowing what was coming.

"Yes, Papa," Patty Ruth said.

"And the Bible says if I love you I will spank you, doesn't it?"

Her lower lip began to quiver. "Yes, sir."

"And I will do this so you will grow up to be a good girl and a lady. Do you understand?"

"I…I think I could do that even if you didn't spank me, Papa."

"God loves you more than I do, and He says if I don't discipline you when you're naughty, you will be spoiled and turn out bad. Now let's go out on the back porch."

Patty Ruth began sobbing pitifully. Biggie followed a few steps, then decided to stay where he was.

The last words the others heard were, "This is going to hurt me as much as it does you, Patty Ruth," and a quivering reply, "Then, why aren't *you* cryin'?"

Five minutes later, father and daughter came through the door. Patty Ruth was in her father's arms, leaning her head against his.

"Everything all right, now?" Hannah asked.

"Yes, Mama," Patty Ruth said. "I got spanked because I broke the rules, and even more because I lied to Papa. Lyin' is a sin. But I won' do it no more."

Breakfast resumed with Biggie beside Patty Ruth's chair. This time she looked down at him and said, "Even if you starve to death, Biggie, I'm not feedin' you at the table ever again."

Everyone ate quietly until Patty Ruth said, "Mama, are you still gonna take me to the Square today, even if I was bad?"

"Of course, honey. You've paid for being bad. Mama's promise still holds true."

"That's how God does it, huh, Mama," B. J. said. "When He forgives us, He doesn't keep on punishing us, does He?"

"That's right. When we confess our sins and ask His forgiveness, He forgives us and cleanses us. He doesn't hold it over our heads."

Before breakfast, Mary Beth had told her brothers about their parents' conversation the previous night. Now they looked toward their father eagerly when Mary Beth said, "Papa...Mama...I overheard some of your conversation last night. Are we going to move west?"

"Well, dear," Hannah replied, "let's just say that Papa and I are seriously praying about it. We want the Lord's will in our lives...and by 'our,' I include you children, too."

"Papa," Patty Ruth said, "how come In'ians masker white people?"

"How come they what?"

"Masker 'em. You know, kill 'em. Lots of 'em."

"Oh, massacre them. Where did you hear about Indians massacring white people?"

"From me, Papa," Mary Beth said. "After I heard you and Mama talking about the Indian problems out west, I went back to our room and found Patty Ruth awake, and we talked about it."

"I'll explain about the Indians later, sweetheart," Solomon said.

"So what about it, Papa?" Christopher asked. "Do you think we'll buy a covered wagon and move to Oregon? Or California?"

"Or Colorado?" B. J. asked.

The head of the Cooper household finished off a gravy-drenched biscuit before replying. "Like your mother said, Chris, we're praying about it. It's a big step. It would mean selling the farm and the store. Might be pretty hard to do."

"We won't have any problem selling the farm and the store if the Lord wants us to move west, Papa," Mary Beth said. "If that's what He wants, He will provide the buyers."

Patty Ruth chewed a mouthful of scrambled eggs and waited to see her father's reaction to Mary Beth's wise words.

Solomon deeply appreciated his oldest daughter's faith in the Lord. He loved each of his children the same, but he had a different relationship with each one. Mary Beth was his "buddy." She often came to the store to spend time with him, and sometimes they would take walks together and talk about spiritual things. He smiled at her and said, "The Lord certainly can supply the buyers, Mary Beth."

Christopher, who was lanky and tall for his age, spoke up. "I think we'd better pray a whole lot before we get serious about moving from Independence, Papa. We've had the store since I was two years old. And we've got our church here, and all of our friends."

Patty Ruth didn't even wait to swallow the mouthful of eggs before she said, "I know why you don't want to move west, Chris. You don't want to leave Lula Mae!"

Chris's face went pink, and he looked at his father.

"Young lady, that's enough," Solomon said. "What did I tell you last night about teasing Chris?"

"Well, I was jis—"

"I know what you were doing. Now, there's nothing wrong with Chris liking Lula Mae. She's a fine Christian girl. Her parents are both good Christian people."

Patty Ruth knew she was walking on dangerous ground, but she gambled a little further. "But he likes Lula Mae because she brags on how good he rides Buster."

Solomon's eyes were stern as he spoke. "I said that's enough."

Patty Ruth wilted under her father's eyes, and Chris smiled at B. J., who smiled back.

"Patty Ruth," Hannah said, "what have I told you about talking with food in your mouth?"

"I'm s'posed to swallow it 'fore I talk."

"Then let's remember that."

"Yes, Mama."

Solomon ran his gaze over the faces of his children and said, "As Mary Beth heard in her eavesdropping last night—"

"Papa, I wasn't exactly eavesdropping. I was just wanting to hear what you and Mama were saying about moving west."

Solomon chuckled. "Anyway, as Mary Beth heard last night, your mother and I are talking seriously about joining a wagon train and heading west to make us a new home. You know we've talked about it before, but last night we decided to pray in earnest about it. Since the government came up with the Homestead Act, it's pretty tempting to go to new territory and pick up a hundred and sixty acres of free land. But we'll only do it if that's what God wants for us."

"What about the Indians, Papa?" Mary Beth asked. "I wouldn't want us to be massacred like those people in Kansas last year."

"I don't either, sweetheart. But from talking to those wagon masters who come into the store, I've learned that the Indians don't bother wagon trains that have fourteen or fifteen wagons or more. The wagon masters said that once in a while the Indians will try to frighten the people in the trains by riding close with war paint on. But they usually just want some food."

"So the people the Pawnees killed were attacked because there were only five wagons in their train, right, Papa?"

"That's right. It's asking for trouble to travel in such a small convoy."

"Papa," Patty Ruth said, "couldn't you just real quick tell us why the In'ians kill white people? Did we do somethin' bad to 'em?"

Solomon glanced at the clock on the kitchen wall. "Well, honey, to put it real quick...I'm sorry to say that when white men started moving west several years ago, they stole land from the Indians and killed their deer, elk, and buffalo. This made the Indians angry. Now many of the tribes make war against all white men who travel through their land or move in and settle on it."

"But they won't make war on white people if they're in big enough wagon trains, right, Papa?" B. J. asked.

"That's right, son."

Patty Ruth had come to her own conclusion. "Then if Jesus tells us He wants us to go out there where the In'ians are, He will protect us, won't He, Papa?"

"He sure will, darlin'. He sure will." Solomon looked around at the others. "All right, it's time for Bible reading and prayer."

Solomon's Bible lay on the cupboard within reach. As he picked it up he said, "We're going to pray every morning and every night about moving west until the Lord gives us a yes or a no."

"How will we know, Papa?" B. J. asked. "God doesn't come and talk to His children today like He did in the Old Testament days, does He?"

"No, son. But He has a way of letting us know His will. Sometimes by something we read in His Word. Sometimes by circumstances. Sometimes by both."

"Papa, what's circum— circum—"

"Patty Ruth, circumstances are things that happen in our lives that show us what the Lord wants for us."

"Oh. Like if Chris falls off of Buster while he's showin' off in front of Lula Mae, it means God doesn't want him to do that."

"I haven't fallen off of Buster ever, little sister," Chris said, "so God must want me to—"

"That's enough," Solomon said. "Both of you."

Mary Beth looked at both of her parents. "Mama... Papa...what about Grandpa and Grandma? From what Grandpa has said, nobody's going to budge him from

Independence. Can we just go off and leave them?"

Solomon answered. "Well, sweetheart, Grandma and Grandpa are Christians, so God has His will for their lives. It may not be the same as His will for our lives. The Coopers will do what God wants, and I'm sure the Singletons will, too."

After Solomon had gone to the store and the three older children had gone to school, Hannah and Patty Ruth walked into town to see the wagons and people gathered in Independence Courthouse Square. The Square was quite large, and afforded room for as many as four normal-sized wagon trains to form at the same time.

Their route took them down Main Street and past Cooper's General Store. The business section of Independence took up six blocks, with the huge Courthouse Square in the middle.

Patty Ruth was all eyes, watching the wagons coming into town from the east. As they walked past the store, Hannah looked in and saw her Solomon and Randy Chase waiting on a great number of customers.

"Looks like Papa and Randy are going to have a busy day," Hannah said.

Soon they neared the Square. The area was a hubbub of activity.

"Oh, Mama! Look at all the wagons...an' mules...an' oxes...an' people!"

Dozens of white-canopied wagons were jammed into the Square. Hammers pounded, dogs barked, and children laughed and played together. Two girls ran by screaming as some boys chased them with frogs in their hands.

Men were leading ox and mule teams through the crowds, and riders moved along the periphery on horseback. You could tell who the wagon masters were by all the people standing around them, asking questions.

Patty Ruth clutched Ulysses close to her chest, and tried to take in every detail as she walked with her mother among the wagons.

"Oh, look, Patty Ruth!" Hannah said. "It's Betty Wilson!"

Patty Ruth had always liked the Wilsons, but she liked Raymond Wilson even more since he had saved her from the big horse's hooves yesterday.

As they came close to Betty, who was casually strolling among the wagons, Hannah called to her. Betty turned and smiled. "Hannah," she said, "I'm glad to see you—I've been dying to find out if it's true."

"What's that?"

"Well, Ray told me that after the incident yesterday, Patty Ruth asked if you and Solomon were going to buy a covered wagon and move west. He said your answer was rather vague. Now, c'mon, honey. Your ol' friend, Betty, here, wants to know if there's anything to it."

Hannah smiled. "All I can tell you at this point is that we're giving it serious consideration and praying for the Lord's guidance. I read an article about the emigration west in the *Kansas City Sun* a couple of weeks ago. I haven't said anything to Solomon about it, but the article pointed out that for the men, the move west is a great adventure. It appeals to their male self-esteem, and they enjoy the challenge and excitement of conquering the rugged frontier. For women, however—"

Betty cut in, nodding in a knowing way. "Mm-hmm...just a lot of hard work and frustration."

"That," Hannah said, "and many fears. They leave all they hold dear, except for the family members going with them. It's hard to face leaving home and going off to some strange, unfamiliar place where there are dangers on every side."

"Oh, I agree, honey. Plus the men don't have to tend to

the children on the trail like the women do…or give birth traveling in a prairie schooner."

"That's for sure, Betty. But despite it all, if the Lord gives us peace about striking out west, I'll back Solomon all the way."

"Of course you will, Hannah, because that's the kind of woman you are." Betty drew in a short breath and said, "Ray and I have talked about doing the same thing."

"You have?"

"Yes. But, of course, there are a lot of things to consider. We'd have to sell the house and the shop…and the shop is doing quite well for us."

"Well, it's certainly not anything to hurry into," Hannah said with a sigh.

Just then the women noticed a young mother with two small daughters coming their way. One child, who looked to be about two years old, was in her mother's arms. The other was about Patty Ruth's age.

"Good morning," Hannah said, flashing her winsome smile.

"Hello," the young mother said. "I'm Darlene Watson, and these are my daughters, Emily and Eliza."

"I'm Hannah Cooper. This is my youngest daughter, Patty Ruth, and this is Betty Wilson."

Eliza, who was exactly Patty Ruth's size, was eyeing Ulysses.

Patty Ruth felt a slight unease with her bear under such scrutiny.

"Hi," Eliza said. "I like your bear. What's her name?"

"It's not a her, it's a *him*. His name is Ulysses." As she spoke, Patty Ruth clutched the bear tighter.

"He's cute," Eliza said. "Can I hold him?"

Patty Ruth froze. All she could manage was a shake of her head.

"Please?"

The two girls now had their mothers' and Betty Wilson's attention.

"No," Patty Ruth said. "Ulysses only wants me to hold him."

"All I want to do is hold him. I won't take him anywhere. I promise."

Patty Ruth turned herself so that Ulysses was farther away from Eliza's reach and snapped, "No! He doesn't want you to hold him!"

Hannah had seen and heard enough. "Patty Ruth," she said, "why are you talking to Eliza like that? She asked you in a nice way if she could hold Ulysses."

Patty Ruth's lower lip protruded as she looked at Eliza, then back at her mother. "He's my bear."

"Patty Ruth, what have I told you about being selfish?"

"That it's naughty."

"Then you're being naughty, aren't you? I heard Eliza very politely ask you if she could hold Ulysses. Now you let Eliza hold him for a few minutes."

"Mrs. Cooper," Darlene Watson said, "it's all right. Eliza understands."

Hannah smiled and turned back to her daughter. "Patty Ruth, let Eliza hold Ulysses."

When she saw the stubborn look in Patty Ruth's eyes, Hannah set her jaw. *"Now."*

Patty Ruth extended the bear and said, "Don't drop him."

Hannah cleared her throat.

Patty Ruth looked at Eliza and said, "Please. Don't drop him, *please.*"

"I won't," Eliza said, pressing Ulysses to her cheek then holding him at arm's length to study his shiny black eyes. She adjusted him in the cradle of her arm and traced the bear's smile with the tip of her forefinger.

The little redhead watched her closely.

Eliza looked up at her mother. "He's really a nice bear, Mommy. I like him."

"I'm sure Ulysses likes you, too, honey. Now give him back to Patty Ruth."

Eliza smiled warmly and handed the stuffed bear back, saying, "Thank you, Patty Ruth."

Patty Ruth managed a weak smile and said, "You're welcome."

While Hannah and her youngest were walking home, Hannah said, "Honey, I know you love Ulysses very much, but you mustn't be selfish with him. Eliza just wanted to hold him and get a good look at him."

Patty Ruth didn't reply.

Hannah let a few seconds pass, then said, "If Eliza had been holding a doll, and you liked the looks of it, would you want to hold it and see it up close?"

"Maybe."

"Well, if you did, would you hurt it?"

"Course not."

"Well, Eliza wouldn't either. You need to remember what happened today and understand why it's important to share with others. Understand?"

"Yes, ma'am."

"Patty Ruth...Mama wants you to grow up to be generous and loving. You know that, don't you?"

"Yes."

"Do you think I can be proud of you if you're selfish?"

"No."

"Well, let me tell you something I've observed in my years on this earth."

"Okay."

"Selfishness in a person's heart eventually makes her very miserable and unhappy. Life is much happier for people who are generous and not selfish. Do you understand what I'm saying?"

"Yes, Mama. I won't be selfish anymore."

"That's my girl. Both Papa and I will be proud of you, too."

CHAPTER FIVE

M ary Beth Cooper listened intently as Miss Powers stood in front of a large map and showed her students the three main routes west. All routes, she pointed out with pride, started right in Independence at Courthouse Square.

Mary Beth's thoughts drifted to her parents and their prayers about whether or not to sell out and go west. Oregon sounded like a nice place, as did California. But Mary Beth was having mixed feelings. If they did go west, they would have to act soon, or wait until next year. It was already the last week of April, and Papa had said the wagon trains never left Independence later than the last week of May. That meant the Cooper family might be gone within a month!

At that very moment, Miss Powers was explaining the length of time it took the wagon trains to reach Oregon City or Sacramento. If all went well, and there weren't any unusual delays, they could make it to Oregon City in twenty-two to twenty-three weeks. The main thing was to get over the mountain ranges no later than the last week of October to safely beat the snow.

Mary Beth's best friend, Belinda Martin, sat next to her. Mary Beth glanced at Belinda from the corner of her eye. She wanted to move to the exciting frontier, but she didn't want to leave her friends. She didn't want to leave Miss Powers, either. Even though she would be in Mr. Barrick's class with Christopher next year, she could still see Miss Powers at school every day.

But even more than that, Mary Beth didn't want to leave Belinda. They belonged to the same church and had been best friends since the Martins came to Independence from Indiana six years ago.

Miss Powers was pointing out the spot on the map some sixty-six miles northwest of Fort Bridger where the Oregon and California Trails divided, explaining that it was known as the Parting of the Ways.

Mary Beth felt a painful lump in her throat. How could she leave her best friend? It would be like going off and leaving her sister.

At that moment, Belinda turned to look at Mary Beth. She could tell something was wrong with her friend. She would just have to wait until recess to ask her about it.

Miss Powers took the rest of the period to discuss the four wagon trains that were forming in Courthouse Square. At ten-thirty, she dismissed the class for the half-hour recess.

Mary Beth rose slowly from her desk as Belinda waited beside her. When their eyes met, Belinda flicked a glance at Miss Powers, who was answering a student's question, then leaned close to her best friend and whispered, "Mary Beth, what's wrong? I saw tears in your eyes."

"Let's go outside," Mary Beth said.

They walked outside and made their way to a back corner of the white frame building.

Mary Beth's lips quivered slightly as she said, "Belinda, Mama and Papa are getting serious about joining a wagon train and moving west."

"Oh, no! I couldn't stand it if you moved away!"

"It's bothering me, too. I...I know my parents won't make

the move unless the Lord leads them. But if He does, then we'll never see each other again. Not in this world, anyway."

Now there were tears in Belinda's eyes too. She shook her head and said, "I'm going to pray that the Lord will keep you here."

"I'm not sure how to pray, Belinda. I'm just praying that if it's God's will for us to go, He'll give me the grace and strength to handle it. It will mean leaving my Grandma and Grandpa, as well as you and all my other friends. I would just flat pray that God won't let us go, but Papa seems to really have his heart set on it."

When school let out that afternoon, Mary Beth reminded Chris and B. J. that this was her day to go to the store and do paperwork for Papa.

Fifteen minutes later, Mary Beth moved along the boardwalk in town, noting the wagon train people on the street. As she entered Cooper's General Store, she had to thread her way through the men, women, and children to reach the long counter where her father and Randy Chase were selling merchandise.

When she rounded the end of the counter and headed for the small desk next to a filing cabinet, Randy looked up and greeted her.

"Oh, hello, honey," Solomon said, diverting his attention momentarily from the line of customers. "Everything's ready for you there. Invoices on the last shipment from Chicago are in the top drawer."

"Okay, Papa."

While Mary Beth made entries in her father's record book, she couldn't help looking up periodically to watch the people from the wagon trains. She could see the excitement in their eyes and hear it in their voices.

The desk sat beside a window, and outside on the street, Mary Beth could see and hear the children laughing and playing while men and women loaded their wagons with supplies purchased at the store. Inside, as women made their way among the long rows of goods, picking and choosing supplies, she listened to their talk.

The women didn't show the same enthusiasm about the upcoming journey as the men and children. They talked about their fears, yet underneath their words, Mary Beth could see some degree of anticipation of building a new life on the frontier.

Twelve-year-old Mary Beth told herself that women were just more level-headed than men and children when it came to these things. By the end of the afternoon, she understood better why her mother was somewhat reluctant to sell out, pack up, and move west.

On Saturday morning, a small crowd of citizens gathered at Courthouse Square to watch the first wagon train pull out. The second one was scheduled to depart on Monday, and the other two would leave later in the week. Even before the last trains were gone, there would be more trains forming.

Christopher and Mary Beth were working at the store with Randy Chase so that Solomon, along with others, could help put the finishing touches on the Beatty house.

The new house was really shaping up, and the wives gathered inside the house at eleven-fifteen to begin preparing a hearty lunch for their hardworking men.

The children who were old enough worked right alongside their fathers. B. J. was picking up chunks of wood after Solomon sawed boards for trimming the windows of the two-story house and piling it behind the house to be used for firewood.

Patty Ruth was playing with some other little girls in the front yard, the ever-present Ulysses cradled in one arm.

Pastor Dan Chase and his wife, Miriam, were there, too. The pastor was high at the top of the sharply-pitched roof, helping Jack Lennox finish nailing trim along the peak.

Jack Lennox's wife, Lucinda, was Hannah Cooper's closest friend. They were the same age, and of much the same temperament. They often spent time together sewing, making fancy things for their houses, and just enjoying each other's company. They also prayed and studied the Bible together.

In the kitchen, Hannah was working at one end of the cupboard with Lucinda and Miriam Chase, cutting vegetables. The other seven women were busily working in twos and threes, each little group in its own conversation.

"I sure don't envy those poor women," Miriam said. "I've read a lot about the wagon trains. I can understand why some of the families turn around and come back before they even get two or three days out. It's just too hard for those wives and mothers to cope with crying babies, cranky children, weary, footsore husbands, the Indians, living in a wagon, cooking over a campfire, sleeping on the ground, and on and on…"

"Yes," Lucinda said, "and for half a year or so."

"And not to mention the heat and the dust," Miriam added, "plus trying to launder clothes for the family in some half-dried-up stream, or in a buffalo wash where the water is filthy."

Lucinda noticed Hannah's quietness and eyed her cautiously. "Hannah, Solomon hasn't been pressing you again about packing up and going west, has he?"

Hannah paused after cutting an onion in half. "Well, honey, the two of us have talked about it some more. But he's not pressing me. Solomon would never try to force such a thing on me. If such a decision were ever made, it would be *our* decision."

Miriam frowned. "But the two of you are considering it, Hannah?"

Hannah attempted a noncommittal tone. "Well, we've been discussing it, yes. But we've also been praying about it. We're in total agreement that—"

"Mama!" B. J. burst into the kitchen, holding up his left hand. "I've got a splinter!"

The eight-year-old had everyone's attention as Hannah took hold of his hand, focusing on the dirty forefinger that held a thin, needle-like piece of wood. It was angled in for about an inch, and blood was welling around it.

While B. J. gritted his teeth, Hannah pulled him over to a chair. "Sit down here, son. I'll see if I can get it out."

Helen Beatty moved in. "I have some tweezers, Hannah."

"Let me see if I can pull it out without breaking it off. If it breaks, I'll use the tweezers."

Hannah grasped her son's wrist and slowly and delicately slid out the splinter. "There! That wasn't too bad, was it, B. J.? Helen, if you have a cloth I can use to wrap this, I'll take him home and clean the wound."

"I have everything you need right here," Helen said, heading for a cabinet at the end of the kitchen.

When Hannah had finished and B. J. had gone back outside with his finger bandaged, Miriam looked at Hannah and chuckled. "I do declare, Hannah, that boy is an accident looking for a place to happen. Have we ever had a church get-together of any kind, but what B. J. didn't scrape something or cut something or break something?"

Hannah laughed. "Not that I can remember!"

Up on the roof, Jack Lennox and the preacher had finished their task at one end and were carrying their materials toward the other.

Solomon looked at them briefly and then glanced toward the rear of the house. B. J. should have been back by now, he thought. Less than a minute later, B. J. approached, pushing the empty wheelbarrow. When Solomon saw the white bandage, he stopped sawing. "What happened, son?"

B. J. explained and told him that Mama had taken care of it.

"Well, B. J., you need to be more caref—"

Solomon's words were cut off by the sound of a cry, accompanied by the rumble of materials bouncing off the roof. Pastor Chase, who was on the opposite end of the roof from Jack Lennox watched helplessly as Jack pitched headlong, arms flailing.

Solomon dropped his saw and limped toward the house as fast as he could, trying to get underneath the falling man and break his fall.

But Jack peeled off the edge of the roof and fell to the ground head-first before Solomon could get there. Other men on that side of the house dashed toward the spot where Solomon had dropped to his knees beside Jack.

Glenn Beatty reached Solomon first and dropped down next to him. Solomon, who was cradling Jack's head, looked up sorrowfully. "He's dead, Glenn."

The other men arrived and watched the preacher coming on the run. They could already see by the way Jack's head was bent that he had broken his neck.

The women had just come out on the porch, trying to see what had happened, when Lucinda bounded off the porch, crying, "Jack! Jack! What's happened to him?"

Pastor Chase rose to his feet and intercepted Lucinda,

gripping her arms. "You don't want to see him," he said. "He's dead, Lucinda. The fall broke his neck."

The knot of men blocked Lucinda's view, and she stared at them with a wild look and screamed, "No-o! Jack!" and broke free. She fell to her knees beside her husband and wrapped her arms around him.

Hannah knelt down and gripped her friend's shoulders. Lucinda's wails filled the air as the other women ushered the children inside the house. Miriam Chase stood next to her husband, looking on in shock.

"Solomon…Hannah…," the pastor said, "as soon as she calms down, we need to take her home. Two of the men have gone for the undertaker."

"I'll go home and stay with her," Hannah said.

"Miriam and I will go, too, and tell the boys."

"We can trade off staying with her until the shock is over," Helen Beatty volunteered. "I'm sure there are plenty of ladies in the church who will be glad to take a turn."

On Sunday morning, Lucinda Lennox and her sons sat with the Coopers. Hannah had planned to stay with Lucinda and the boys all day Sunday, not expecting that Lucinda would feel like attending church services. But Lucinda said she wanted to be in church on the Lord's day.

Hannah's parents, Ben and Esther Singleton, sat in the same pew with Chris and B. J. on one side of them, and Mary Beth and Patty Ruth on the other.

When the final hymn had been sung, Pastor Chase walked to the pulpit and looked around at the somber faces of the congregation, then said, "All of us have been shocked to have one of our finest men taken from us. As I'm sure most of you have heard, I was on the roof with Jack Lennox yesterday when he fell.

"Miriam and I have spent much time with dear Lucinda and her sons since yesterday morning, and have prayed and read Scripture with them. Mrs. Cooper stayed the night with them, and also spent much time in prayer and the Word.

"Now, those of you who have your Bibles, turn to the Book of Job, chapter fourteen."

The sound of fluttering pages filled the place.

"First," Chase said, "look at verses one and two. 'Man that is born of a woman is of few days, and full of trouble.' You will note that at best our time on this earth is spoken of here as *few days*. A full lifetime on this earth is but a blink of God's eye. Let's read on.

"Of man, it says, 'He cometh forth like a flower, and is cut down: he fleeth also as a shadow, and continueth not.' I believe you can see here the brevity of human life underscored for our minds by the hand of our Creator. This is why Moses said to God in Psalm 90, 'So teach us to number our days, that we may apply our hearts unto wisdom.'

"Now, look at Job 14:5. Scripture says, 'Seeing his days are determined, the number of his months are with thee, thou hast appointed his bounds that he cannot pass…,

"When the sun came up yesterday morning, our brother Jack Lennox did not know it, but it was the Lord's appointed day to take him home to heaven. We don't understand God's ways, nor are we expected to. All He asks of us is that we trust Him…trust that He doesn't make mistakes, and that He knows what He is doing.

"Let us not weep for Jack Lennox, for he is now in the presence of the One who went to the cross for him. Let us weep for ourselves, for we are still in this sin-cursed world of heartaches, tears, trials, and testings. And to Lucinda and the boys, I say, don't wish him back. He's had a glimpse of Jesus' bright face. This world would be too dark for him now.

"If you are sitting within the sound of my voice and cannot

give testimony that you are a born-again, blood-washed child of God, then you have no way of knowing but what this very day is your last to settle this most important issue. Don't trifle with Almighty God, and don't trifle with your feeble hold on life."

When the message was finished, and the invitation was given, several people responded by coming down the aisle to receive Christ, and many Christians came to the altar to dedicate their lives afresh to the Lord.

Many of the women had signed up to spend a night with Lucinda and the boys, but Hannah would stay with them through Tuesday—the day of the funeral.

That night, after Lucinda had prayed with her boys and tucked them in bed, she came to the kitchen, where Hannah was pouring two cups of hot tea.

She placed the teapot on the stove and turned around to find her friend looking at her with tears streaming down her cheeks. Lucinda wrapped her arms around her friend and sobbed. "Oh, Hannah, I miss him so much! How am I ever going to make it without Jack? My heart hurts so much!"

Hannah held her tight for a long moment, then said softly, "Honey, I want you to sit down and drink some hot tea. It'll make you feel better. And I have something I want to show you from God's Word."

Hannah opened her Bible and said, "Honey, I've read this verse to you for the past three nights. I want to read it to you again. God's Word says that we can have His perfect peace, and I'm praying that He will make it real to you. Jesus says, 'My peace I give unto you: not as the world giveth, give I unto you.' The peace this world gives is a false peace. It isn't real, and it doesn't last. But the peace Jesus gives is real and it doesn't fade away. And He follows that truth with, 'Let not your heart be troubled, neither let it be afraid.' Real peace is found only in Him because it is His own peace."

Tears were spilling down Lucinda's cheeks now, and her face began to mirror the truth Hannah spoke of. "Then I must claim that peace right now," she said.

Hannah rejoiced as Lucinda prayed for that peace and her heart was flooded with it. Though she still grieved over Jack's death and missed him terribly, she had the "peace that passes all understanding."

Lucinda squeezed Hannah's hand and said, "Honey, you'll never know what your friendship means to me, nor how very much you have helped me in these days since the Lord took Jack home. I love you for being my friend. But now I want you to go home to your family. They miss you and they need you."

Hannah looked at her friend in surprise. "But...well, I'll stay the night, so if you need me—"

"No. I want you to go home. I'll be just fine. The Lord is so close to me, it's as if He's almost bodily in this room, Hannah. Please. Your family needs you. I'll hitch up the wagon and take you home."

Hannah smiled radiantly and said, "It's only a little way. I can walk. There's no need to go to all the trouble of hitching up the team."

Hannah quickly packed her things and stepped out onto the front porch. She embraced Lucinda once more and moved out into the moonlight.

Lucinda stood tall and watched until her best friend passed from view, then went inside and quietly closed the door.

CHAPTER SIX

A chill came on the night breeze, a reminder that winter
had not been gone long, as Hannah walked the dusty
road toward home. She pulled her shawl tighter and
picked up her pace.

As she walked Hannah had a private praise service within
her own heart. "Thank You, Lord, for what You did for Lucinda
tonight. It was so wonderful to see the tranquil look that came
over her face when You put Your peace in her heart."

She sniffed, and wiped her tears. "Thank You, Lord Jesus,
that Your Word is true, and when applied by faith it will never
fail to meet Your child's needs. I love You. Thank You for being
so good to Your children."

The Missouri countryside was aglow with a soft silver
light from the clear-edged moon. Soon Hannah could see her
house as it nestled under the elms near the road. Smoke was
lifting skyward. Solomon had built a fire to take the night chill
off the house, she thought. Soft orange light came from only
the downstairs windows, so the children were already in their
beds.

An owl hooted as Hannah approached the house.
Through the window, she saw Solomon lay down his Bible and
leave his chair. He had heard her footsteps.

The door came open and he was silhouetted against the

brightness inside. "Sweetheart! I didn't expect you home tonight."

Hannah smiled and raised up on tiptoe to kiss his cheek. "I didn't expect it, either, but after Lucinda and I spent some time in the Word, the Lord filled her heart with His perfect peace, and she sent me home."

"Well, praise the Lord! I'm glad the Lord used you to help her, and I'm glad to have you home. This house is like a mausoleum when the kids are asleep and you're not here."

She smiled to herself and set down her overnight bag. "Put on your light jacket, Sol, and come out on the porch with me. It's a bit cool, but it's such a beautiful night."

Solomon hurried to the hall closet, saying over his shoulder, "When the most beautiful woman in the world asks me to go outside in the moonlight with her, I'm not going to pass up the opportunity!"

Hannah felt a warmth all through her as her love for him stirred afresh. They stepped to the railing, and Solomon slid his arms around her and bent to kiss her neck. Hannah reached back and stroked his cheek. "I love you, Solomon Cooper," she said.

He captured her hand and kissed it, saying, "And I love you, Hannah Cooper."

Neither one spoke for several minutes until Hannah said, "I'm so glad for Lucinda, Sol. You should have seen her face when the Lord almost literally poured that peace into her heart."

"Must be a horrible thing to lose your mate...especially for a woman to lose her husband. Suddenly the responsibility to provide for the household is on her shoulders."

"Yes. Lucinda has peace about that, too."

"I know it's the Lord who gives the comfort and peace, honey," Solomon said, tightening his hold on her, "but He used you to guide her to the place where she could find it."

"I'm glad I could do it."

Solomon sighed, then said softly, "One of the million things that I adore about you, sweetheart, is the lovingkindness and compassion you have for others."

"I'm glad you see me that way, darling," she said.

Solomon kissed her forehead, then the tip of her nose, then her lips.

Soon the Coopers were in their moonlit bedroom, under the covers. They held hands as Solomon prayed. All was quiet when the prayer was finished, and they lay there, savoring each other's presence.

After a while, Solomon said, "Honey, one concern I have about going west is that there might not be a good Bible-believing church where we decide to settle."

"I've thought about that ever since the subject of a move came up," Hannah said. "I was waiting for you to mention it."

"It isn't that we can't have family altar and study the Bible together, but we need a good church to go to. We need the preaching of a real man of God, and the fellowship of other Christians."

"I agree," Hannah said. "We must take this into serious consideration."

"Well, God won't lead us wrong, honey. We'll just trust Him to lead us concerning a church, too."

Daylight came with a brilliant sun rising in a cloudless sky. After Hannah had sent her husband off to the store and her three older children to school, she went to work washing clothes behind the house. Patty Ruth was "helping" her, with Ulysses lying close by on the back porch.

A fire burned beneath the cast iron pot, heating additional water, while Hannah scrubbed clothes on a washboard partially immersed in a large galvanized tub. It was Patty Ruth's job to stir the clothes with the end of a broom handle in a second galvanized tub of cool water used for rinsing.

When all the clothes were washed and rinsed, Patty Ruth carried the clothing to her mother, and Hannah hung them on the line.

As Hannah was pinning up the last piece, she heard Patty Ruth's excited voice say, "Grandma! Grandpa!"

Ben Singleton would turn seventy on his next birthday, and Esther would be sixty-nine. Ben had a thick head of white hair beneath his wide-brimmed hat, and a round, cheerful face to match his portly body. He had been an astute businessman in Kansas City, and had retired financially well off.

Hannah, his only child, had been the apple of his eye since the day she was born. When his grandchildren came along, each one found a special place in his heart.

Esther Singleton had been slender until she reached her mid-sixties, then had put on a little extra weight. Anyone could see that as a younger woman she had been a beauty. And she still was in a soft, faded way. She was tender of heart, and she adored Hannah, Solomon, and her grandchildren.

Hannah embraced them both, puzzled by the looks on their faces. "Mother...Daddy...you look upset. Is there something wrong?"

"We'd like to talk to you, honey," Ben said.

"Well, certainly. Let's go in the house."

It took Hannah only seconds to realize that word had reached her parents about them.

As they reached the back porch, Hannah said, "Patty Ruth, you stay out here and play with Ulysses while I talk to Grandma and Grandpa."

"All right, Mama."

Hannah led her parents into the kitchen. "Sit down here at the table, Mother...Daddy. Would you like some coffee or tea? I can start a fire in a jiffy, and—"

"That won't be necessary, Hannah," her father said, hanging his hat on a wall peg. "We just want to talk to you."

Hannah had hoped this conversation wouldn't come until—and *if*—it had to.

"Honey," Ben said, clearing his throat, "word is spreading through the church and around town that you and Solomon are probably going to go west."

"Well, Daddy, we have been discussing it more seriously than when we talked to you and Mother about it several months ago. Solomon has a big dream about beginning a new life. He—"

"*Solomon* has this dream."

"Well, yes, but—"

"Hannah," Esther said, "I want to know your feelings about this. Is Solomon trying to force this move on you?"

"No, of course not."

"Well, how do you feel about it? Is it your dream, too?" Ben asked.

Hannah swallowed hard. "I...I have some reservations about it, Daddy. I've discussed them with Sol, and he understands them. We're praying about it every day."

Ben Singleton's expression turned grim. "Hannah, somebody's got to talk some sense into that husband of yours. I told him before that the idea was foolish, and I thought maybe he was seeing it my way. There hasn't been any talk about it for a while. Now, we hear it's more than talk."

"No it isn't. It hasn't come to the planning stage, Daddy. We aren't going to make any plans until the Lord reveals His will about it."

"Sounds to me like Solomon's got plans, and he's just trying to slowly persuade you," Esther said. "Hannah, don't you let him talk you into it."

"Mother, listen to me," Hannah said, her voice taking on a

slight edge. "Solomon is not trying to persuade me. He's told me how he feels, but he has also said we won't make one move in that direction unless we get the unmistakable approval of the Lord. Please don't make me have to defend him to you. You, either, Daddy."

Ben sighed. "Hannah, you know your mother and I love Sol. We know he's a good husband and father. We just think maybe he's let this 'go west' fever get a grip on him, and it's downright foolishness. You and Solomon must consider the children. You shouldn't take them out there on the plains and subject them to blood-hungry, hostile Indians."

"That's right," Esther said. "Our grandchildren should not only be spared the danger of the Indians, but also the hardships that go with wagon train travel, let alone the hardships they will face in Oregon or California once you get there. It isn't right."

"Hannah," Ben said, "I've read a lot about those wagon trains. Children and adults alike come down with cholera and typhoid fever. The dust is horrible, and by July the heat is unbearable. Some people die just from the heat. Sometimes they run out of water and die of thirst. Do you know there are graves all along the Oregon Trail?"

"I know about them, Daddy. But there's a graveyard south of this town, too."

Ben passed a hand over his face. "And even if you don't consider the dangers, Hannah, it isn't fair to take our only daughter and our only grandchildren away from us."

"That's right," Esther said, her voice breaking. "Your father and I are getting up in years. We should have our daughter and grandchildren—yes, and our son-in-law—near us. Solomon isn't considering us at all. We—"

"Mother, Sol only wants to give his family the best life he possibly can. Sometimes there's sacrifice to do that. But how can you say Sol isn't considering you and Daddy at all? Didn't he say if we went, you would be welcome to come along?"

"Well, yes, but we're just too old to make a trip like that."

"Lots of people older than you make the trip. We've had many in the store in the past few days."

"It's not for us, honey," Ben said. "It isn't good for anybody, and we sure aren't going to do it."

"Daddy, there are many good things about a westward move. Think of the thrill it must be to have a part in settling this country somewhere beyond the Missouri River...all the way to the Pacific coast. I know the Homestead Act wouldn't interest you, but think of all the people who are making their living on their free one hundred and sixty acres. Such an opportunity is never possible on this side of the Missouri."

"Bully for them, but to me it wouldn't be worth it...making that long trip in a wagon with Indians breathing down my neck and fighting all the storms and the dust and possible sicknesses...and having to fight off Indians to keep them from killing my family and burning down my house. No thanks. Man's a fool who crosses the Missouri. Don't you or Sol either one ever bring it up to your mother or me about going with you. We're staying right here in Independence till we go home to glory."

Esther was sniffling now and wiping tears with a hanky she carried in her sleeve.

Hannah reached across the table and took hold of her hand. "Don't cry, Mother. Solomon and I don't mean to cause heartache over this situation. We just—"

"Mama," came Patty Ruth's tiny voice, "what's wrong with Grandma?"

Hannah turned to see her little girl at the back door, peering through the screen.

"She's just a little upset, honey," Hannah said.

"Can I come in and hug her?"

"Yes, of course."

With Ulysses under her arm, Patty Ruth dashed in and let

the screen door slam behind her. "Please don't cry, Grandma," she said, crawling up into Esther's lap.

Esther wrapped her arms around Patty Ruth and wept all the more.

Ben looked at Hannah with pleading eyes and said, "Honey, if you and Sol need money to expand your business or start another one so you'd be happy staying in Independence, just name the amount. Mother and I will give it to you."

Hannah patted his hand. "Thank you for such a generous offer, but money isn't the issue."

Esther held Patty Ruth tight and dabbed at her eyes. "Hannah," she said, with a quivering voice, "you've got to talk Sol out of this nonsense. It isn't right to take these grandchildren away from us."

On the verge of tears herself, Hannah said, "Mother, as I've told you, Sol and I won't make any kind of a move unless the Lord makes it clear that the move is His will. I understand why you and Daddy are upset, and I've tried to put myself in your place. I know you love us and want to be with us in your golden years. Please try to understand that we have our own lives to live, and God's will may separate us."

"I can't believe God would do that," Ben said.

Hannah's face took on a pinched look. "Daddy, God called Abraham out of his homeland and sent him into a different country. He had a purpose in doing so. The move was God's will, wasn't it?"

"Yes, but Solomon Cooper isn't Abraham."

"No, but he's a child of God as much as Abraham was."

Ben rose to his feet and took his hat off the peg. "Let's go, Mother. We did what we came to do."

Esther squeezed Patty Ruth once more and kissed her cheek. As she rose from the chair, still sniffling, Hannah went to her father and said, "Daddy, please don't be angry. Sol only wants to do what's right for his family."

Ben embraced her as he said, "I'm not angry, honey, just upset. The whole thing is foolish. We'll see you soon."

Hannah knew there was nothing more she could say. She stood on the porch with Patty Ruth as they climbed in their buggy and drove away.

Patty Ruth looked up at Hannah. "Mama, I don't like to see Grandma and Grandpa unhappy."

"I don't either, sweetheart. I don't either."

It was early afternoon when more wagons rolled into Independence to form another wagon train. Cooper's General Store was a beehive of activity.

Solomon was adding up a large number of items at the counter next to Randy, who was taking care of his own customers. Solomon looked up at the man and his wife who were buying such a large amount of food and supplies.

"So where are you folks from?" he asked.

"Springfield, Illinois," the man replied.

"Oh. Abraham Lincoln territory."

"Yes, sir, but I never had the privilege of meeting him."

"Well, where you folks headed?"

"Oregon."

"Going to homestead up there?"

"Sure are. Amy and I are really excited about it."

"I can imagine. My wife, Hannah, and I have—"

"Soldiers are comin'!" came the voice of a teenage boy at the front door.

The store was packed with people, but all attention went to the street. "Wonder why the army's coming in here?" one man asked.

"Probably just passin' through," another said, craning his neck to see out the door.

There was a large window directly behind the counter, and Solomon excused himself to the people from Illinois to take a look for himself. From what he could see, there were units of twelve cavalry riders, four abreast, interspersed at even intervals by covered wagons with "U.S. Army" emblazoned on their sides. The wagons were driven by uniformed men, but some of them were occupied by women and children.

People on the street were cheering the soldiers, waving and calling out to them. Solomon was about to turn back to his customers when he saw the faces of the two officers in the lead. One was Colonel Ross Bateman, who had been his commander in the Civil War. The other was Captain Darrell Crawley. He and Solomon had fought side by side in many a battle. The last time Solomon had heard about both men, they were stationed at Fort Benson, Illinois.

Solomon limped hurriedly to the door, working his way through the crowd on the boardwalk as he attempted to get the two officers' attention. They were too far past him; to call out would be useless.

Solomon stepped off the boardwalk and approached a trooper on horseback. "Hello!" Solomon said.

"Hello, yourself, sir!" came the friendly reply.

"My name's Cooper. Solomon Cooper. I own the general store right here."

"Yes, sir?"

"I was a captain in the Union Army in the War. I fought under Colonel Bateman, and alongside Captain Crawley. I just happened to see them as they were passing by. I know you're from Fort Benson, Illinois. Where are you going?"

"We're on our way to Fort Bridger, Wyoming, sir," the trooper said. "Colonel Bateman has been commissioned as commandant of the fort. He's taking his entire Fort Benson regiment with him. Three hundred and sixty-seven men, along with the wives and children of all our officers."

"That include Mrs. Bateman?"

"Yes, sir. She's in the first wagon up ahead. And, by the way, sir, it is *Major* Crawley now."

"Oh! I only got a glimpse of him. Didn't see the insignia on his uniform. Well, good for him! Does Colonel Bateman plan to halt the column, or are you going to keep moving?"

"We've been moving steadily, except at night, since we left Fort Benson. We're going to stay just outside of Independence for a couple of days and let everybody rest, including the animals."

"Good!" Solomon said, his limp becoming more pronounced as he tried to keep up with the trooper. "Would you do me a favor?"

"Sure."

"When you haul up out there at the edge of town, would you remind Colonel Bateman and Captain—I mean, Major Crawley that I am proprietor of Cooper's General Store, and ask them to please come see me?"

"Will do, sir."

"Thank you."

"My pleasure."

Solomon returned to his customers and steady sales. While they worked side by side, Solomon told Randy some of his experiences with Colonel Bateman and Major Crawley in the War.

Some two hours after the regiment had passed through town, Solomon was waiting on a family from Wisconsin when he looked up to see Colonel and Mrs. Ross Bateman come through the door, followed by Major and Mrs. Darrell Crawley.

"Hello!" Solomon said. "Wonderful to see you! Let me take care of these customers and I'll be with you in a jiffy!"

Bateman raised a palm. "Take your time, Sol. We'll just browse around."

Ten minutes later, Solomon joined his old friends and fellow soldiers.

Early in the Civil War, Hannah, Chris, and Mary Beth had left Independence to live at three different forts with Solomon, who served under Colonel Bateman the entire time. They were at Fort Detrick, Maryland, then were transferred to Fort Bedford, Pennsylvania, where B. J. was born. The last year of the War, they were at Fort Benson, Illinois. When the War was over, and the Coopers returned home, Hannah was expecting their fourth child.

Now Solomon gripped Crawley's shoulder and said, "Hey, Darrell! Congratulations on making major!"

"Thank you...you'd have been a general by now if you'd stayed in the army, you know."

Solomon snorted. "You know better than that!"

Sylvia Bateman said, "Sol, we never did know whether Hannah had a boy or a girl when you left Fort Benson."

Solomon's grin widened as he said, "A girl...Patty Ruth. Hard to believe she's five years old now. And let me tell you, she's a pistol!"

Christel Crawley laughed. "Well, when do we get to meet her and see Hannah and the other children?"

"I imagine the kids have grown a lot since we saw them last," put in the colonel.

"You won't know them, sir," Solomon said. "Hannah and I can bring the children to your camp tonight, if that's all right."

"Of course it is."

"Oh, yes, we must see them!" Sylvia said.

Solomon flashed her a smile and said, "Believe me, ma'am, Hannah would be very disappointed if she didn't get to see all four of you!"

"We'll look forward to it," Colonel Bateman said, stepping to one side to let two women in hoop skirts squeeze past.

Solomon glanced toward Randy Chase to make sure he was still keeping up with the customers, then turned back to the colonel. "The trooper I talked to told me you're heading to

Fort Bridger, Wyoming, to become its commandant."

"That's right." Bateman nodded and brushed a hand over his handlebar mustache.

"How did the appointment come about?"

"Well, the present commandant, Colonel George Sanford, is retiring. There have been some serious Indian problems in that part of Wyoming Territory of late—Cheyenne, Sioux, Arapaho, and Blackfoot. So the big brass in Washington planted the commission on me and told me to take my entire regiment to beef up the number of troops at the fort. They're building more barracks and officers' quarters to accommodate us right now."

"Sounds like you'll be busy."

"You're right about that. Only I'd rather fight Rebels than Indians any day. Men can usually figure out what Rebels are going to do, but Indians...now they're something else."

"That's what I hear," Solomon said with a chuckle.

The old friends chatted for a few more minutes, then the officers and their wives left, saying they would see the Coopers at the camp that evening.

CHAPTER SEVEN

S everal campfires winked against the darkness as Solomon
and Hannah approached the army camp. Uniformed
men milled about, and they could hear the sound of
women's and children's voices.

"Oh, Sol, I'm so excited!" Hannah said. "It's been so long
since I've seen them!"

"Well, none of them have changed much. The colonel's
hair is completely silver now. But it was close to that when we
left Fort Benson. Mrs. Bateman has either found some marvelous make-up, or she just hasn't aged. Christel's only a year
older than you, and like you she still looks the same."

"I guess you haven't noticed the crow's-feet at the corners
of my eyes."

"Guess I haven't."

"Well, just keep it that way, okay?"

Solomon chuckled and gave her a quick hug as they
entered the camp.

Two soldiers, standing beside a wagon, looked at the
Coopers with curiosity. Solomon stepped close and said,
"Excuse me, gentlemen. We're looking for Colonel and Mrs.
Bateman, and Major and Mrs. Crawley. They're expecting us.
Where might we find them?"

The shorter soldier pointed in the direction of a wagon on

the other side of a large fire. "Right over there, sir. The wagon with the white wheels."

Hannah's heart was throbbing with anticipation as she held onto her husband's arm and walked toward the designated wagon.

Christel Crawley spotted the Coopers first and sprang out of her chair, shouting, "Hannah!"

The others were quickly on their feet as Christel and Hannah met in a warm embrace.

Sylvia crowded in, playfully saying, "My turn, Christel!"

When the hugging was done and the two officers had greeted Hannah, Colonel Bateman looked around. "Where are the children?"

"Well," Hannah said, "we left them home so we could use them as bait for tomorrow night."

"Pardon me?"

Hannah's laugh tinkled in the chill night air. "Well, it's our understanding that you'll not be pulling out until day after tomorrow. Is that correct?"

"Correct," the colonel said with a nod.

"Then Solomon and I would like to extend a formal invitation to Colonel and Mrs. Bateman, and Major and Mrs. Crawley to attend dinner at our humble home tomorrow evening."

"Oh, we'd love it!" Christel said. "Wouldn't we, Sylvia?"

"Consider the invitation accepted," Sylvia replied.

Bateman raised his eyebrows in mock surprise at the women. "Without checking with your husbands?"

"We both know how well our husbands liked Hannah's cooking in the past," Christel said. "Certainly it can't be anything but just as good now!"

Hannah smiled her pleasure and said, "We figured if you hesitated to accept the invitation, we'd tell you that unless you came for dinner tomorrow night, you wouldn't get to see the children!"

Bateman laughed. "Well, even if your cooking was horrible, Hannah, I'd come and eat it just to see those three younguns again...and to meet the little one."

"Good," Hannah said. Then, putting on her best English accent, she said, "Dinnah will be suhved at seven."

Everybody laughed, remembering what good times they'd had together around Hannah's table.

The Coopers spent a few more minutes talking with their old friends, then Solomon gave directions on how to find the farm and offered to come in the family wagon and pick them up. The colonel refused, saying they would come in an army wagon, and they would be there promptly at fifteen minutes before seven.

At half past six the next evening, darkness was settling over the land when Colonel Bateman and Major Crawley helped their wives into the army wagon. The air was cool, as it had been for the past few nights.

The women rode on the second seat while Darrell Crawley held the reins and Ross Bateman sat beside him.

The moon was beginning to cast its silvery spell over the hills, creating shadows in the low spots. When the wagon turned off Main Street and headed north, Sylvia said, "I wonder if Hannah has her house fixed up as darling as she kept their quarters at the forts."

"I would imagine so," Christel said. "She has such a way of tastefully putting things together."

When the wagon turned off the road into the Cooper yard, the four were greeted with bright lanterns on posts that illuminated the front of the white two-story house.

"Just as I figured," Christel said. "You can see Hannah's personality all over it."

The house had a wide porch across the front and on one side, forming an L. Bright potted plants adorned the porch railing, and comfortable red-and-white gingham padded chairs looked inviting.

The black shutters contrasted with the soft yellow glow of lanterns from inside that flowed through snow-white lace curtains.

"Beautiful, isn't it?" Darrell said, pulling the wagon to a halt in front of the porch.

The front door swung open, and the entire Cooper family came out on the porch, the children preceding their parents. Patty Ruth stayed close to her mother, holding Ulysses in the crook of her arm.

Chris and Mary Beth remembered their guests, and B. J. smiled as the visitors marveled at how all three had grown so much in the past five years.

Then all attention was turned to the little redhead looking on with big blue eyes.

"So this is Patty Ruth!" Colonel Bateman said, bending low and placing his hands on his thighs. "My, aren't you a pretty little thing!" The others made over Patty Ruth, commenting on how much she resembled her mother and sister.

Patty Ruth smiled, curtsied politely, and thanked them.

"My, what a sweet child!" Sylvia Bateman said, while the others nodded in agreement.

Unnoticed by the adults, Chris and B. J. exchanged glances, as if to say Mrs. Bateman's comment about Patty Ruth was absurd. The little redhead saw them and stuck out her tongue.

Inside, the guests looked around appreciatively at the decorations and furnishings. The parlor was so warm and cozy with a cheerful fire reflected in the polished hardwood floors.

While the men talked to Solomon and the women chatted animatedly with Hannah, Patty Ruth edged closer to her father.

When she reached his side, she looked up at the two army officers and smiled.

The conversation broke off and Colonel Bateman looked down. "Hello, Patty Ruth. My, that's some bear you have there. Does it have a name?"

"Yes, sir. He's not an it, he's a he. His name is Ulysses."

Bateman's head bobbed. "Ulysses?"

"Yes, sir."

"Did you hear that, Major Crawley?"

"Yes, sir." The major bent down to Patty Ruth's height and said, "Did you name him, honey?"

"Sort of. My papa helped me. He's named after President Ulysses S. Grant, who was the gen'ral my papa fighted for in the Cibil War."

"That's wonderful, honey," Bateman said. "Major Crawley and I fought for General Grant, too."

"Oh," she said, adjusting Ulysses in her arm. "Did you and Major Crawley help Papa when he won the Cibil War?"

Solomon's face turned pink. "Honey, Papa didn't win the War."

"I heard B. J. tell Tommy Nelson that you won the Cibil War almos' all by yourself."

Everyone was in on the conversation now. Solomon sent a sharp glance at his second son, who gave him a blank look and shrugged his shoulders.

"Dinner's ready," Hannah said, eager to change the subject. "Let's eat."

The guests laughed and followed the family to the dining room.

B. J. took the opportunity to lean close to his little sister and whisper, "Blabbermouth!"

Patty Ruth gave him an innocent look. "I jis' tol' 'em what you tol' Tommy."

It was Mary Beth's job to show the guests where they would

sit at the big dining table. When everyone was seated, Solomon led in thanking the Lord for His bounties, and the meal began.

Hannah had prepared roast beef, succulent and tender, with thick gravy, golden-brown roasted potatoes, and green peas and baby onions in a creamy white sauce. There was applesauce with cinnamon and yeasty homemade dinner rolls with freshly churned butter. There was steaming hot coffee for the adults, and milk for the children. And for dessert, they would all enjoy her scrumptious pies, both cherry and apple.

Everyone was eating with gusto when Colonel Bateman looked across the table and said, "So, tell me, Sol, how's the store doing?"

"Very well, sir. Especially right now. It's wagon train season. You saw a little of what it's like in the store, although it had slowed some by the time you came in."

"Lots of people moving west, eh?"

"Yes, sir." Solomon glanced at Hannah.

"We're maybe gonna go out west, too," Patty Ruth blurted.

The guests looked at her, then at Solomon and Hannah. Solomon shifted uneasily on his chair.

"That so?" Bateman asked.

Solomon glanced at Hannah again. "Well, we've been talking some about it. Kind of caught the 'go west' fever. The lure of the frontier is strong."

Hannah laughed, "The lure is stronger for Sol than it is for me. But, then, I guess it's that way with all husbands."

"If I might speak, here," Christopher said, "I sure would like to go west."

"Me, too," B. J. said.

Mary Beth and Patty Ruth just looked at their mother without speaking.

"What part of the West are you considering, Sol?" Bateman asked.

"We've talked about California, but then we agreed that if

we do it, maybe Oregon would be better. We could make a good living up there on a hundred and sixty acres of free land."

"You just want to farm, eh?" Crawley asked.

"Well, they tell me Oregon is a virtual paradise. Beautiful valleys of rich black soil, plenty of water, and heavy with timber. One old wagon master who came through here last year told me that in Oregon the cattle feed on such thick green grass that they run around fat and already cooked, with knives and forks sticking out of them so you can cut off a slice whenever you're hungry."

Patty Ruth giggled. "O Papa, that's silly!"

There was a round of laughter, then Bateman said, "Sol, are you wanting to get out of the general store business? I mean, you think you'd like farming better?"

"I love the general store business, but Hannah and I have talked farming because of the Homestead Act and all that free land. I don't know how the business would do out there. Maybe in a few more years, when the population grows, we could get back into it."

"Would you be interested in going west and bypassing the free land in order to do a powerful lot of business with a general store?"

Hannah looked at Bateman, then at her husband. Solomon quickly swallowed a mouthful of potatoes. "Would you run that by me once more, sir?"

Bateman smiled, winked at Sylvia, and said, "Sure. You can go west right now and go into the general store business. And believe me, you can do well."

"You're not talking about Oregon."

"No. Your trip would be much shorter. I'm talking about Fort Bridger."

"I don't understand, Colonel. Are you talking about a sutler's store?"

"No, Sol. You see, a town is forming outside the walls of

the fort. They're calling it Fort Bridger after the name of the fort. At present, there's a sutler's store in the fort, and that's where the townspeople are doing their trading. But the way the town is growing, they need a general store. You could make a good living there."

Hannah saw a light come into her husband's eyes. The others saw it, too.

Bateman took a sip of coffee, then said, "Let me explain what I mean by a 'good living.'"

"Please do," Hannah said. "Certainly the town is quite small."

"Yes, it is, Hannah. But it's growing fast. And think of this. All the wagon trains going either to California or Oregon pass through Fort Bridger."

"That's right, Mama...Papa..." Mary Beth said. "Miss Powers has been teaching us about the Oregon and California Trails at school."

"Mr. Barrick has too!" Chris said, his voice full of enthusiasm. "And he says there's every indication that people will be moving west for many years to come."

"That's right, Chris," Bateman said, then turned to Sol. "While the town is growing, Sol, you'd be doing right well, just with the wagon trains coming through. I realize the wagon train business is seasonal, but you can make enough on your sales in the spring and summer months to easily carry you through the fall and winter."

Solomon grinned. "You're right about that, sir. I can make it here just by what happens in wagon train season."

"Ah, but there's more," Bateman said, his smile getting wider. "I happen to know that the man who runs the sutler's store in the fort is wanting to get out of the business. If you come in there and open up a general store for the town, he'll gladly close down the sutler's store. That would give you all the army business, too."

Solomon looked at Hannah, who smiled back weakly.

Chris and B. J. exchanged glances, the light of adventure shining in their eyes.

Mary Beth knew that what the colonel was saying to her father was making the desire to go west even stronger within him. She couldn't help but think of her grandparents...and Belinda. How could she ever tell them good-bye?

"There's more, yet," Bateman said. "Wells Fargo is making plans at this very moment to put a stage stop in the town. That would certainly bring in more business for your general store. A hotel is being built right now, along with a café, and a tonsorial parlor. A family by the name of Williams from St. Joseph, Missouri, has seen the opportunity and will operate all three."

"Sounds like a good set-up, Sol," Darrell Crawley said. "You'd get business from the stage riders, no doubt, and from the people who stay in the hotel."

"Right," Bateman said. "And as the town grows, the store would do even more business. The Coopers would make a better living in Fort Bridger than they would at farming a homestead."

Hannah could tell by the look in her husband's eyes that Bateman's words were appealing. To help keep things on an even keel, she said, "What about the Indian problem, Colonel? You're taking your entire regiment out there to strengthen the fort. Are the Indians posing a threat to all this?"

"Not to the town, Hannah. It's the settlers in the area and the wagon trains that come through who are in danger of Indian attack. That's exactly why we're beefing up our troops at the fort. We're going to keep those hostiles in line. Though the fort has patrols out all day long every day, there are always plenty of troops at the fort to keep any hostiles from coming against the town."

"May I ask, Colonel Bateman," Mary Beth said, "if there are some friendly Indians who live close by the fort?"

"Yes, honey. The Shoshones are quite friendly. They are avowed enemies of the Cheyenne, Sioux, Arapaho, and Blackfoot. The Shoshones come in and out of the town all the time. In fact, if you decide to run the store there, Sol, they'll give you plenty of business, too. Of course, you'll have to trade goods for goods with them, but they make some pretty nice jewelry and pottery, which you can turn around and sell, and make a profit from it."

Chris grinned at Mary Beth. "Wouldn't it be neat if we could make friends with some Shoshone Indian kids?"

Patty Ruth twisted her mouth around for a few seconds, then said, "Papa, would the Sho— Sho— uh...them kind of In'ians take our scalps?"

"No, honey. Like Colonel Bateman said, they are friendly to white people. They don't take scalps."

As silence descended on the table, Hannah said, "Colonel..."

"Yes, Hannah?"

"There's something else Sol and I have discussed. We've agreed that we wouldn't move anywhere unless there was a good Bible-believing church there. What's the church situation in Fort Bridger?"

Colonel Bateman glanced at Solomon, then gave his attention to Hannah. "It's interesting you should say this. We just happen to have Reverend Andrew Kelly and his new bride, Rebecca, in one of our wagons. I can guarantee you, he believes the Bible. He's been preaching some of it to me on this trip."

"Good for him," Solomon said.

"Tell you what, Sol, he's almost as good at it as you," the colonel said.

Solomon grinned and glanced at Hannah. She seemed more relaxed, having heard about Reverend Kelly.

"Here's the situation," Bateman said. "Right now, there's an elderly retired preacher holding services in the town hall, which was built just recently. The services are for both civilians and military. The townspeople and the military people who attend the services are all aware that Reverend Kelly is coming. Kelly, I understand, will actually organize a church and be its pastor. He's a young man. Twenty-seven, I believe. Didn't Rebecca tell you, Sylvia, that she's twenty-two?"

"Yes. They got married about six months ago. And she told me that Andy—as she calls him—is very eager to get to Fort Bridger and preach the gospel."

"This is sounding better all the time," Solomon said. "Colonel, could we meet the Kellys? We'd like to talk to them."

"No problem. I decided just this afternoon that we'd stay another day before pulling out. Already announced it to everybody in the column. You can come to the camp and meet them anytime tomorrow."

"Good! We'll do that!"

During the rest of the meal, the women exchanged stories about what had happened since the Coopers had left Fort Benson, and the men talked about the War and some of the men Solomon had known.

When both pies had been devoured, the adults moved to the parlor, and the Cooper children—having previously volunteered—did the dishes.

As the Batemans and Crawleys were preparing to leave, Darrell Crawley laid a hand on Solomon's shoulder. "Sol, if the words of an old friend have some import, you and Hannah give some real serious thought to coming to Fort Bridger. We'd love to have you there."

Solomon grinned. "Thanks, ol' friend."

"You'll need to make up your minds pretty soon, Sol," the colonel said. "As you know, the last wagon trains heading that way will leave in a month."

"Yes, sir. Hannah and I are aware of that. You've given us a lot to think about tonight. We'll discuss it and pray about it."

After the Batemans and Crawleys had driven away and Solomon had closed the door, Chris and B. J. cornered him.

"Papa," Chris said, his eyes sparkling, "can we go to Fort Bridger? Boy, it sure would be neat to be around all those soldiers!"

"I can't say for sure yet, son. Like I told Colonel Bateman, we'll pray about it."

"I want to see those friendly Indians!" B. J. said. "I've never seen an Indian before."

"I wanna see 'em, too!" Patty Ruth piped up. "Long as they don' take my scalp!"

Everybody laughed except Mary Beth. Hannah laid a hand on her shoulder and looked into her eyes. "Honey, it's bothering you, thinking about leaving your friends, isn't it? Especially Belinda."

Mary Beth put her arms around her mother and laid her head on her shoulder. "Yes. And Grandma and Grandpa, too."

"I know how you feel, sweetie. I have my best friend, Lucinda. And all of us have Grandma and Grandpa. If the Lord wants us to move to Fort Bridger, He'll give us the grace to leave those we love here in Independence."

Mary Beth leaned back to look into her mother's eyes. "Mama…"

"What, honey?"

"Do you feel better about us going to Fort Bridger than you did about Oregon?"

All the other Cooper ears waited to hear her reply.

"Yes…yes, I do. In fact, the thought of living in the town next to the fort and having our store there sounds real good."

CHAPTER EIGHT

I t was midmorning when Hannah and her youngest daughter entered the store. Randy Chase glanced up and greeted
them, and Solomon nodded as he continued what he was
doing.

"You sure you can get away, Solomon?" Hannah asked.
"Looks awfully busy."

"Randy says he'll handle it by himself. I told him we
wouldn't be gone too long."

Randy chuckled and said, "I can get more done with him
out of the way, Mrs. Cooper."

The customers grinned when Solomon quipped, "Just
don't you forget who's boss around here, pal!"

As Randy was stuffing goods into a box he looked down
at Patty Ruth. "You wouldn't fire me, would you?" he asked.

"I wouldn't fire you, Randy," Patty Ruth said with a giggle.
"I ain't the boss, here. Ulysses is!" As she spoke, she held up the
bear toward his face.

This time the customers laughed out loud.

The Coopers left Patty Ruth with Randy and moved
quickly along the boardwalk.

"Did you tell Randy what we're doing?" Hannah asked.

"No details. Only that we were going out to the army
camp at the edge of town to talk to some people."

"You think he suspects anything?"

"Sure. Too many people in town already know what we're considering. One thing is for sure: If we sell the store, we won't sell to anyone who won't agree to let Randy keep his job."

"Solomon...we really need to talk to Pastor Chase. At least let him hear it straight from us that we may leave."

"I'll go see him tonight."

"Another thing...we didn't think to ask about a school in Fort Bridger. If there's no school, I'll have to teach the children."

"Let's ask that when we get to the camp."

When they reached the army camp, they found Colonel Bateman, who took them to the Kellys and introduced them.

The Coopers and the Kellys warmed to each other instantly. The Kellys love for Jesus was quite apparent as they talked.

They explained the plans for a church in Fort Bridger. Andy Kelly had graduated from seminary at the age of twenty-one and had been pastoring a church in Cincinnati, Ohio, since that time. He and Rebecca had married the previous October, and though things were going well in the church, they both were feeling a "stirring in the nest," knowing that God was preparing them for a move.

Through a relative of a close friend, Andy was approached about establishing a church in Fort Bridger. He corresponded with the elderly retired preacher who was holding services there, and after much prayer and deliberation, an agreement was made that Kelly and his bride would come to Fort Bridger.

"Well, this all sounds good to me," Solomon said. "Do you mind if we ask you some doctrinal questions?"

When the questions had been asked and answered, the Coopers were satisfied they had a real man of God with spiritual backbone, a tremendous grasp of the Scriptures, and the vision to do a great work for God in the growing town of Fort Bridger.

Kelly smiled and said, "So, when will you be coming to Fort Bridger, folks?"

"Well, we haven't made a decision yet," Solomon said. "We're still praying about it."

"It took a lot of prayer for us to make the decision, Mr. Cooper," Rebecca Kelly said.

"Tell you what," Solomon said, "talking with you two has helped a lot. At least we know there's going to be a church in Fort Bridger if the Lord leads us there. You see, up until last night, we had thought of going either to California or Oregon. But when Colonel Bateman started telling us about Fort Bridger, Hannah and I liked what we were hearing. Now that we've talked to you, we like it even better."

Solomon looked at Hannah as he spoke. He was relieved when she nodded in agreement.

"Well, I've got to get back to the store," Solomon said.

"Would you have time to pray with us?" Kelly asked.

"Sure. We have time for that," Solomon said.

The young preacher led in prayer, earnestly asking God to guide the Coopers every step of the way. When Kelly had finished, Solomon shook his hand and Hannah embraced Rebecca.

"One other thing," Solomon said. "What do you know about the school situation in the town?"

"Well, since Rebecca and I don't have any children yet, we haven't asked about it, but according to what we've picked up by listening to the officers' wives and children, there's a school there. It has one teacher for all twelve grades. I'm sure as the town and the fort increase in size, they'll add more teachers."

At supper that evening, Solomon told the children about talking with the Kellys, and how much he and their mother liked the young couple.

"So have you made a decision yet?" Chris asked.

"Not yet, son. But I think it's time we hear from each of you. Although the final decision lies with your mother and me, I'd like to hear what each of you thinks about this Fort Bridger situation."

Mary Beth spoke first. "I think I've seen a change in Mama's attitude about going west since we talked to Colonel Bateman last night. Is that right, Mama?"

"Yes, honey. I like the Fort Bridger idea a whole lot better than striking out for Oregon or California."

"Then if you like it better, so do I, Mama."

"But what about leaving Belinda? And Miss Powers? And Grandma and Grandpa?"

Mary Beth spoke without hesitation. "I've prayed about this a lot, myself. And I feel that if you and Papa are sure in your hearts that we should go to Fort Bridger, it's because the Lord is leading you. Though it will be very hard to say good-bye to Belinda, and Miss Powers, and all my friends at school and at church, the Lord will give me the grace to do it. The hardest to leave, of course, will be Grandma and Grandpa."

"Bless your heart, sweetie," Hannah said. "Papa and I deeply appreciate your attitude."

"Maybe Grandma and Grandpa would go with us, since we'd be going to Fort Bridger instead of Oregon," B. J. said.

"I'm afraid not," Hannah told him. "Independence is their home, and older people have a hard time making changes. I realize that we've seen people even older than them in the wagon trains, but I know my parents. Mother might consider it if Daddy showed an inclination in that direction, but he won't."

"I'll say this much," Solomon said, "we'll sure offer to take them along with us. At least let them know we love them and want them to go with us."

"Since you want to hear what us kids feel," Chris said, "I want to go to Fort Bridger."

"Me, too!" B. J. said.

All eyes went to Patty Ruth. She was looking down at Biggie, who sat beside her chair. Then she looked up and said, "As long as Ulysses and Biggie can go to Fort Bridger with us, I want to go."

Solomon smiled at Hannah. "Well, sweetheart, it looks like the young ones in this family are in agreement that we go to Fort Bridger."

"Does that mean we'll go?" Chris asked.

"Not for sure, son," Solomon said. "Your mother and I have to talk about it some more. But it helps to know what you children think about it."

When supper was finished, Solomon rose from his chair and said, "Well, I've got to go see the preacher and let him know where we are on this whole thing. It's not right that he should hear only rumors."

Chris shoved his chair back. "Can I go with you, Papa?"

"Not this time, son. It's best that I talk to Pastor Chase alone."

Suddenly Biggie began to bark and headed for the front door.

"I guess we've got company," Solomon said. "I'll see who it is."

When he opened the door, Pastor Chase was just raising his hand to knock.

"Hello, Pastor. Come in. I was about to saddle up Nipper and come see you."

"Oh? Hello, Hannah...children. Guess I saved you the trip, Sol," Chase said with a chuckle. "What did you want to see me about?"

"I wanted to fill you in on what you may have been hearing about the Coopers."

"That's exactly why I'm here. Rumors have been flying for the past few days, and I wanted to see how much truth there is to them."

Mary Beth spoke up. "Papa, Mama, we'll do the dishes and clean up the kitchen. You go ahead and talk to Pastor."

Solomon let Hannah precede him and then ushered the pastor into the parlor. As soon as they took their seats, Solomon explained that they had not talked to Chase about it yet because it wasn't definite. They planned to tell him as soon as they were sure.

When the whole plan had been laid before the pastor, he told them he hated to lose them from the church, but he understood their desire to be a part of the growing frontier. After praying with them about it, he went to the kitchen and told the children goodnight, then left.

Later that night, as Solomon closed the bedroom door, Hannah put her arms around him, and said, "Darling, for the past twenty-four hours I've been getting peace in my heart about going to Fort Bridger. I'm not looking forward to telling Mother and Daddy, but I really think the Lord sent Colonel Bateman through here so that we could learn about it and He could lead us in that direction."

Solomon's eyes lit up. "Honey, do you really mean it? I...I mean, you're not just saying this because you know my big dream has been to go west?"

Hannah looked him square in the eye and said, "No, I'm not just saying it because I know your big dream has been to go west. It's what I feel the Lord would have us do, Sol. Understand?"

He kissed her several times and hugged her hard, and said, "Hallelujah! Fort Bridger, here we come!"

There was a sudden burst of laughter in the corridor. Solomon let go of Hannah and jerked open the door. All four of the Cooper children tumbled in, laughing and jumping up and down. In one voice they shouted, "Hallelujah! Fort Bridger, here we come!"

When the excitement had died down a bit, the children were ordered back to bed. Alone once more, Solomon and Hannah knelt beside their bed and asked God to guide their every step, and to provide buyers for the store and the farm in His own way and in His own time.

At breakfast the next morning, three of the children talked excitedly about the new Cooper family venture.

Mary Beth was quieter. Though she was all for the move, she still was having a hard time about telling certain people good-bye.

Hannah understood. She reached across the table and squeezed Mary Beth's wrist. "None of us are looking forward to the day of parting with our friends and loved ones, Mary Beth, but the Lord will see us through it."

Patty Ruth waggled her head and said, "How about *you*, Chris? Are you really gonna be able to tear yourself away from Lula Mae?"

"I can handle it, little sister," Chris said with a scowl.

Patty Ruth giggled. "Well, how about—"

"Patty Ruth, that's enough," Hannah said. She sighed and looked at Sol. "I want to get the chore of telling Mother and Daddy over with, Sol. Will you stop by their house on your way to the store this morning and invite them for supper tonight?"

"All right. And don't let it ruin your whole day, sweetheart. The rest of us will be here with you. And for that matter, I'll be the one to tell them, okay?"

"You really shouldn't have to be the one to do it. They're my parents."

"And I'm your husband. Let me take care of it. We'll eat supper, then I'll break it to them, along with the invitation to go with us. I'll go to the camp as soon as Randy and I open the store. Colonel Bateman told me they'd pull out about ten this morning. I'll let him know we're coming to Fort Bridger and give him enough money to buy a piece of land to build the store on and pay for labor and materials to have the store built. From what he said, they've got construction people there already."

Hannah set down her coffee cup. "But won't you have to draw him a sketch of how we want the store laid out?"

Solomon looked a bit sheepish. "I…ah…already drew one up."

"Oh, you did, eh?"

"Yes'm."

"And just when did you do that?"

"Yesterday. During the slow times."

"Pretty sure of yourself, weren't you?"

"Well, not exactly. Just…ah…thinking ahead in case it went this way."

Patty Ruth giggled. "Papa's smart, isn't he, Mama?"

"Yes, honey, that he is. Anyway, Sol, dear, are we going to have the same type of store we have now?"

"Not exactly. Since we plan on doing more business, I think we should have more square footage. And instead of a false-fronted building, we'll build a two-story one. We'll have living quarters on the second floor and stay there until our house gets built. We'll buy the land for that when we get there."

Hannah smiled. "You really have it all planned out."

"Just doing my job, honey."

"So, how soon will we put a 'For Sale' sign on the farm and the store?"

"Today. I'll paint them during the slow times."

Breakfast was finished, and just as prayer and Bible reading time ended, Biggie started to bark.

"I'll see who it is, Papa," Chris said, shoving back his chair.

Solomon rose to his feet. "I have to get going. You kids study hard in school today."

Chris's voice came from the front of the house, "Papa! Mr. Wilson's here to see you."

"Good morning, Ray. To what do we owe this early morning visit?"

"Word is that it's pretty definite you folks will be heading west before too long. Betty and I have changed our minds about going, and we know if you go, the store will be up for sale. Betty and I agreed I should catch you right away and tell you we'd like to buy the store. I'm sure we can agree on a price."

Solomon looked at Hannah, their expressions showing that they were thinking the same thing: God was already putting his seal of approval on their decision.

"Yes, we've decided to go, Ray," Solomon said. "And I'm sure we can get together on the price. But there's one stipulation."

"And what is that?"

"The new owner must agree to let Randy Chase keep his job."

Wilson laughed. "No problem there. I was planning on doing that very thing if Randy wanted to stay on."

Hannah's voice had a lilt in it as she said, "This is how it works when the Lord is in it, Sol!"

Solomon nodded. "Tell you what, Ray, I've got to go to the army camp outside of town right now, but I'll come over to your shop later this morning and we can talk price and details."

Solomon stopped at the Singletons and invited them to supper, then stopped at the store and left a note for Randy Chase, telling him to open the store at eight o'clock as usual. He would be back after he ran some errands.

When Solomon arrived at the camp, the soldiers were busily preparing to move out. He saw Colonel Bateman talking to a couple of captains who moved away as Solomon drew near. Bateman smiled a greeting.

"Good morning, Colonel," Solomon said. "Do you have a minute?"

"Why certainly."

"I just wanted to tell you that we've decided to take your advice and open up a general store in Fort Bridger."

"Great! Now what can I do to help?"

"You mentioned that it wouldn't be a problem to hire a construction outfit to build the store before we get there."

"I'm sure I can get it done for you."

"All right. I've brought enough money to pay for it all. And I've made a sketch of what I want built. I'll want the store on the town's main street, of course."

"Certainly. I've been there twice, Sol. I already know the layout. I'll get you a choice spot."

"Fine, sir. I appreciate your help."

"My pleasure. I sure hope you'll be able to sell the store and the farm quickly."

"Tell you what. The store is as good as sold already. The man who owns the saddle shop next door to the store wants to buy it."

"That's a stroke of good luck, I'd say."

"Not luck, Colonel. It's the hand of my God."

Bateman's face stiffened slightly. "Oh. Yes, of course. So you're...ah...planning to pull out in one of the last wagon trains of the season, I take it?"

"Yes, sir. Even if the farm hasn't sold, we'll go. I'll get someone to sell the farm for me. Of course, the way the Lord's working, he'll probably send me a buyer right away!"

"So you'll leave here the latter part of May?"

"Yes, sir."

"That means I can expect you about the second or third week of August. Shouldn't take you more than fourteen or fifteen weeks. I'm sure the store will be ready by then."

They shook hands on it, and Solomon headed back to town. As he turned onto Main Street, he told himself he must take food and supplies to stock the store. He would order from the Kansas City people in the future, but he wanted to be sure to have plenty of stock to open the new store.

He'd have to buy four wagons besides the one for his family, plus oxen to pull them. Those people going to Oregon or California, Solomon knew, would use six oxen per wagon to get over the mountains, but since South Pass in central Wyoming was the only high spot they would have to travel, he would only have to put four oxen to a wagon.

When he reached the town's business district, he stopped at the telegraph office and ordered food and goods to fill four wagons from his supplier in Chicago. The shipments came by rail and would arrive in Independence within two to three weeks.

Next Solomon stopped at the office of the agent who booked the wagon trains. He booked passage on the last train of the season, scheduled to leave May 25. Ezra Comstock was the wagon master. Ezra had been leading wagon trains west for many years and had been in the store to buy supplies before every trip. He was a widower in his late fifties, a fine Christian, and Solomon knew his family would enjoy traveling with Ezra.

Solomon then hurried to the stockyards and reserved twenty head of oxen and five wagons, which he would pay for and pick up on May 24.

On his way to talk with Ray Wilson, he saw another wagon train forming in the Square. He stopped at the store and found Randy working hard but not overloaded, and then went next door to the saddle shop.

Ray was at his workbench, making a fancy Mexican-style saddle with bridle to match.

"Hi, Ray. Have time to talk business?"

"Sure. Been expecting you."

It was nearly 10:30 when Randy Chase looked up with relief as Solomon entered the store. The place was packed with customers, many of whom were waiting patiently in line to purchase their goods.

As Sol threaded his way through the crowd, he looked around the store and realized that soon it wouldn't be his anymore. A wave of emotion rushed through him. He loved this store. It would be hard to walk away from it.

He forced his thoughts to Fort Bridger and the new life he and his family would have there.

The sun had disappeared below the horizon, leaving only brilliant orange clouds with purple edging, as Solomon limped up the road toward his farm. He noticed a buggy, and by the horse that was hitched to it, he knew that Lucinda Lennox had come to visit.

As he turned into the yard, he saw Chris and B. J. at the barn, doing their chores. Suddenly the front door opened, and Lucinda emerged with Hannah a step behind her. They had seen Solomon but didn't speak to him. Instead, they wrapped their arms around each other in a tight embrace.

When they let go of each other, there were tears on their cheeks, and Solomon could tell by the redness of their eyes that they had been weeping for some time.

"Hello, darling," Hannah finally said. Then to Lucinda:

"We'll spend as much time together as possible in the next four weeks."

"Yes," Lucinda said. "How about sewing together tomorrow afternoon?"

"Fine. I'll be there about two o'clock."

"Couldn't you come for lunch?"

"Well, yes, I could do that," Hannah said, wiping at her tears.

"All right. See you at noon. Hello Solomon."

Solomon moved close to Hannah as Lucinda climbed into the buggy and drove away.

"Did she learn by the grapevine, Hannah?"

"Yes. I told her that it might happen. But when she heard it was for sure, she came right over."

"That grapevine sure is speedy. Everybody in town and all around Independence must know by now that we're moving to Fort Bridger."

Hannah reached up and locked her wrists behind Solomon's neck. "I'm sure you're right, darling," she said with a smile. "The news moved so fast that we already have a buyer for the farm."

CHAPTER NINE

Hannah Marie Cooper, are you joshing me?"

"No! Isn't the Lord wonderful? When He decides to make a move…"

"Well tell me about it, honey! Who—?"

"Hyram and Florence! They came by about three hours ago. Said they heard we were moving to Wyoming and asked if we wanted to sell the farm."

Hyram and Florence Donaldson were in their late twenties and had three children. They had moved to Independence from Kentucky about eight months ago, and were regular customers at Cooper's General Store. The house they now lived in was quite small.

"Sweetheart, Hyram doesn't make a lot of money. How can they afford to buy this place? We have to get our money out of it so we can buy land in Wyoming and build a new house."

"Tell him, Mama!" Mary Beth said.

"Yeah," Patty Ruth said. "Tell him, Mama!"

"I had the same thoughts when they showed up here this afternoon, Sol. They didn't tell me at first how they could afford it. They said they wanted to raise their children in the country. They've admired our place, and you'll remember they visited us once, so they knew what the house looks like inside.

"Then, right out of the blue, Hyram said—well, wait a minute. How much did you say we would have to get out of the farm?"

"Sixty-five hundred. No less."

Mary Beth's eyes danced as she looked on. Patty Ruth didn't really comprehend it all, but she was excited because her sister and mother were excited.

"Are you ready for this, Sol?" Hannah said.

"Ready as I'll ever be..."

"Hyram offered us seven thousand."

"Great! We'll take it! But—"

Hannah grinned. "But you want to know where he's going to get the seven thousand..."

"That's my next question."

"He already has it! A wealthy uncle died in Kentucky and left Hyram and each of his four siblings twelve thousand dollars! He and Florence have the money in the bank right now!"

"So what did you tell them?"

"I said we'd take it! They'll be back to talk with you this evening."

"Glory to God!" Solomon said, grasping Hannah by the waist and lifting her off the floor. "Praise the Lord!" he shouted, whirling her around in a circle.

"Sol, put me down!"

As Hannah's feet touched the floor, he kissed her soundly and said, "Everything is working out, honey. We're going to have a wonderful life out west!"

At that moment, the boys came in. They knew of Hyram Donaldson's offer and had heard their father's voice clear out at the barn.

Solomon gathered his family in a circle and led them in prayer, thanking God for the marvelous way He was guiding them to Fort Bridger.

Hannah then said, "Sol, you did remember to invite

Mother and Daddy to supper?"

"Yep. They acted a bit frosty, but they'll be here."

"I'm really nervous about this."

"It's okay. As I told you last night, yours truly will break it to them."

"I'm still nervous."

"Me, too," Mary Beth said. "I don't want Grandma and Grandpa mad at us."

"We'll just have to take that as it comes, honey," Solomon said.

"Sol…"

"Yes, my darling wife?"

"Something occurred to me about our taking four extra wagons to Wyoming. Who's going to drive them?"

He grinned and said, "When I made reservations for the last wagon train today I talked to Fred Brinton about it. By the way, we're going with Ezra Comstock."

"Oh, wonderful! He's a dear man."

"Fred said the wagon trains always have several young men who switch off driving with their parents or brothers. They're eager to do more driving. He says I'll be able to get drivers without even having to pay them. If, however, I have to pay them, I'll do it gladly. We'll know more when Ezra gets here. So far, he's got thirteen wagons signed up in addition to ours. The agent is sure there will be more."

"And just when are we leaving?"

"Oh! I'm sorry. On Wednesday, May 25. I've got the oxen and wagons reserved."

"Good. Now, if we just had this thing with Mother and Daddy settled." Hannah touched her forehead.

"Headache?"

"Yes. It's just now coming on."

"Honey, don't let your parents' attitude upset you."

"I'm trying not to, but I hate having them angry and hurt.

I'm glad you're going to break it to them. You will wait until after supper?"

"Yes."

"All right, girls," Hannah said, "we've got to hurry and get supper on the table. Grandma and Grandpa will be here in about twenty minutes. You boys get your hands washed."

"I guess that includes you, Papa," Chris said with a laugh.

Ben and Esther Singleton pulled up in their buggy and parked in front of the house. Chris and B. J. bounded out the door, shouting, "Grandma! Grandpa!"

"Hello, boys," Ben said. He wrapped the reins around the metal tube that held the buggy whip. "Supper about ready?"

"Sure is!" Chris said, stepping close to the passenger side and holding out his hand. "Here, Grandma, I'll help you down."

Ben put an arm around B. J. and watched Chris walk Esther up the porch steps.

Solomon appeared at the front door with a smile on his face, though it felt as if he had hot rocks in his stomach. "Evening, folks. Hope you're hungry. Hannah has a beautiful meal prepared."

They gave him a bland look and focused their attention on their granddaughters. Patty Ruth came charging out the door to hug them, and Mary Beth followed more sedately. Hannah stepped onto the porch last, feeling a sickish flutter in her stomach.

When she embraced her mother, she felt a definite coldness between them. It was even worse with her father. "Mother...Daddy...what's wrong? You seem upset."

Ben swung a piercing look at Solomon, then turned it on his daughter and said, "I want to hear it straight from you,

Hannah Marie. It's all over town, but I'll call it rumor until you tell me straight out that you and your husband have decided to take our grandchildren and make that irresponsible, foolish move west. Please tell me, Hannah, that it's not true."

Solomon stepped forward. "Ben, it's not rumor. That's why we asked you to supper tonight. We wanted to have a nice meal together, then I was going to tell you about it, and—"

"We don't want to hear it!"

"I was going to show you how we know our decision is the Lord's doing."

Ben's features molded into a rigid mask. "Don't you tell me, Solomon Cooper, that God would lead you into anything so utterly senseless! You're making a big mistake! I don't want to hear any of your 'God's leading us' tripe!"

The children looked on in confusion, anxiety showing on their faces.

Hannah had an arm around her mother and could feel her tremble. "Daddy," Hannah said softly, "if you will let us, we'll tell you some marvelous things the Lord has done to show us—"

"I'm not listening!" he said. "And neither is your mother!"

Hannah's head began to throb. "Daddy, please…let's go in and eat supper. Let us tell you how the Lord is working."

Ben's mouth drew into a hard line. "I wanted so much to hear that it was only rumor, but you're really going to do it, eh?"

Esther spoke up. "Why would God lead you out there amongst those wild Indians, Sol? And why would He lead you to subject Hannah and these precious children to that uncivilized wilderness? And why would He lead you to take our daughter and grandchildren away from us in our old age? We don't have a lot longer in this world, you know. I agree with Ben. You're making a big mistake."

"Mother, don't lay it all on Sol," Hannah said. "This is as

much my decision as it is his. If you and Daddy will just let us explain how we know it's the Lord's will that we go to Fort Bridger, you will understand."

"That's right," Solomon said. "And if you'll let us tell you about it, maybe you'll just change your minds and go with us. We don't have to be separated. We can still be together."

Ben's features almost rippled with anger. "I told you before, we're not going to do any such thing!"

"Daddy, supper's getting cold," Hannah said. "Let's go in and eat. We can talk about it some more, and—"

"We're not talking about it any more! And we're not eating with you, either. C'mon, Esther. We're going home."

Esther was surprised at Ben's command, but she nodded and turned away from Hannah toward the buggy.

Tears welled up in Hannah's eyes and her voice caught as she said, "Mother…Daddy…please don't treat us like this! We love you."

Ben, who was walking behind his wife, looked over his shoulder and delivered a parting shot. "If you loved us, you wouldn't be so eager to go off and leave us! I'm telling both of you, you'll be sorry you did this foolish thing. It'll backfire on you! You're making the biggest mistake of your lives!"

Solomon pulled Hannah close, and the children drew up on both sides to watch in stunned silence as their grandparents drove away. In the dusky light they saw Esther look back, her cheeks wet with tears.

Solomon kept his arm around Hannah as they moved inside, and said, "If this has put any doubts in your mind about going west, honey, you just say so. We'll call the whole thing off right now."

Hannah shook her head. "No, Sol. What just happened here doesn't change anything. The Lord has made it quite clear that we're supposed to move to Fort Bridger. Let's eat supper."

❦   ❦   ❦

During the next four weeks, the Cooper family prepared for their trip. The supplies for the four wagons came in, and everything was moving along on schedule.

The Singletons remained aloof, nursing their deep hurt that their daughter and her family could so easily leave them behind. Hannah's heart felt heavy, but she didn't let it spoil the excitement that was building as the days passed.

On Saturday, May 21, Solomon was behind the counter in the store when he recognized a small, wiry man among the customers. "Well, hello, Ezra!" he said.

"Howdy, Sol." Ezra Comstock grinned and looked around the store. "Would you be havin' time to talk this mornin'?"

"Sure. Soon as I finish up with these folks, I'll have Randy take over and we can chat."

The sun and wind had weathered Ezra's skin to a mahogany color. He stood slightly over five feet seven inches, and there wasn't an ounce of fat on him. He wore an old hat with a mashed-down, discolored crown, and a sweat-stained band.

Solomon pointed toward the back of the store and said, "Come with me; there's a place to talk back here."

The two men sat beside a small table that held a checkerboard game, near the pot-bellied stove.

"What's this I hear?" Ezra asked. "The Cooper family's gonna be in my train?"

"That's right."

"And you're goin' only as far as Fort Bridger?"

"Yes, sir. Fred told me you were taking this train to Sacramento."

"Correct. Now, I hope you'll pardon this old man's curiosity, but how come you're goin' to Fort Bridger?"

"Well, it'll take a few minutes to explain."

"I'm all ears."

Solomon told Ezra how he had been stirred, watching the wagon trains form in Independence and seeing the people so excited about beginning a new life on the frontier. Now Hannah had caught the "bug," and so had the children. And the Lord had confirmed the move to them in so many ways.

"Well," Ezra said, "sounds like everything's workin' out for you. You know that we're pullin' out on Wednesday?"

"Yes, sir."

"We'll have a little meetin' with everybody in the train on Tuesday evenin'."

"All right. How many wagons are signed up now?"

"Sixteen, not includin' yours. That'll make twenty-one. I like havin' that many. It'll tend to keep the Indians off our backs. Now, Fred told me you need drivers for those four extra wagons. I've already got 'em lined up."

"Good! I'll pay them whatever they want."

"No need. They don't want pay. They're glad to have the wagons to drive. All young fellas. Oldest is twenty-six. When do you want to meet 'em?"

"Well, I think we need to load the wagons sometime on Tuesday. The goods are in the storage shed behind the store."

"You open up at eight, don't you?"

"Mm-hmm."

"How about I bring the boys by at eight on Tuesday mornin' to load?"

"Fine. My family and I will spend the last night in our house on Tuesday, and join the train with the other covered wagons on Wednesday morning."

"Sounds good, Sol. I have to say I hate to see you leave Independence, but it'll sure be a pleasure havin' you in my train."

Hannah and the children were at the store on Tuesday morning when Ezra Comstock brought the four young men who would drive their wagons. The oldest was twenty-six-year-old Tony Cuzak. The others, Perry Norwood, Bob Lander, and Buck Mylan, ranged in age from nineteen to twenty-three.

While Hannah helped Randy at the store, Solomon and his drivers picked up the oxen and wagons and brought them back to load the food and supplies. Then the drivers took the wagons to Courthouse Square.

The people in Ezra's wagon train gathered in Independence Square that night after supper. When the Cooper buckboard pulled up, Solomon's drivers were standing near the fire. The young men waved and called out a special greeting to little Patty Ruth.

When everyone had gathered in a circle around the fire, Ezra asked all the men to introduce themselves and their families and say where they were from.

There were four wagons that carried only men, and they were all in the Cuzak family. Walt Cuzak, from Scranton, Pennsylvania, introduced himself and pointed out his sons, Frank, Gordon, Dwight, Edmund, and Tony. He bragged that he and his boys were going to dig gold in California and get rich, and woe to anybody who got in their way.

Solomon and Hannah heard a man behind them whisper, "I'm from Scranton, too. The four older brothers are just like the old man. Tony's the only decent one."

When everyone had been introduced, Ezra ran his gaze over the crowd. "Now, folks, you all know that when we pull out of here tomorrow morning, we'll be heading northwest across Kansas toward Nebraska. This is the beginning of the rainy season. There's no doubt we'll encounter some heavy rainstorms. Most of the time, I'll be riding my horse back and forth along the train. When the storms get real bad, I'll call for the wagons to make a circle and wait it out.

"I'm glad to see that most of you have done as I suggested and hooked your wagons to mule or oxen teams."

Walt Cuzak's four wagons were the only horse-drawn wagons. He stepped away from his sons and came within a few feet of Comstock almost as if to challenge him. "Since I'm the only one with horses pullin' my wagons, does that make for a problem, Ezra? I mean, it was only a suggestion that we use oxen or mules. I don't like oxen, and I don't like mules."

Ezra looked back at him steadily and said, "Horses have proven to wear out sooner than oxen or mules, Walt. But I leave the choice to the wagon owners. The biggest problem is that Indians like to eat the big draft horses. Lots of meat, you see. So they're more likely to attack wagon trains and wipe them out to get their hands on horses in the harness."

"Well," Cuzak said, "since there will only be four wagons out of twenty-one pulled by horses, I doubt any of those savages would chance attacking our train."

"Let's hope not," Ezra said. "There is one other problem. Like I said, we're going to have some storms. If they're severe, I'll call for the wagons to make a circle. We've got to keep the animals in control when lightning is popping all around us. The mules sometimes will panic and bolt...the oxen never. But horses are especially skittish. If they're not controlled, they'll bolt. If we stay in a circle, with the horses' faces against the wagon in front of them, it will usually keep them in check.

"I must also caution those of you with saddle horses. When I call for a circle, place your saddle horses inside the circle. There's no place for them to run if the circle is tight."

The fire was dying down and Ezra looked toward the

edge of the group. "Micah, how about throwing some more wood on the fire?"

A clean-cut young man picked up some wood from a small pile behind him and carried it to the fire.

"Folks," the wagon master said, "for those of you who haven't met him, this is my nephew, Micah Comstock. Micah drives my wagon on all my trips."

Sparks flew up toward the star-bedecked sky as Micah tossed wood on the fire.

Ezra waited for a moment and then continued to speak. "Now, folks, I noticed that some of you flinched when I mentioned Indians. Ordinarily a train the size of ours has too much firepower for the hostiles. I can't guarantee it, of course, but our chances are good that we won't have any trouble with them. Which brings to mind what I put in the brochure about firearms. As far as I can see, every man here except my friend Solomon Cooper is wearing a sidearm."

"I'll have mine on in the morning, Ezra," Solomon said.

Ezra explained that he wanted every wagon to have at least one rifle for every adult, and plenty of ammunition. They would use the rifles to shoot game…and if Indians attacked.

Everyone in the train had to obey his orders without question. It was for their own good. And if any wagon got into trouble while crossing streams, or had any other kind of problem, everyone would pitch in to help. There must be absolute cooperation among the people at all times.

Anyone who deliberately broke the rules would be put out of the train and left to fend for themselves. Ezra then opened up the discussion for questions. In a few minutes he dismissed the meeting and reminded everyone that the train would pull out two hours after sunrise.

Ray and Betty Wilson were waiting when the Coopers arrived at the store. Solomon had told them he would bring the family by after the meeting at the Square and officially turn over the store to them.

When the Cooper buckboard pulled up, they saw that Ray had already put up a new sign across the store front:

WILSON'S GENERAL STORE AND SADDLE SHOP

Hannah felt a lump rise in her throat as she greeted the Wilsons and entered the store for the last time. She casually drifted away from the rest of the family and walked between the stacks of shelves. A shadow of doubt started to descend. No! she told herself. You know you're doing the right thing.

She moved past the old pot-bellied stove and looked toward the rear of the store, letting memories flood her mind. Although she felt a deep ache in her heart at leaving these familiar surroundings, there was also a mysterious feeling of peace and excitement at doing God's will and starting this new adventure.

Hannah was wide awake at the crack of dawn. She slipped into her robe and left the bedroom, taking care not to awaken Solomon.

She felt the same way she had felt last night at the store, only worse. This was her home. They were leaving all of the furniture behind for the Donaldsons. A prairie schooner couldn't hold much more than a few boxes of clothing, some personal items, bedding, and food.

Hannah descended the stairs and went from room to room, gazing at every wall and piece of furniture. In the dining room, she lovingly caressed the long table, the backs of the chairs, and the beautiful glass-encased china hutch. Her fine china was packed and already in the covered wagon. She remembered the day Solomon brought the entire dining set home as a surprise.

In the parlor, Hannah touched each piece of furniture and wall tapestry. A hot lump rose in her throat when she approached her grandmother's piano—her most treasured heirloom. She knew Solomon would have bought more wagons to take the piano to Wyoming, along with her furniture, but the journey would have been too hard on them. They probably wouldn't have survived all the way to Fort Bridger.

Solomon had bought this house when they became engaged. Hannah turned slowly and looked at the staircase, recalling how Solomon had carried her up the stairs on their wedding night.

All of her children, except B. J., had been born in this house. It had always been such a happy place, filled with laughter and joy. Now she must leave the farm behind. A flood of sorrow washed over Hannah and she began to sob.

Suddenly two strong hands took her by the waist and Solomon's voice said, "Darling, are you all right?"

Hannah pivoted and threw her arms around his neck. She drew a shuddering breath, and sobbed all the more.

"We can still back out of this deal," he said tenderly. "I can send a wire and tell Colonel Bateman we changed our minds."

"No...no! I'll be all right. It's just...this house...this place has been my life for so long. When we left it during the War, I knew we'd be coming back. But this time..."

Solomon held her until the sobs turned to little shudders and her body began to relax.

Just as the Coopers finished breakfast, friends from church, and neighbors from all directions began arriving to say good-bye. Between their arrivals, Solomon and the boys carried the last boxes to the covered wagon.

The wagon was almost totally loaded when the Singletons drove into the yard. They were still somewhat cool toward Hannah and Solomon, but they cried as they embraced their grandchildren.

Hannah asked her mother if she would write. Esther's expression softened and she nodded yes. The Singletons hugged and kissed Hannah last, then climbed into their buggy and drove away.

Hannah knew it was possible she had just seen her parents for the last time. A powerful wave of emotion churned inside her, trying to force its way up through her throat and out her mouth. Suddenly an unseen Hand seemed to reach into her heart and calm the storm.

Pastor Chase and his family waved to the Singleton buggy as they passed it and pulled into the yard. There was a deep bond between the Coopers and the Chases, and emotions ran high as they spoke their parting words.

Before the Chases left, Pastor Chase gathered everyone into a circle for prayer. Patty Ruth happened to be standing between Mary Beth and B. J. It was bad enough that she had to lay Ulysses down to free both hands. Now she had to put her hand in B. J.'s! She couldn't remember the last time she'd seen him wash!

Solomon noticed the break in the circle and said, "All right, you two. We're all holding hands while the pastor prays."

Patty Ruth curled her lip. "I don't want to hold B. J.'s hand, Papa. It's dirty." When she saw the stern look in her papa's eyes, she reluctantly slipped her fingers into B. J.'s hand.

"All right, Pastor," Solomon said.

When he could see no one was looking at them, B. J. whispered, "It oughtta be me refusing to hold your hand, Patty Ruth. You've got a wart on your finger!"

Patty Ruth squeezed his fingers as hard as she could.

B. J. jerked, trying to free himself from her grasp, but Patty Ruth had a firm grip. When the prayer was finished, B J. whispered, "I'll get you for that!"

Patty Ruth smiled sweetly and wiped her hand on her dress, then picked up Ulysses.

The Cooper wagon rolled out of the yard with Hannah at the reins and Chris and Solomon on saddle horses. Hannah gave the house one last look, then urged the oxen forward. Mary Beth sat beside her mother, holding an excited Biggie, and Patty Ruth held her best friend. To her, Ulysses seemed excited, too. B. J. rode in the back.

When they arrived at the Square, Hannah's attention was drawn immediately to Ezra Comstock astride his horse, calling for everyone to make ready. They would pull out in exactly twenty minutes.

The Coopers' personal wagon was ninth in line behind Ezra's lead wagon, which was driven by Micah Comstock. The four supply wagons were directly behind the Cooper wagon. When the wagon was in place, Hannah and the children climbed down. They mingled with the others in the wagon train for a few minutes, then Ezra called for everyone to get ready to move out.

Mary Beth helped Patty Ruth and Ulysses onto the wagon seat while B. J. climbed in from the rear with Biggie licking his face.

Chris came trotting up on his horse, his eyes sparkling with excitement. Solomon smiled at Hannah. "I'll tie Nipper to the back of the wagon, honey, then help you up."

"Sol, are you going to start right out walking alongside the wagon?"

"Sure. That's what most of the husbands in the train are doing."

"But…your leg…"

"I'll get in the saddle when it starts to bother me."

The early morning light danced on Hannah's dark-brown hair, giving it a coppery sheen. She flashed Solomon a smile as he took her hand and led her a few steps from the wagon to a spot where they could see the western horizon. "Out there, Hannah," he said, "under the distant sky, is our new home and our new life."

CHAPTER TEN

P recisely on schedule, Ezra Comstock trotted his horse past the line of wagons. When he reached the lead wagon, he stood up in the stirrups and thrust his arm forward. "Wagons, ho-o-o!"

As Hannah held up the reins, eagerly awaiting her wagon's turn to move, she glanced down at Patty Ruth. The little girl's eyes glinted with excitement, and she squeezed her best friend "Hang on, Ulysses. Here we go!"

Mary Beth held on to Biggie, who was yapping as if he understood that he and his family were starting the biggest adventure of their lives.

When the wagon in front of Hannah lurched forward, she snapped the reins and mimicked the other drivers, shouting, "Yee-haw! Yee-haw!"

It was a beautiful sight—the long line of white-covered wagons stretching westward, men walking beside their wagons, and riders sitting tall and straight on their mounts. The happy laughter of children rode the air, along with the barking chorus of dogs.

Chris rode beside his father, who limped along with a smile on his face.

Hannah twisted around on the seat to look at Independence one last time. The lump in her throat came back as she thought of her parents.

Suddenly a tidal wave of doubt washed over Hannah, filling her mind with questions. Were her parents right? Were the Coopers making a big mistake? Would they be miserable and unhappy at Fort Bridger?

She steeled herself and looked down at Solomon as he walked beside the wagon, remembering his words of a few moments ago: "Out there, Hannah, under the distant sky, is our new home and our new life."

Hannah shook her head as if to clear it, and squared her shoulders. Her parents were wrong. They weren't making a mistake. They were doing God's will. Out there under that distant sky lay the fulfillment of their dreams. They would be superbly happy at Fort Bridger, Wyoming.

Soon the rising dust from the hooves of oxen, mules, and horses took over Hannah's nose, and she decided a good rain would be a blessing.

Half an hour after the wagon train had pulled out of Independence, B. J. asked if he could walk beside his father. He dropped to the ground at the rear of the vehicle and waved at Tony Cuzak, whose wagon followed thirty feet away.

Hannah glanced back to look at B. J., then her eyes settled back on Solomon. His limp looked more pronounced. "Sol, don't overdo it, now."

"I won't."

"So how does the leg feel by now?"

"Not too bad."

Biggie was still on Mary Beth's lap, but when he saw B. J. on the ground, he barked and wagged his tail. "Papa," Mary Beth said, "Biggie wants to come down and walk with you and B. J. Is it all right?"

"Sure. Go get him, B. J."

Chris, who was riding Buster, said, "Mama, what's for supper tonight?"

Hannah laughed. "I'm not sure whether it will be beans

and hardtack, or hardtack and beans."

"Really? I thought you'd cook on the trail like you do at home."

"I'll do better as we go along, son, but I'll need a day or two to get used to this traveling all day and cooking a big meal at night."

"That's okay," Chris said with a grin. "If you fix it, it'll be good, no matter what it is."

"Why, thank you, son."

The dust billowed as the wagon train moved slowly westward. When they had been on the trail for nearly three hours, the lead wagon began to veer in a northerly direction. Solomon looked up at Hannah, who was talking to her girls, and said, "Sweetheart, I think maybe I'd better ride for a while. This leg is starting to hurt."

"I'm glad you're going to give it a rest," she said, a note of relief in her voice. "You want to ride in the seat or in the back?"

"I figure maybe you'd like some relief from holding the reins. I'll come up there and drive."

The girls moved to the wagon bed and Hannah scooted over as Solomon climbed up. He gave her a quick kiss and took the reins.

Hannah moved close and placed her hand in the crook of his arm. "I love you, Mr. Cooper."

"And I love you, Mrs. Cooper."

"And I love *you*, Mr. and Mrs. Cooper," Patty Ruth said with a giggle.

The other children joined in with "I love yous," and Solomon laughed heartily.

"Well, Mrs. Cooper and I love all four of you, too!" he said. "Right, Mama?"

"More than they'll ever know!" Hannah said, brushing a loose lock of hair from her forehead.

Biggie yapped and looked up at the wagon.

"Biggie loves you, too!" Mary Beth said.

Patty Ruth held up her bear. "So does Ulysses!"

Hannah squeezed her husband's arm. "Darling, we're going to be so happy at Fort Bridger!"

Ezra Comstock was pushing to reach the Blue River by the end of the day. His goal was fifteen miles a day, or as close to it as possible while they were on level ground. Once the train reached the Sierra Nevada Range, they would be down to only six or seven miles a day.

The fifteen-mile goal would be out of reach if they stopped for a noon meal, so the people snacked on whatever provisions they had brought and kept moving.

Soon B. J. and Biggie were back in the wagon as the long train rolled northwest.

All afternoon, Ezra rode up and down beside the wagons, talking with people. The only exceptions were Walt Cuzak and his four oldest sons, who had no interest in getting better acquainted.

Toward sunset, the Blue River came into view. Ezra trotted along the line, letting everyone know they had reached their goal and would make camp on the bank of the Blue. Three miles on the other side of the Blue was the Kansas border.

Soon, fires were winking around the inside of the wagon circle. The Coopers shared their fire with the people in the wagon just ahead of theirs, an elderly couple named Maudie and Elmer Holden, and their twenty-one-year-old grandson, Curtis. The Cooper children gravitated to the elderly Holdens, finding in them a resemblance to their own grandparents. The Holdens responded, especially to Patty Ruth, who charmed them with her sweet smile and winsome ways.

When the meal was over and the women were washing dishes with river water, one man started to play a fiddle. Within minutes a banjo player joined him, and Tony Cuzak brought out his harmonica.

Off to one side of the circle, children were chasing fireflies as the little insects flitted about, lighting in their hair and on their clothing. Several family dogs yapped and barked excitedly, trying to catch the fireflies in their mouths.

While the music and fun was going on, a little girl sidled up to Patty Ruth and smiled. She was exactly Patty Ruth's size and had bright blue eyes and blond hair.

"Hi. My name's Polly Winters," she said. "I'm five. What's your name?"

The little redhead smiled warmly and said, "Patty Ruth Cooper."

Polly set her gaze on Ulysses. "What's your bear's name?"

The smile left Patty Ruth's face as quickly as it had come. She shifted Ulysses to her other arm and said, with a cool note in her voice, "Ulysses Cooper."

"He's a nice bear. Where'd you get him?"

"My grandma who went to heaven gave him to me before she went."

At that instant, Biggie loped up to Patty Ruth and raised up on his hind legs, wagging his tail. She bent over to pat his head, and Polly said, "Is that your dog?"

"Mm-hmm."

"What's his name?"

"Biggie Cooper."

"Could I pet him?"

"Sure. Go ahead."

Biggie enjoyed the attention and wiggled all over and licked Polly's hand. Patty Ruth steeled herself for what she figured would come next. But it never did.

After a few minutes, Polly said, "My mommy said I could

come and talk to you, but I have to go back to her and Daddy now. See you later."

"Okay. See you later."

Patty Ruth decided she liked Polly Winters very much.

At the Cooper wagon, Hannah and Solomon sat on a small bench and held hands as they listened to the music and watched the children play.

Solomon squeezed Hannah's hand and looked into her chocolate-brown eyes. "You all right, sweetheart?"

Her lips parted in a soft smile. "Yes. I'll have Mother and Daddy on my mind quite often, and I'm sure my heart will feel some pain because of their attitude, but the Lord will give me the grace to handle it. As for Independence and everything we left there, I'm sure time will get me over it. When we get to our new home in Wyoming, I'll be so happy, it won't bother me anymore."

Soon it was bedtime for the youngest members of the train, and they reluctantly scattered to their wagons. The Cooper children chattered about their new friends and how much fun it was to be traveling like this.

Hannah put an arm around her youngest. "Honey, who was that little girl I saw you talking to?"

"Her name is Polly Winters, Mama...an' I like her."

"She's about your age, isn't she?"

"Uh-huh. She's five."

"Well, it's wonderful that you've found a playmate so soon."

"Yeah! An' I really like her! She likes Biggie, too. She petted him."

"That's nice. Did she like Ulysses?"

Patty Ruth stiffened slightly and said, "Mm-hmm."

"Did you let her hold Ulysses?"

"Huh-uh. She didn't want to. I really like her."

Solomon and Hannah exchanged glances.

Before leaving home, the Coopers had discussed with the children the sleeping arrangements. Everyone had bedrolls, so they would rotate who slept in the wagon and who slept underneath the wagon. On the first night out, Solomon decided they would all sleep under the wagon.

While Mary Beth and her little sister were inside the wagon getting into their nightgowns, B. J. was feeding Biggie and Chris fed oats to Buster and Nipper.

When the boys had gotten into their nightshirts, Solomon tossed more wood on the fire and called the family together for Scripture reading and prayer. Biggie snuggled between Mary Beth and Chris, and Ulysses lay safely in Patty Ruth's arms.

Solomon was heating coffee over the fire and was about to say something to Hannah when a young couple walked up. They were accompanied by a girl of about eighteen or nineteen, who was carrying a baby.

"Good evening," the young man said. "My name is Lloyd Marlin. This is my wife, Suzanne, and Suzanne's sister, Deborah Smith. Aunt Deborah has our little son, James, here. He's ten months old."

The Coopers introduced themselves, explaining that they were from Independence. Then Solomon asked, "Where are you folks from?"

"Virginia," Lloyd said. "Near Roanoke. We're going all the way to Sacramento."

"We're only going as far as Fort Bridger," Solomon said."

Hannah smiled at the baby. "Would you mind if I hold him, Deborah?"

"Of course not," she said, handing James to her.

Hannah held the baby close and kissed his fat little cheek. "We don't have any babies in our family any more. Our youngest is five."

"We saw the children with you a little while ago," Suzanne said.

"So many names being reeled off last night," Lloyd said. "Too hard to remember them all."

"That's for sure," Solomon said with a chuckle. "You folks like some coffee?" He went to the wagon and brought out some extra tin cups. Hannah declined a cup, saying she was having too much fun getting to know little James.

"Maybe you should have another baby, Mrs. Cooper," Suzanne said. "You sure have a way with them. That's the first time James has smiled all day."

Hannah glanced at her husband.

"I'd love to have another baby in the family," Solomon said, "but I guess you have to stop sometime. Won't be too many more years till Chris gets married. Guess we'll have to wait for babies till then."

Hannah smiled, but didn't comment.

"The...ah...reason we're here, Mr. Cooper," Lloyd said, "is that when we passed by a little while ago, we noticed you were reading the Bible to your family. We decided you must be Christians."

"You've got that right—the born-again, blood-washed kind," Solomon said.

"Well, amen. Us, too."

There was an immediate bond between the families as they talked about how wonderful it was to know the Lord. Then Suzanne explained that Deborah was going with them to California because their parents had died within a month of each other about two years ago. Deborah had moved in with her sister and brother-in-law, and since she had no other family, she was going to make her new life in California, too. Lloyd was going to homestead land in the valley just east of Sacramento.

Solomon told them of their general store in Independence and explained that they would open up a new one in Fort Bridger. After chatting for a few more minutes, Hannah reluctantly gave the baby back to his aunt, and they said goodnight.

It was a good ending to the first day out, and when Solomon and Hannah finally got into their bedrolls, they fell asleep peacefully.

At sunrise the next morning, Ezra Comstock gathered the people around and explained that even though the Blue was little more than four feet deep where they would cross, they would do it at an upstream slant to lessen the current against the wagons.

He noted the Colt .45 revolver on Solomon Cooper's hip and said, "Now, folks...just three more miles after we cross the river, we'll be in Kansas. Beyond law and order. Its up to us to protect ourselves. We're also movin' into Indian territory. It's the Comanches we have to worry about. The other three tribes who inhabit this area are the Kaw, the Potawatomi, and the Pawnee. For the most part, they're friendly toward whites. The few times I have known them to attack whites is when the whites have done something to rile them.

"When we get into Nebraska Territory, the dangerous ones are the Sioux, the Crow, and the Blackfoot. There's no way to tell which tribe they are from a distance, so we'll just have to keep a sharp eye for *any* Indians. If they gallop toward us, whooping and barking like dogs, it's an attack. Anyone who spots Indians, no matter what they're doin', let me know immediately. I'll decide what we should do. But keep your weapons within reach at all times."

With that, Ezra said, "All right! Let's get ready to move out in five minutes!"

True to his word, Comstock was in the saddle five minutes later, shouting, "Wagons ho-o-o!"

There was a chorus of "Yee-haws" and the sound of cracking whips as the wheels began rolling once more.

They crossed the Blue River without incident and reached the Kansas border two hours later.

The travelers soon realized the difference between Missouri and Kansas. Now they were on the wild prairie, heading almost due north toward the Kaw River, where they would cross near a small settlement known as Topeka.

Ezra Comstock and his nephew were the only ones who had been this far west before. The others were amazed at the vista before them. They had not imagined there could be so much space. The sky seemed much bigger here, like a huge bright-blue lid set down over the earth.

Grass waved in seemingly endless fields in the stiff prairie wind, reminding those travelers who had been on the Atlantic coast of great ocean waves. Meadowlarks flitted about, landing on grassy mounds, while broad-winged hawks rode the airwaves high above.

The fields were dotted with spring flowers, pink, purple, blue, and yellow, that rippled in the wind as far as the eye could see.

When the dust began to rise in clouds, Ezra trotted along the length of the train, instructing everyone to stagger their wagons so that none followed directly behind another.

As point man, Ezra rode ahead and scanned the prairie, looking for any sign of Indians. He knew the hostiles would not be seen unless they wanted to be seen, but any attack would be quite visible as they came thundering against the train. All was quiet in every direction.

Solomon walked longer than he had the day before, with B. J. at his side. After four hours, he and B. J. returned to the wagon, and Solomon relieved Hannah at the reins.

In the late afternoon he returned to the ground with Mary Beth at his side. Mary Beth and her father liked to talk about the Bible together. Her questions pleased him and showed him that she was reading her Bible and thinking about what she was reading.

That night, as they mingled with the other travelers, Solomon and Hannah met William and Martha Perryman and their six children, who were from Joplin, Missouri. The Perrymans introduced them to Stuart and Tracie Armstrong, newlyweds from Toledo, Ohio.

As the Coopers moved on, they encountered another pair of newlyweds, Lafe and Vanessa Tolliver, from Racine, Wisconsin. Hannah's eyes strayed to the next wagon, where she saw one of the Cuzaks leaning against a rear wheel, eyeing Vanessa. The look in his eyes had nothing to do with admiration of beauty.

As Hannah and Solomon moved on to meet more of their fellow travelers, Hannah held fast to Solomon's arm. When they were out of earshot from anyone, she tugged him to a halt.

"Sol...did you notice one of the Cuzak brothers at the wagon next to Tollivers'?"

"I saw a man leaning against the rear wheel..."

"He was ogling Vanessa, Sol, and I didn't like the look in his eyes."

Solomon casually turned and looked back. The Cuzak brother was still there, but now he was checking the ties that held the canvas bonnet. "I think that's the one they call Dwight."

"I've got a bad feeling about the Cuzaks, Sol."

"Me, too. They're a mean-looking bunch. That is, except for Tony."

"Should we say something to Ezra?"

"Don't think we need to, darlin'. Ol' Ezra is a sharp cookie. He's got his eye on them."

At the Cooper wagon, two girls Mary Beth's age had stopped to introduce themselves—Corrie Weathers and Becky Croft. The Weathers and the Crofts were from the same town in Delaware.

Patty Ruth held Ulysses and listened to how the big girls talked together.

Corrie pointed toward the sky and said, "I've never seen so many twinkling stars. You can't see them like this in Delaware."

Patty Ruth moved Ulysses from one arm to the other and said, "My sister knows a whole lot about the stars, don't you, Mary Beth?"

"I know a little, Patty Ruth, but not a whole lot."

"Well, show Corrie and Becky what you were showin' me an' Chris last night."

Patty Ruth looked on proudly as her sister pointed heavenward and said, "All right, follow my finger. See that brilliant star right…there?"

It took Corrie and Becky a few seconds to focus on it. When they saw it, Mary Beth said, "That's Sirius, the brightest star of all. It's in the constellation Canis Major, and is known as the Dog Star. My teacher at Independence, Miss Powers, taught me about Sirius and Canis Major."

"Tell 'em some more, Mary Beth."

Solomon and Hannah were just walking up as Mary Beth guided the girls back to Sirius and said, "See those three bright stars real close together to the right of Sirius? That's Orion, the Hunter."

"My sister is the smartest girl in all the world," Patty Ruth said.

Mary Beth blushed. "Patty Ruth, that's sweet of you, honey, but I'm not the smartest girl in the world."

"You are, too. Isn't she, Mama? Isn't she, Papa?"

Mary Beth hadn't seen her parents' approach, and she turned to them in surprise.

"She's pretty smart, all right," Solomon said.

Mary Beth introduced her parents to her new friends, then Becky looked down at the stuffed bear in Patty Ruth's arms and said, "That's some bear, Patty Ruth. What's it's name?"

"He's not an *it*," Patty Ruth said. "He's a *he*. His name's Ulysses Cooper." At the same time, she gripped Ulysses hard, turning her body to put the bear out of Becky's reach.

"Patty Ruth, maybe Becky would like to hold Ulysses for a minute," Hannah said.

"Oh, yes! That would be nice!" Becky said.

"Go ahead, honey," Solomon said. "Let Becky see Ulysses."

Though Patty Ruth didn't want to obey, she handed the bear to the older girl.

"Oh, isn't he cute?" Becky giggled and turned to show the bear to Corrie.

"He sure is," Corrie agreed, stroking Ulysses' head. "I love his smile…and those big black eyes!"

When Patty Ruth had the bear back in her arms, she pressed him tightly to her chest.

As the girls walked away, telling Mary Beth they would see her tomorrow, Hannah turned to her youngest daughter. "Patty Ruth, you were on the verge of being selfish again, weren't you?"

"Huh?"

"I saw the look in your eyes. Now, honey, Mama's trying to teach you that you must not be selfish. Do you understand?"

Patty Ruth's features reddened and her chin jutted as she said, "Ulysses is *my* bear! Nobody else has any business holdin' 'im!"

Solomon took hold of Patty Ruth's arm and said, "You don't talk to your mother that way, young lady!"

The little redhead started to cry as her father ushered her

outside the circle for a spanking. Hannah and Mary Beth could hear her trying to talk her father out of it, but to no avail.

On this night, Hannah and the girls would sleep inside the wagon while Solomon and the boys slept outside. As the cool night breeze brushed against the canvas walls, mother and daughters slipped into their strange new beds. It was somewhat crowded among the trunks and barrels and a big washtub. But even though Mary Beth's elbow poked into her little sister's ribs and everyone's breathing was all mixed up together, Patty Ruth and Ulysses felt snug and safe.

Hannah lay awake for a long time, listening to her daughters' breathing and the night sounds outside. She missed her comfortable feather bed and Solomon's closeness. When doubt started to descend once more, she fixed her mind on Jesus. Almost instantly she felt the answer to her prayer, and sleep came easily.

CHAPTER ELEVEN

I t was late morning the next day when the Comstock wagon train arrived at a single post that marked the fork of the Santa Fe and Oregon Trails.

As the wagons rolled to the north, the Coopers noticed that Chris was spending a good deal of time riding alongside the lead wagon. During supper that night, they learned from Chris that he and Micah Comstock had a lot in common. Both were Christians, they both loved horses, and they were interested in soldiers and things military.

B. J. spoke up to tell everyone he had struck up a friendship with Billy Perryman, who was his age. Billy wanted to know if B. J. could ride in his wagon tomorrow, and play alongside it while the train was moving.

Solomon told him he would talk with Mr. Perryman about it.

On Saturday, Chris tied Buster behind the lead wagon and spent most of the day riding on the seat next to Micah. B. J. and Billy Perryman walked alongside the Perryman wagon and played "cowboys and Indians."

Patty Ruth sat on the wagon seat beside her mother and received another loving lecture on selfishness, while Mary Beth and Biggie walked with Solomon. Father and daughter talked about the future. Mary Beth still held to her desire to become a teacher and spoke of how she missed Miss Powers. She hoped she would like her teacher at Fort Bridger.

The fifth day out was a Sunday. The wagon train was now just thirteen miles south of the Kaw River.

Before pulling out that morning, Ezra Comstock called for everyone to gather for a brief church service. Ezra led them in a few well-known hymns, then beckoned Solomon Cooper forward to bring the message.

While he was speaking, Solomon noticed that young Tony Cuzak, who stood next to Chris and Micah, was listening intently to the message on the death and resurrection of the Lord Jesus Christ. Solomon filed that observation away for later pursuit.

Ezra closed in prayer and then dismissed everyone to their wagon, saying that the train would pull out in ten minutes.

As Tony headed for the wagon he was driving for the Coopers, he heard his father's voice. "Tony, wait up. I want to talk to you."

Tony stopped and turned around. "Sure, Pa. What about?"

"I watched you when that Cooper idiot was preachin'. You were drinkin' it in like it was somethin' good."

"It *is* something good, Pa."

"Well, I don't want you listenin' to that Bible and Jesus stuff, y'hear?"

"It makes sense to me," Tony said. "I've heard you talk against it all my life, but people like the Coopers have something you and I don't have. You have to admit that they're different."

"Yeah, they're different, all right. Fool fanatics is what they are. That lame-brained wagon master and his nephew, too. I'm tellin' you, Tony, stay away from 'em. And don't listen to that tommyrot they put out anymore. Ain't no such thing as heaven and hell. When a man dies, he dies like a dog. That's the end of 'im."

"You're wrong, Pa. And deep down inside, you know you're wrong. Like Mr. Cooper said, the very fact that Jesus Christ broke the bands of death and came out of the grave is proof that there's life after death."

Cuzak released a string of profanity, cursing his youngest son, and stomped away, saying, "You're too much like your mother! They'll make a fanatical fool outta you, too!"

With an ache in his heart at mention of the mother he had never known, Tony slowly moved toward his wagon.

Mariana Cuzak had died giving birth to Tony. When he was a small boy he had learned from neighbors that she went to church faithfully—in spite of Walt's protests—and tried to teach the Bible to her sons. But Walt wouldn't let her.

Tony was convinced that his mother was a Christian like Solomon Cooper described in his sermon. And he was beginning to want the same thing for himself.

The wagon train arrived at the Kaw River, and made its circle just outside the small settlement of Topeka. After supper, the men and boys went around a bend in the river to bathe beneath the stars, and the women and girls chose a more private spot.

When the children were bedded down, the women brought out their washtubs while the men fed wood to the fires and hauled water from the river. The fiddle, banjo, and harmonica provided music while the men greased wagon wheels and the women washed clothing and hung it on rope cords strung from wagon to wagon.

The next morning, Ezra stood before the people and said, "Now, folks, as you can see, the river is a long way across. The spring thaw up north has it running pretty deep. It's about twelve feet deep in the middle. Your wagons are made to float, and your animals can swim. However, you'll find that the oxen and mules don't know that. Back there at the Blue, they could see the bottom, so they didn't balk. It's gonna be different here.

"Everybody get out your whips. We'll cross at an upstream slant, just like we did at the Blue. Only this time, we'll have ropes tied to your wagons, and men standing on the opposite bank, holding the ropes. I'll be right here on this bank. Just follow my instructions when it's your turn to cross, and you'll do fine."

Ezra's oxen had crossed many a river. When Micah guided the lead wagon to the bank, they moved in without hesitation, and soon were pulling the wagon up the bank on the other side.

It was totally different with the next wagon. The mules in the harness laid back their ears, dug in their hooves, and hee-hawed in protest. A few cracks of the whip over their heads, and they took the plunge. Seconds later they were swimming across.

One by one, the wagons made the crossing. When it came time for the Coopers' personal wagon to cross, Solomon was at the reins with a whip in his hand. Nipper and Buster were tied behind. The three oldest Cooper children and Biggie rode in the bed, and Patty Ruth was in the seat between her parents, Ulysses safe in her arms.

The wagon creaked and groaned as it floated across, rocking like a boat. In spite of their father's insistence that the wagon wouldn't tip over, the children clung to each other. Suddenly the wagon gently nudged against the north bank, the oxen found footing, and the wagon emerged onto dry ground.

The wagon train was thirteen miles north of the Kaw River when Ezra guided it to a spot beside a small creek. They had lost a little time in the river crossing, and he would have pushed them to make another mile, but both men and animals were showing signs of weariness.

After supper, Solomon sought out his drivers to thank them for the good job they were doing. As he headed back toward his wagon, a familiar voice called, "Mr. Cooper!"

Solomon looked over his shoulder to see Tony hurrying toward him.

"I have some questions about your Sunday morning sermon, sir. Ever since that service, I've been thinking about what you said."

"I'll be glad to answer your questions, Tony. Do you want to come to my wagon so I can get my Bible?"

"Sure."

At the wagon, Hannah and the children were nowhere in sight, and Solomon invited Tony to sit down on the bench near the fire. "All right, Tony. How can I help you?"

"Well, sir, if I understood right, you said that the only way to have my sins cleansed and forgiven is by putting my faith in Jesus Christ."

"That's right, my friend. If there were some other way of salvation and forgiveness, God wouldn't have sent His Son to die that awful death on the cross. He would have let people lay hold on salvation through their various religions. But religion isn't the answer. It was because He preached against the religions of His day that Jesus was hounded and crucified by the religious leaders and their followers. They were actually doing what God had planned before the foundation of the world."

Tony looked as if a light had gone on inside him. "So the crucifixion was planned by God before He ever created the world?"

"Exactly," Solomon said, flipping pages. "Listen to Jesus' words in John 10:17-18:

> Therefore doth my Father love me, because I lay down my life, that I might take it again. No man taketh it from me, but I lay it down of myself. I have power to lay it down, and I have power to take it again.

"Do you see what he said? Not only did He have power to release His spirit into the Father's hands, but He had power to raise Himself from the grave. All of this, Tony, was to provide the only way of salvation for sinners like you and me. Jesus satisfied the Father's holiness and righteousness. Only Jesus Christ had spotless blood, and only Jesus Christ was sinless. The rest of the world—throughout the ages—could not qualify. Understand?"

"Whew! This is all new to me, but it sure makes sense. So it's not religion a person needs, it's Jesus Himself."

"That's right."

"Mr. Cooper, you wouldn't happen to have a spare Bible I could borrow, would you?"

"Sure. We've got several."

"Would…would you write down some places I could read to help me understand it better?"

"Be happy to. When you've read them we'll talk about it some more, okay?"

"Yes, sir!"

Tony was gone when Hannah and the children returned to the wagon. They were elated to hear of Tony's interest, and they prayed together right then, asking the Lord to enlighten him and bring him to salvation very soon.

The next morning, the sky was heavy with clouds, and a brisk wind was blowing.

B. J. and Billy were playing alongside the Cooper wagon when B. J. happened to notice movement to the west. He studied it for a moment and realized he was looking at a band of mounted Indians.

He ran toward his father, who was on Nipper, and shouted, "Papa! Papa! There's Indians out there!"

Solomon looked in the direction B. J. pointed. "I'll go alert Ezra!" he said, and goaded Nipper forward.

"Ezra! Indians!"

Ezra adjusted his battered old hat and said, "Yeah, son. I spotted 'em about ten minutes ago. Looks like about fifteen of 'em. That few ain't gonna attack. They may just be watchin' us, or they might want somethin'. I was about to ride back and calm everybody."

At that moment, the Indians trotted off the mound and made a beeline for the wagon train.

Solomon told Chris to stay with Micah and headed back the way he had come as Ezra hurried along the line, admonishing the people to stay alert but not to panic. The Pawnees were not attacking. They wanted to talk, and Ezra would do the talking.

Solomon was at his own wagon, talking to Hannah, when the wagon master called for him and Becky Croft's father, Dave, to come to the lead wagon. As Ezra reached the front of the line, he signaled for the train to stop.

The Pawnees came within twenty yards of the train and halted. Three of them nudged their mounts closer. With Dave and Solomon flanking him, Ezra raised his hand in a sign of peace. The lead Indian, whose long-tailed headdress identified him as a sub-chief, made the same sign, although his features remained stony. A stiff wind plucked at the feathers of his head-dress.

By now, the occupants of the wagon train looked on with a mixture of fear and curiosity.

At the Cooper wagon, Patty Ruth watched, wide-eyed. "Are the In'ians gonna scalp us, Mama?"

"No, honey. Everything will be all right. You'll see."

Ezra spoke to the leader in the Pawnee language. While they talked, Dave Croft whispered, "Sol, look who's coming."

Walt Cuzak and his four oldest sons were walking toward them with rifles in hand. It wasn't until the Pawnee leader clipped off his words and stared past Ezra that the wagon leader turned to see the Cuzaks. He looked back at the Pawnee sub-chief, said something appeasing, then set hard eyes on Walt Cuzak.

"Stop right there," Ezra said. "I didn't call for you and your boys. Get back to your wagons."

Walt stared back belligerently. "Whatta they want?"

"I said get back to your wagons, Cuzak. You walkin' out here brandishin' those rifles can give 'em the wrong idea."

"We're part of this train," Dwight said. "We gotta right to be out here."

"Whatta they want?" Walt asked again.

"Food."

"We ain't gonna give 'em no food. Why should we feed these redskinned skunks? Tell 'em to go beg somewhere else."

Solomon scowled down at Walt and said, "Do as Ezra told you, Cuzak."

"Don't you tell me—"

Solomon interrupted. "It's a good thing for you these Pawnees don't know English. If they did, your life wouldn't be worth the dirt it would take to cover your body. Do what Ezra told you. Get back to the wagons."

Anger spilled from Cuzak's dark eyes. There was a steely

quality in his voice as he said, "Who's gonna make me, Cooper? You?"

"If I have to."

"Well, you—"

"Walt, shut up!" Ezra said. "When I want your help, I'll ask for it. I'm tryin' to keep peace with these Indians. Now, butt out! If you get Chief Big Cloud angry, there'll be bloodshed."

Ezra turned back to the sub-chief and talked to him for several minutes. When Chief Big Cloud nodded, and the shadow of a smile touched his coppery face, Ezra turned to Solomon and Dave and said, "I'm going to ask the people if they'll share some food with the Pawnees."

The Indians waited patiently while the wagon master met with the people and explained the situation. He advised them it would be best to give the Pawnees the food they requested.

Ezra nodded his approval as the people agreed, and then lifted his voice. "All right. I want everyone who will donate food for the Pawnees to raise a hand."

All hands lifted except those of Walt, Frank, Dwight, Gordon, and Edmund Cuzak.

"Hey, Walt!" Stuart Armstrong called from the midst of the crowd. "What is it with you Cuzaks? Aren't you part of this train?"

Walt's features hardened. "Yeah. So what?"

"Seems to me if you guys are going to enjoy the protection of this train, you ought to do your part. None of us want to give away our food, but it's better than dying in a Pawnee massacre."

Walt's jaw jutted out defiantly. "You don't know what you're talkin' about, Armstrong! We give 'em food, those savages will keep comin' back for more. When we run out they'll attack the train and kill us all."

"You're the one who doesn't know what he's talkin' about, Walt," Ezra said. "I've been dealin' with Indians on these plains for a long time. The smartest thing to do is treat 'em like human bein's and show 'em some compassion. If we give 'em food, they'll treat us real good."

"Well, they ain't gettin' no food from me and these boys o' mine."

Ezra and the others left the Cuzaks to stew over the situation and gathered several gunnysacks full of food.

The Pawnees rode away happy and the Cuzaks stomped back to their wagons.

Ezra shook his head and mumbled, "Walt Cuzak must have been born under a black cloud."

That evening after supper, the women went to the creek to wash clothes. Curtis Holden told his grandmother to rest; he would wash the clothes for her. In the light of the rising full moon, he came upon an open space next to Deborah Smith. He had noticed her on several occasions and liked her fresh-scrubbed farm-girl look.

"Hello," he said, as he knelt down beside her.

"Hello yourself," she said.

Curtis grinned. "I know we all had our names called out the night before we left Independence, but I don't expect you to remember mine. However, I do remember yours. You're Deborah Smith."

She flashed him a smile and said, "And you're Curtis Holden."

A little ripple of pleasure ran through Curtis as he realized she'd noticed him. "Miss Deborah, I don't have near as many clothes to wash as you do. I'll carry yours back to your wagon when you're finished. That is, if I may."

"Well, of course, Curtis. I appreciate that very much. You are indeed a gentleman."

While they worked side by side, Curtis said, "You're from Virginia, right? Farm girl?"

"I'm from Virginia, yes. But I never lived on a farm. I just have that farm-girl look."

"Well, it sure becomes you."

Deborah blushed. "Thank you. And you're from Arkansas."

"Sure am. That sort of gives us something in common, doesn't it? I mean being Southerners, and all."

"Guess you could say that...and unless I'm mistaken, we have something else in common."

"What's that?"

"My brother-in-law, Lloyd Marlin—you've met him, I believe?"

"Yes."

"He told me that he's noticed you reading your Bible quite often."

"That's right."

"Do you believe it?"

"From cover to cover."

"When and where did you get saved?"

"At a revival meeting in Hot Springs, Arkansas, when a hellfire-and-brimstone evangelist came to our church. I was nine."

"Well, isn't that a coincidence? I came to the Lord in a revival meeting in Roanoke. And guess what? I was nine years old, too."

"Wonderful, Miss Deborah. We really do have a lot in common!"

"You can just call me Deborah," she said, smiling warmly.

By the time the clothes were all washed, both young people knew they wanted to get to know each other much better.

On the opposite side of the circle, at the Tolliver wagon, lovely Vanessa Tolliver was sitting on a straight-backed wooden chair, doing some sewing while she chatted with a young woman named Katherine Oakley. After a while, Katherine jokingly said she needed to go find her husband. It would soon be time to spank him and put him to bed.

Vanessa was still giggling when a beefy male figure came out of the shadows as if he had been waiting there. She recognized Walt Cuzak's third eldest son, Dwight, in the firelight.

"I'm sorry, Vanessa," Dwight said. "Didn't mean to scare you."

Vanessa gave him a wary glance and said, "I don't recall giving you permission to call me by my first name, Mr. Cuzak. I'm *Mrs. Tolliver* to you."

Dwight scratched at his beard and chuckled. "No sense standin' on ceremony, Vanessa. Let's be honest. I've noticed you, and you've noticed me."

"Pardon me?"

"Aw, come on…you know it, and I know it."

"You can be on your way now, Mr. Cuzak."

"I ain't brushed off that easy. Now, warm up a little."

Curtis Holden had carried Deborah Smith's wet clothing to the Marlin wagon and was heading for his own wagon when he passed by and heard Vanessa say, "I told you to leave, mister! Now, do it!"

"Is there a problem here, Mrs. Tolliver?"

Vanessa looked at Curtis with relief and said, "Yes, there is, Mr. Holden." She put down her sewing basket and rose to her feet. "Mr. Cuzak, here, seems to have his ears full of wax. I told him to leave, but he insists on being a pest."

Curtis sized up Cuzak—at least two inches taller and about forty pounds heavier. But Curtis knew how to box and was good at it. He fixed Dwight with steady eyes and said, "Best thing for you to do, mister, is grant Mrs. Tolliver's wish."

The rising full moon and the firelight revealed a smoky glare in Dwight Cuzak's eyes. He looked Curtis up and down and sneered, "And just what are you prepared to do if I don't, pee-wee?"

"If you don't leave on your own power, I'll be forced to use mine."

CHAPTER TWELVE

Curtis Holden gracefully sidestepped Dwight's swinging fist, causing the bulky man to stumble.

"Now, Dwight," Curtis said, still holding his wet wash rolled up in a bundle, "you heard what Mr. Comstock said about fighting. You want to get thrown out of the train?"

"There won't be any fight, pee-wee, if you mind your own business."

"As a gentleman, I am minding my own business—looking out for a lady who's being annoyed by a rodent."

"Rodent, eh?"

"That's what I said. Now, go find your rat hole and jump in it. Mrs. Tolliver's husband isn't going to be very happy when he learns about you pushing yourself on his wife."

"I can handle him! And I can handle you, too!"

Curtis dropped his wet wash, dodged a hissing fist, and countered with a solid blow that split Dwight's upper lip. The big man staggered backward and put a hand to his mouth. When his fingers came away crimson, his features contorted with anger.

By this time, a few people had gathered around.

"I'm gonna kill you, pee-wee!" Dwight roared.

"I don't think so."

Curtis's words had a ring of challenge, and Dwight

charged like a maddened bull.

Curtis sidestepped again and landed a chop to Dwight's temple. The big man fell in a heap, shaking his head.

Now people were coming from every direction as Dwight struggled to his feet, cursing Holden and going after him again. Curtis met him with a stiff jab to the nose, a left jab to the mouth, and a hissing right cross.

Just as Dwight went down, his brothers Frank and Edmund and his father piled on Curtis from behind, taking him to the ground.

Suddenly Ezra Comstock's voice cut through the night. "Hold it right there! Frank! Edmund! Walt! Stop it!"

The Cuzak brothers rose to their feet. Curtis got up, too, brushing dirt from his hair. When Walt stood up, he swore at Curtis and surprised him with a punch to the jaw. Suddenly Walt felt powerful vise-like arms around him, lifting him off the ground.

"That's enough!" Solomon Cooper said into Walt's ear, squeezing so tight that Walt could barely breathe.

Lafe Tolliver pushed his way through the crowd to his wife's side. Vanessa gripped his arm with trembling hands, and told him how Dwight Cuzak had accosted her and Curtis Holden had stopped to help. Lafe charged toward the man who had dared harass his wife.

Ezra jumped in front of him, throwing up his palms. "No, Lafe! No more fightin'!"

Lafe stopped with great effort. "Only because it's you saying it, Ezra," he said, breathing hard.

Ezra turned toward Walt Cuzak, still held tightly by Solomon, and said, "You know the rules, mister, and so do your boys! I made it clear before we started this trip that there would be no fightin'."

"Don't blame us!" Walt said. "I'm sure Dwight didn't start the fight!"

"Oh, yes he did!" Vanessa said. "I told him to leave me alone. Curtis Holden was passing by and heard me. He told Dwight to do as I said and disappear. It was Dwight who started the fight."

Tony Cuzak listened but said nothing. He was so weary of the ways of his father and brothers.

Walt struggled to free himself, but to no avail.

"You just cool down," Solomon said. "I'll let you go when you cool down."

Ezra stepped closer to the head of the Cuzak clan. Biting off each word, he said, "Walt, you and these four are no longer part of this wagon train. Get your wagons and go your way."

"But Ezra, you can't put us out! We paid you in advance for the whole trip!"

"So did everybody else. You and your oldest four broke the rules. Be gone."

"Wait a minute, Ezra!" Dwight said. "Hey, I'm sorry. I didn't mean Vanessa no harm."

"It's *Mrs. Tolliver* to you!" Lafe said, his arm draped protectively around his wife.

Dwight nodded at Vanessa. "Yes, ma'am...*Mrs. Tolliver.*" Then to Ezra: "If Holden hadn't butted in, there wouldn't have been no fight."

Again Vanessa spoke up. "Curtis was being a gentleman, Mr. Comstock. When he heard me tell Dwight to leave, he stepped in to take my part. It was Dwight who swung first."

"Well, he called me a rodent!" Dwight said.

"You were pushing yourself on a married woman," Curtis said. "It's bad enough to be that way with *any* woman, but you sure shouldn't be bothering a married woman!"

Ezra looked at the senior Cuzak, who was still in Solomon's powerful grasp. "Like I said, Walt, be gone."

Walt struggled to get free of the crushing arms. "Make him let go of me, Ezra!"

The wagon master nodded. "Turn 'im loose, Sol."

Solomon eased the husky man to the ground and released him.

"You can't do this, Ezra," Walt said in a wheedling tone. "Me and my boys jumped Curtis because he was fightin' Dwight. We didn't know any more than that. It was an honest mistake. I apologize for what Dwight did."

Ezra was silent for a moment, then said, "That ain't good enough. I'll consider lettin' you stay if Dwight sincerely apologizes and promises not to cause any more trouble."

Walt was still trying to get his breath as he fixed his third son with a hard, meaningful look.

Dwight bristled then looked at Vanessa. "I...I'm sorry, Mrs. Tolliver. I really meant no harm, but I'm sorry."

Dwight turned to Curtis Holden. "I'm sorry. Didn't mean no trouble. Just don't like bein' called a rodent. 'Specially a rat."

"Vanessa...Curtis...," Ezra said, "do you accept his apology?" Both nodded.

"I've got one coming, too! It was my wife you were flirting with!"

A stubborn look etched itself on Dwight's bearded face.

"Do it," Walt said.

Dwight managed to ease the stubborn set of his features and said, "I'm sorry, Mr. Tolliver. All I was doin' was just bein' friendly. I really didn't—"

"Don't you ever go near her again!" Lafe cut in. "Best thing for you to do is leave *all* the women alone!"

"He won't bother any of the ladies," Walt said. "Married or not. Will you, Dwight?"

"No," Dwight said. "No, I won't."

Silence settled over the crowd as everyone waited for Ezra to speak. "Dwight, do I have your solemn promise you won't cause any more trouble in this wagon train? I mean, all the way to Sacramento?"

Dwight didn't look at his father, but he could feel the heat of his look. "Yeah. You got it."

Ezra was silent for a long moment. "Okay, Walt. I'll let you and your wagons stay in the train. But the five of you had better toe the line. There won't be a second chance. Understand?"

"Yeah…I understand."

Ezra told the crowd they'd best get to bed…tomorrow was another long day.

Elmer and Maudie Holden had waited for their grandson, and now watched him look around on the ground for the clothing he'd dropped when the fight started. "I…I dropped the wash around here somewhere. I'll take it back and wash it again."

Just then, Deborah came toward them, carrying the wash and smiling. "I picked up the clothes and rinsed out the dirt."

"Why, thank you," Curtis said. "You didn't have to do that."

"I know. But it's my way of saying how much I appreciate what you did for Mrs. Tolliver. You are a real gentleman."

Curtis blushed and introduced Deborah to his grandparents.

"Would you like me to help you hang them up?" Deborah asked.

"That would be great," he said.

When the wash had been hung on a line strung from the Holden wagon to a nearby tree, Curtis said, "Thanks a lot. Girls are better at this kind of thing than fellas are."

"I won't disagree with that," she said. "Well, I'd better be going."

Curtis stepped close, wanting to take hold of her hand, but refrained. His heart was banging against his rib cage. "See you tomorrow, Deborah."

"Sure will." Deborah turned and took a couple of steps, then turned and said, "I want to say again that I appreciate what you did for Mrs. Tolliver."

Curtis grinned. "I'd do the same for you."

On the thirteenth day out, Ezra announced they were near the
Nebraska border. The hot sun bore down out of a cloudless sky,
causing tempers to flare, but no fights broke out.

It was quite evident to Elmer and Maudie Holden that
Curtis and Deborah had a powerful attraction for each other.
Others in the train saw it, too. Elmer offered to ride in the back
of the wagon for a while that day, so Curtis could invite Deborah
to ride with them. Deborah gladly accepted the invitation.

Because of the intense heat, everyone was drinking more
water. It had been two days since they had come to a stream,
and the water barrels were getting low. Ezra assured everyone
that they would reach a stream the next day.

The wagons lumbered slowly over an undulating sea of
wind-blown grass, and trees had become scarce. When they
came to an area where there were large patches of earth with no
grass, Ezra ordered the wagons to spread out once again, so the
people didn't have to eat each other's dust.

Hannah sat next to Solomon and wiped her sweaty dirt-
streaked forehead, longing for a good soak in a stream. Her hair
was full of dust, and like everyone else, there was grit in her
mouth.

As the wagon rocked and creaked, and the heat and dust
tormented her, Hannah thought of the home she had left in
Independence and the convenient place to bathe, unlike this
journey between streams, when all they could manage were
"spit baths."

At midafternoon, Solomon handed the reins to Hannah and
swung into the saddle on Nipper. The three oldest Cooper children
were riding in different wagons with their friends, but Patty Ruth,
who had been crabby and quarrelsome since she'd awakened, rode
inside the Cooper wagon with only Ulysses for company.

Ezra rode from wagon to wagon to say they would stop at

sundown and were coming back to grassy fields where they could graze the animals. He pointed out that according to the guidebook published by John C. Fremont in 1846, they were now 209 miles from Independence. They had averaged sixteen miles a day, and he was pleased.

As the sun was setting, there was a welcome sight on the western horizon. Heavy clouds were gathering, blocking the sun, and the air began to cool down.

However, the cool air had not eased Patty Ruth's fussiness. At supper, she toyed with her food, and when corrected by her mother, she sassed back. Solomon took her behind the wagon and spanked her. When she returned to supper, her lower lip protruded, and though she gave no more sass, she was quite obviously still in a bad temper.

Solomon and Hannah realized that it wasn't easy for their little girl to stay cooped up in the wagon all day, especially in the heat, and they were giving her the benefit of the doubt. But when she only stared at her food and refused to eat, Solomon told her to get inside the wagon and stay there until she could straighten up.

With Ulysses in hand, Patty Ruth went to the back of the wagon where a couple of wooden boxes were stacked high enough for her to climb up to the tailgate. Biggie, who had already had his supper, welcomed her.

Just as the Coopers were finishing supper, Buck Mylan, who drove one of the Coopers' supply wagons, and his parents were passing by. The Mylans had taken a liking to the Coopers.

Rosalie Mylan greeted the Cooper children, then looked around and asked, "Where's that sweet little Patty Ruth?"

Chris and B. J. looked at each other and snickered.

"That's enough, boys," Solomon said.

"Patty Ruth is in the wagon," Hannah said with a sigh. "She...ah...she's been a bad girl today."

"Why, I can't imagine that," Rosalie said. "Don and I have

talked about what a charming little thing she is."

"Oh, she's got her charm all right," Solomon said, chuckling. "But along with all that charm lives a very stubborn will. She's a precious little girl, and very loving, but periodically she has to be dealt with."

Don Mylan snorted, then laughed. "Who does that sound like, Rosalie? Buck's big sister, Donna, was just like Patty Ruth when she was her age. It's Donna and her family that we're joining in California. Donna was a charmer, but had a stubborn streak. She needed a lot of correcting. But let me encourage you, she's turned out okay. She married a fine man, and they have two wonderful children."

"Well, that is encouraging," Solomon said. "I guess there's hope for us, honey."

Hannah laughed. "I've never doubted it. I'll admit that the little one is very different from her sister, here, but she'll turn out all right."

As the Mylans moved on, Solomon said, "Sweetheart, I told Cecil Oakley I'd come over after supper and help him repair one of his wagon wheels."

"All right, darling. Better head on over there then."

As Solomon limped among the campfires, he came face to face with Walt Cuzak. Cuzak just stared at him and started to move past when Solomon turned and said, "Walt…"

"Yeah?"

"Look, there's no need for you and me to be at odds. Here we are, traveling in this wagon train together with a long time to go. Being enemies is foolish. How about we bury the hatchet, and—"

"You're the one who put the bear hug on me, Cooper. I didn't do it to you. So, who started it, anyway?"

"I was only helping Curtis, Walt. I didn't start anything."

"Another thing…you stay away from Tony with your religious stuff."

"Tony will tell you that he approached me," Solomon said.

"Well, you stay away from him. I don't want him hearin' all that Jesus stuff."

"If Tony's willing to listen, I'm going to talk to him about being saved until he opens his heart to the Lord. Would do you some good too, Walt. Not only will Jesus give Walt Cuzak a place in heaven, if you'll let Him, He'll take that sour attitude out of you and give you real joy."

Anger suffused Cuzak's face. "I don't want anything to do with Jesus Christ!"

Solomon kept his voice low and looked at Walt with compassion. "You will have plenty to do with Jesus Christ one day, whether you like it or not. Every Christ rejecter is going to stand before Him at the White Throne Judgment and be cast into the lake of fire."

Cuzak swore again, and said, "I don't believe that!"

"It's your very unbelief that will land you in hell forever. By saying you don't believe what I said about the Lord Jesus Christ, you're telling me that you're headed for hell."

Tony stepped out of the shadows just as Walt turned to walk away. When father and son came face to face, Walt stopped long enough to say, "You stay away from that fanatic!" With that, he moved stiff-leggedly across the circle.

Tony lifted his hat and ran his fingers through his hair. "I'm sorry for Dad's behavior, Mr. Cooper, and I appreciate the kindness you showed him in spite of his attitude."

"You were listening?"

"Yeah."

"Well, what about you, Tony? Do you want to escape the lake of fire?"

"Of course."

"You can be saved right now, if you will. I'll be glad to help you."

Tony wiped a nervous hand over his mouth. "I...uh...I'm not ready yet, Mr. Cooper."

"Are you ready to die?"

"Well, no—"

"Then you'd best turn to Jesus right now."

"Mr. Cooper, I appreciate your concern for me, but...well, I need some more time."

"Are you reading those Bible passages I marked for you?"

"Yes, sir."

"Well, keep it up. And Tony..."

"Yes, sir?"

"Read Luke chapter 12—the part about the rich man who thought he had many years to live. See what happened to him on the very night he assured himself he had a long life ahead of him."

"I'll read it right now, sir."

"Good. I'm always here for you, Tony. Don't ever hesitate to come and find me when you need help with this."

"I won't, Mr. Cooper. Thank you."

At the Cooper wagon, Hannah and Mary Beth were drying the dishes and cookware. Hannah turned to her sons, who were sitting by the fire talking, and said, "Would one of you boys go inside the wagon and bring the box that the cooking stuff goes in?"

"I'll get it, Mama," B. J. said, and darted away.

Hannah turned to her other son. "Chris, throw some wood on the fire. We'll need more light when Papa returns for Bible reading before bedtime."

Chris went to the small pile of broken tree limbs and bent to pick some up just as B. J. came running back, saying, "Mama! Patty Ruth's not in the wagon!"

"What? Of course she is. She was told to stay there until she was ready to straighten up."

"No, she isn't. Biggie's in there, but she and Ulysses are gone."

Chris dropped the wood and followed his mother as she rushed to the rear of the wagon. Biggie made little whining sounds, wagging his tail.

As Hannah searched, panic rose within her. She returned to the rear of the wagon and climbed down, looking around the circle. There was no sign of her youngest daughter.

She went to the outer perimeter of the circle and called Patty Ruth's name repeatedly. When there was no response, she turned to Chris. "Go get Papa! Mary Beth…B. J.…split up and go around the circle and ask if anyone in camp has seen your little sister. I'll wait here for Papa."

Chapter Thirteen

The brilliant moon spread its silver light over the prairie as the wind picked up, popping the wagons' canvas covers.

Cecil Oakley looked skyward and commented, "Those clouds in the west are getting closer, Sol. I think we're about to get some rain."

"Papa! Papa!"

Solomon glanced up to see his oldest son running across the open circle.

"It's Patty Ruth, Papa! She's disappeared!"

Solomon dropped his tools and lay aside the wheel. "What do you mean, disappeared?"

"You sent her to the wagon during supper and told her not to leave it till she was ready to straighten up...well, she's gone. Mama asked me to come and get you."

Solomon turned to his friend. "Cecil, I'll have to finish this later."

"I'm coming with you," he replied. "Katherine, would you bring me the lantern from inside the wagon?"

Ezra Comstock was already at the Cooper wagon with several other men when Solomon arrived, and Micah Comstock's voice could be heard in the camp, recruiting men for the search.

Ezra nodded encouragement and said, "Sol, we'll find her. She couldn't have gone far. We'll get every man to help us. We'll spread out with the lanterns."

Hannah's grip tightened on Solomon's arm. "Oh, Sol. You don't suppose she ran away because you sent her to the wagon?"

"Honey, she's been sent to the wagon three times since we left Independence. She didn't run away the other two times."

Hannah brushed a trembling hand across her forehead. "But, maybe she decided this time would be the last time."

"We'll have the answer when we find her. Now, you stay here with the women and children while we go after her."

Micah joined the group with four more men.

Quickly Ezra organized the men into four teams and sent them off in different directions. Before they left he told them, "When you find Patty Ruth, fire three shots in quick succession. The rest of us will converge at that spot."

The wind was getting stronger, carrying the unmistakable smell of rain as it stirred the campfires and made the lanterns flicker.

Ezra glanced at the sky. "It won't be long till those clouds cover the moon...and there's rain comin'. We're all glad to get the rain, but we've got to find that little girl before the storm hits. Let's go!"

Chris had one of the lanterns from the wagon in hand. "Is it all right if I go, Papa?"

"Sure, son. You can be on my team."

"Can I go, too, Papa?" B. J. asked.

"You're a bit young yet, son. I don't want to have to go looking for you, too. Sorry, but I can't let you go."

"But I want to help find my little sister."

"I know, but you'll need to stay here and give strength to Mama and Mary Beth. You'll be a big fella if you do that."

"Yes, sir. I'll take care of them for you."

"Good boy." Solomon turned to Hannah and laid a hand on her shoulder. "I know you're already praying, sweetheart. Keep it up. We'll find her, and she'll be all right, too. I love you."

Hannah nodded, blinking to hold back the tears. She stepped to the edge of the circle of wagons and watched her husband and son move out onto the prairie with the other men. She felt two small bodies press against her and arms go around her waist.

"Patty Ruth will be all right, Mama," Mary Beth said. "Jesus knows where she is, and He loves her more than we ever could. He will take care of her."

"That's right, Mama," B. J. said. "Jesus will take care of her."

Every woman in the wagon train was gathered around Hannah, Mary Beth, and B. J., and took turns speaking words of encouragement.

Twenty minutes had passed when little Polly Winters looked up at her mother and whispered, "Mommy, could I tell Mrs. Cooper that I love her? Maybe that would make her feel better."

"I'm sure it would, honey," Gladys said. "Go ahead."

Hannah was looking toward the prairie once more, praying in her heart.

"Mama..." Mary Beth said. "Somebody's here to see you."

Hannah turned to find the sweet little five-year-old who had become Patty Ruth's friend. "Why, Polly...hello."

"Mrs. Cooper," came the tiny voice, "I love you."

A lump rose in Hannah's throat, and she bent down to pick up the little girl and hug her close. "I love you, too, sweetheart."

Polly wrapped her arms around Hannah's neck and leaned close to whisper, "My daddy and Patty Ruth's daddy and the rest of those men will find her, Mrs. Cooper. Patty Ruth is my friend, and I know God will take care of her."

Hannah bit her lip and held Polly tighter. "Yes. God will take care of her."

Suddenly three shots ripped through the night in swift succession.

Out on the prairie, to the southeast of the circle of wagons, the men were converging on a low spot beyond a grassy rise.

When Solomon limped up with Chris, Lloyd Marlin, and Tony Cuzak at his side, he saw his little daughter sitting on the ground in a circle of lantern light. Donald and Buck Mylan knelt close to her, with Jock Weathers and Dave Croft, who were part of their team, standing over them.

In the crook of Patty Ruth's arm was Ulysses Cooper, and on the ground next to her was a young jackrabbit. She was stroking its long, furry ears.

Solomon went to his knees before his little daughter and said, "Honey, why did you leave the wagon?"

Patty Ruth's lips quivered as the night wind plucked at loose strands of her hair. "Because…because I was mad. I didn' want to stay in the wagon. An'…well, Papa, I was feelin' sorry for myself. I was sorta all mixed up. So I decided to jis' take a walk."

"Mm-hmm. And what about this jackrabbit?"

"I foun' 'im when I was walkin'. When he didn' run from me, I knew he mus' be hurt." She looked down at the rabbit. "He's not very old, Papa. An'…an' I think his hind legs are broke. I was gonna bring him to the camp, but when I tried to pick him up, he scratched me. I didn' want to leave 'im here all alone, bein' hurt, so I stayed with 'im. I figured you would come lookin' for me."

Solomon caressed his little girl's cheek. "You did wrong to

disobey me and leave the wagon, Patty Ruth. Do you under-stand that?"

She blinked. "Yes, Papa."

"Your mother is back at the camp, all torn up with worry that something bad has happened to you."

Patty Ruth's free hand was still stroking the rabbit. The tears spilled down her freckled cheeks in tiny rivulets. Sniffling, she said, "I've been real bad, haven't I, Papa?"

"Yes, you have."

"Are you gonna spank me?"

"Well, that depends. Do you think you've learned your lesson about disobeying Papa when he tells you to stay in the wagon until you can straighten up?"

"Yes, Papa."

"Then there won't be a spanking."

The relief on Patty Ruth's face was almost comical. She looked down at the rabbit. "Can we take him to the camp and take care of him, Papa?"

"Sure, honey. Let's take a look at him."

The men drew closer with their lanterns as Solomon care-fully examined the young jackrabbit. It was frightened and tried to scratch him, but he was able to examine it.

"The legs aren't broken," he said for all to hear. "Somehow the little fella has been injured, but we'll take him with us and nurse him back to health."

Ezra bent down. "Would you like me to carry him, Patty Ruth? I've handled jackrabbits before."

"Uh-huh. Thank you, Mr. Comstock."

Ezra picked up the rabbit by the nape of the neck, and Solomon took Patty Ruth in his arms. They hugged each other tight, and Patty Ruth began to cry again. "I'm sorry, Papa. I'll try not to be bad any more."

"All right, sweetheart. Let's get back to the camp so your mama and Mary Beth and B. J. will know you're okay."

The moon was fully covered by clouds and the wind was blowing hard as the group entered the circle of wagons. There was great rejoicing when the women and children saw Patty Ruth in her father's arms, clutching Ulysses.

Patty Ruth was quickly transferred to Hannah's arms, and she hugged her mother fiercely and wept, saying, "I'm sorry, Mama. Papa didn' spank me 'cause I told 'im I've learned my lesson. I shouldn' have left the wagon. Please forgive me."

"You're forgiven, honey. I love my baby girl."

"I love my mama, too."

Patty Ruth's attention was drawn to Polly Winters, who stood patiently looking up, waiting for a chance to speak.

"Hi, Patty Ruth. I sure am glad God took care of you. Would you like to ride in our wagon tomorrow?"

"Uh-huh. If Mama says it's all right."

"That'll be fine, Polly," Hannah said.

While Polly and Patty Ruth were talking, Ezra held up the jackrabbit and explained to the small crowd that Patty Ruth had found it injured and wouldn't leave it. This broke the tension, and suddenly everyone began talking at once and drifting toward their own campfires and wagons.

"Tell you what, folks," Ezra Comstock called out. "The way the wind is blowin', and the feel I've got in my bones, I'd say we've got a healthy storm movin' in. We'd best make sure our animals are secured and tighten the covers on the wagons."

As people hastened to follow Ezra's advice, Solomon said, "Hannah, our animals are secured right here, and the wagon cover is down tight already. So I'm going to finish my repair job on the Oakley wheel. It will only take another half hour or so."

"All right, darling. I'll get the children ready for bed."

As he started to walk away, Patty Ruth called, "Papa..."

"Yes, honey?"

"Thank you for forgivin' me."

"I love you, sweetie. When you admit you've done wrong, and show you're sorry for it, I would be wrong not to forgive you."

Solomon had just finished his work on the wagon wheel and was putting it back on the wagon when the rain started to fall. Blue-white daggers of lightning lashed the sky and thunder shook the earth as the howling wind accelerated the rain's force.

People dashed to their wagons, bending their heads against the storm. Solomon and Cecil were soaked to the skin by the time they had the wheel back on the axle.

Lanterns shone dully through the canvas-covered wagon walls, giving vague light to the circle. Walt Cuzak's sons Frank, Gordon, and Edmund had climbed inside Walt's wagon to play poker.

"Where's Dwight?" Walt asked, as he turned up the over-head lantern.

"Dunno," Frank said. "He knew we were playin' poker tonight. Maybe he'll be along in a minute."

Walt's features turned stony as he said, "Course, no need askin' about your little brother. He thinks he's too good to hang around the likes of us anymore."

"Too bad about him," Edmund said. "I used to have high hopes for the kid."

Walt nodded. "He got too many genes from your mother, I guess."

Walt had successfully turned his four older sons against the memory of their mother. He had drilled it into them that she was nothing but a religious fanatic ever since she made friends with "Bible-jabbering" neighbors when Frank was their only child. The neighbors had dragged her off to church, and the next thing Walt knew, Mariana was telling him she had become a Christian, and was inviting him to church, too.

From that time on, Walt had felt plagued with Mariana's talk about Jesus Christ, until he angrily told her to shut up about it. He had to admit that Mariana was a better wife and mother after becoming a Christian, but he always felt uncomfortable when she prayed at the table before eating, and came home from church looking so happy. As the boys grew older, she took them to church and taught them Bible verses.

Finally, he put his foot down. His boys weren't going to Sunday school or church anymore, and Mariana was forbidden to teach them any more Bible. It bothered him because she wouldn't lash back at him. She was always so sweet and kind. Periodically, she would slip in a word about Jesus Christ, or heaven and hell. Walt hated it, but he didn't leave her because he needed her to care for the house, cook the meals, and take care of his boys.

When Mariana died giving birth to Tony, Walt was glad she was gone. He hired a nursemaid and housekeeper, making sure, first, that the woman wasn't a religious fanatic.

"Too bad about those genes," Gordon said. "Tony never will be part of us."

Walt opened a deck of cards and started shuffling them. "Yeah. Right now he's probably out there in the rain bein' a Good Samaritan to somebody. Never thinks of himself. Always doin' for somebody else. That's stupid. My philosophy is take care of ol' number one."

"Right, Pa," Frank said with a nod.

Edmund pulled a small wooden box from a larger one and dumped the chips on the small table.

"I'm so ashamed of Tony," Walt continued. "I hate for anyone to know he's my son. He's soft. Not tough like you boys. And now that religious nut, Solomon Cooper, is workin' on him. I'm scared to death he's gonna make a Christian outta that kid. Then he'll be gone, for sure. Havin' your old lady a fanatic was enough. Sure hate to think of havin' another religious fool in the family."

"Maybe you oughtta write him off and disown him," Edmund said. "Send him packin'. Then we won't have to share any of the gold with him."

"Just might do that."

At the Oakley wagon, Solomon and Cecil were getting their tools picked up when Tony Cuzak came dashing up. "Can you men come? The wind just tore the canvas off Maudie and Elmer Holden's wagon! The old folks are getting soaked! Curtis is trying to get the cover back on, but he needs help!"

"Let's go!" Solomon shouted.

Curtis already had Lafe Tolliver helping him when Tony returned with Cecil and Solomon.

Elmer and Maudie sat huddled in their wagon, rain drenching them and everything around them.

"Just hang on, folks!" Solomon shouted. "We'll have the cover back on in a few minutes!"

At the Tolliver wagon, Vanessa was sitting on a wooden box, wrapped in a shawl, hoping the Holden's canvas top could be replaced quickly so that Lafe could get back to her. She hated thunderstorms, and this was a bad one. She was glad, at least, that Lafe had made sure their own canvas was secured.

Vanessa picked up a book and tilted it toward the nearby lantern to read. But the whine of the wind and the pelting rain was too much. She couldn't concentrate. Lightning cracked overhead and thunder boomed.

Suddenly a fierce gust of wind worked the canvas loose and began slapping it against wood. Vanessa strained to grasp the loose cord, but it whipped just beyond her reach as the rain pelted her face. There was nothing left but to climb down from the wagon and tie the flap in place.

The wind blurred her vision as she bent to let down the tailgate. In the same instant she saw the dark form of a man standing no more than three feet away. Her shawl slipped from her shoulders as she straightened and the dripping-wet man pressed himself against the tailgate, taking hold of the flapping canvas cover.

Lightning lit up the sky, illuminating the man's features.

Vanessa's heart jumped wildly as she recognized Dwight Cuzak. "Wh-what do you want?"

"Hello, honey. I saw Lafe over at the Holden wagon. Thought maybe you might be lonely."

Thunder shook the ground as Vanessa cried, "Get away from me!"

"I notice you're having trouble with that flap, honey. I'll fix it for you, then in appreciation you will no doubt invite me in out of the rain, like any good neighbor would do."

"You leave right now or I'll scream!"

Dwight laughed, brushing water from his eyes. "Who's gonna hear you the way this storm is carryin' on? No sense bein' unfriendly, honey. Just a minute. I'll fix that flap for you."

While he tied the flap, Vanessa grabbed the canvas covering and tried to tie it over the rear opening, but her hands were trembling, and she couldn't make a knot.

Dwight jerked the canvas from her hands and grabbed her wrist. "Flap's secured, honey. Are you gonna invite me in?"

She shook her head, struggling against his strong grip. Dwight pulled her closer and bent over the tailgate, curling his other hand behind her neck. She made a mewing sound as he pressed his lips to hers and held the kiss for a long moment. When he released her, Vanessa stumbled back in revulsion, wiping her mouth.

When the loose canvas fell back across the opening, Dwight pushed it aside and held it there, saying, "If you tell your husband, he'll no doubt come after me. But if he does, I'll kill 'im! You'd best be thankful for the thrill you just had and keep quiet about it. Anybody sees me here, I was just bein' a gentleman and tyin' down the flap for you."

Vanessa grabbed the canvas cover from his hand and jerked it into place, leaving him standing in the rain. She held her breath until she heard his steps splashing away, then worked at tying the end cover. It took several minutes for her trembling hands to accomplish the task. At last she turned and went to the lantern, holding her hands over the top of the glass chimney to warm them.

Suddenly the enormity of what had just happened flooded her and she started to gag, wiping her mouth again and again as the nausea came in waves. She trembled all over, but it was more from wrath than from being soaked to the skin.

Vanessa wanted to tell her husband what that obnoxious man had done, but the look in Dwight's eyes when he'd warned her was enough to fill her with fear. Best just to let it go.

CHAPTER FOURTEEN

The next morning, as soon as people were up and building fires, Curtis Holden went about the camp, asking people for a stick or two of dry wood. Everyone knew about the canvas top blowing off his grandparents' wagon and were glad to share their wood.

Curtis had visited four wagons when he came to Walt Cuzak's.

"So what're you doin', Holden?" Walt asked. "Passin' out wood?"

Frank and Edmund chortled.

"No, I'm askin' folks to donate a little so my grandparents can have a fire this morning."

Father and sons exchanged glances. "We ain't got no spare wood," Walt said.

Curtis smiled in a friendly manner and turned away, saying, "Well, thanks just the same. I know you'd share if you had it."

Edmund snorted in derision. "Sure we would," he said in a low voice. "Maybe when the north pole becomes a tropical paradise."

Soon Curtis came to the Marlin wagon where Deborah and her brother-in-law were standing over a smoking fire.

"Good morning," Curtis said, looking at Deborah with adoring eyes.

"Hey, how about me?" Lloyd asked. "Do I get a 'good morning' too?"

Curtis adjusted the wood in his arms and laughed. "Oh, sure, Lloyd. Good morning to you!"

"And how about us?" came Suzanne's melodic voice, as she stood near the rear of the wagon with baby James in her arms.

"Well, good morning to James and his mother, too!" Curtis said with a chuckle.

Lloyd glanced at the bundle in Curtis's arms. "Are you gathering wood for your grandparents?"

"Well, let's say I'm trying. I was just at Walt Cuzak's wagon. Didn't fare too well there."

Lloyd laughed. "You really didn't expect to, did you?"

"Not really. Just thought I'd give those malcontents an opportunity to reform."

"Well, we've got plenty of dry wood. How about I load your arms the rest of the way, then carry another armload to your wagon?"

"Don't need that much, Lloyd. If you could spare enough to fill my arms, I'll get the rest from others."

"No need," Lloyd said.

"I'll help carry wood," Deborah said.

Lloyd smiled knowingly. "Okay. Let's get you both loaded up."

Moments later, Curtis and Deborah were headed toward the Holden wagon.

"Some storm, huh?" Curtis said, smiling at Deborah.

"Sure was. And from what I heard Ezra tell a group of the men, we're liable to get some more just like it. He said severe storms like that run in cycles. Whenever the first one hits, you can look for several before they ease down to simple rain showers."

"Well, I guess we'll just have to tough it through them."

The elderly Holdens had watched the young couple's approach all the way across the open circle, and now greeted them with a big smile. To Elmer and Maudie, it was quite evident that their grandson had found the woman he wanted to marry.

Curtis dropped the wood from his arms and quickly took the load out of Deborah's. "We can get a fire going now," he said to his grandparents. "Most of the wood came from the Marlins."

"You should've hollered," Elmer said. "I could have carried what Deborah's carryin'."

"It's all right, Mr. Holden…it wasn't that heavy."

Soon Curtis had a fire going and Maudie began preparing breakfast. Elmer decided to give Curtis a little push and turned to Deborah. "If you'd like to ride in our wagon today, you're plenty welcome, Deborah. Maudie and I can ride in the back so's you love birds can have a little…ah…privacy."

Deborah's cheeks flushed.

"Elmer!" Maudie said. "You've done gone and embarrassed them!"

The old man snickered. "Well now, Ma, my eyesight ain't what it once 'twas, but I know what young folks look like when the lovebug has bit 'em!"

Curtis cleared his throat nervously. "Deborah, you'll have to excuse Grandpa. He's not much for tact."

"It's all right, Curtis," she said, and smiled.

"Then, would you like to ride with us today?"

"Of course."

"Maybe we could even walk alongside the wagon and let Grandpa hold the reins for a while. Helps the oxen when we lighten the load, you know."

"Certainly. We'll walk as long as you want to."

At the lead wagon, Ezra and his nephew were standing at the tailgate, eating breakfast and talking to Chuck Lander and Hank Norwood, whose sons drove supply wagons for Solomon Cooper.

"So you really think we'll have more storms like the one last night, Ezra?" Hank asked.

"Prob'ly a half-dozen or so, yep."

The four men noticed Mary Beth and Patty Ruth Cooper coming toward them with Biggie trotting alongside. And of course Patty Ruth carried Ulysses.

"Good mornin', ladies," Ezra said. "I think I know why you're here."

"I'm sure you do, Mr. Comstock," Mary Beth said with a smile. "Mama's fixing breakfast. She said it would be best if I bring Patty Ruth over here now."

Ezra bent down and winked at the little redhead. "You want to see your furry little friend, don't you, honey?"

"Yes, sir."

"All right. I already fed him some grass for breakfast." The wagon master leaned over the tailgate and brought out a wooden box with its lid off. Lowering it so the little redhead could see the jackrabbit, he said, "See there? He's doin' just fine."

Patty Ruth reached in and stroked its long ears. "Good mornin', Mr. Rabbit. Do you feel better today?"

"I'm sure he does, honey," Ezra said. "Mr. Rabbit is going to get well, I'll guarantee you."

She smiled up at the old man. "That's good. Thank you for takin' care of him, Mr. Comstock."

"You're welcome. You can see him anytime we're stopped for camp."

Patty Ruth petted the rabbit again. "'Bye, Mr. Rabbit. See you tonight."

Lafe Tolliver lay aside the top layer of kindling and dug deeper into the box to find dry wood. Vanessa stood over him, wanting to tell him about Dwight Cuzak, but she held her tongue. Dwight was the kind of man who would kill if he got angry enough, she thought, and he'd probably do it by stealth.

"I'm sure sorry you had trouble with the canvas last night, Vanessa," Lafe said. "I still don't know how you managed to tie that knot so tight in the corner. It'll hold now, for sure."

"You just don't know how strong your wife really is," she said with a hollow laugh.

Moments later, Lafe was building a fire near the wagon while Vanessa put grounds in the coffeepot and filled it with water. The tailgate was suspended horizontally with short lengths of chain, and she was using its flat surface to prepare breakfast.

Lafe was bent over the fire, fanning the flames, when Dwight Cuzak passed by slowly. He stopped just as Vanessa turned to say something to Lafe. Instantly, her body stiffened.

Lafe felt the tension in his wife and turned to see what she was looking at. He caught the licentious look in Dwight's eyes and leaped in front of Dwight, blocking his path. "I saw that, mister!"

"Saw *what?*"

"The way you looked at my wife!"

"And how was that?"

"The wrong way, that's how!"

"Aw, it's just your imagination."

"Don't stand there acting innocent, you vulgar piece of scum!"

Dwight bristled and doubled up his fists.

"Good!" Lafe said. "You swing first, then I'll finish it!"

"Hold it!" came Ezra Comstock's shout. "What's goin' on here?"

"He was eyeing Vanessa again!" Lafe said, as the wagon master drew up with Micah and Tony at his side.

"That's a lie!" Dwight said.

Ezra held up his hands. "Now, both of you cool down. I'm not gonna tolerate this arguin', nor the fightin' you were about to do!"

"Then you tell this lecher to stay away from Vanessa, Ezra! I know what I saw, and so does Vanessa!" Lafe wheeled around and looked at his wife. "Tell him, Vanessa!"

Vanessa avoided Dwight's eyes and said, "This is the second time Dwight Cuzak has been a source of trouble over me, Mr. Comstock. My husband is right. He was leering at me."

Solomon and Hannah Cooper stood in the half-circle of onlookers beside Deborah and Curtis.

Ezra turned to Dwight, who was standing beside his father and brothers, and said, "You promised me after the other incident that you wouldn't cause any more trouble in this train. I warned you and your father that there would be no second chance."

"Now, look Ezra," Dwight said, "it's their word against mine. Okay, when Curtis Holden and me had trouble, I was talkin' to Van— Mrs. Tolliver, though I meant nothin' bad about it. All I was doin' this time was walkin' past their wagon. Nothin' else. Lafe's imagination is keyed up because of the other thing. I'm tellin' you, Ezra, I didn't do nothin' wrong."

Ezra studied Dwight's face and came to a decision. "I believe the Tollivers. But since it's your word against theirs, I'm givin' you one more chance to stay out of trouble."

Then Ezra moved up close to Dwight, who dwarfed him in size, and said evenly, "I'm gonna say this just once. Are you listenin'? You keep your distance from Mrs. Tolliver. If there's anything...*anything* like what happened the other time, or this time, you and your family are out of the train and on your own. Understood?"

Dwight looked at his grim-faced father. Then to Ezra, he said, "Understood."

Ezra turned to Walt Cuzak. "Understood?"

"Understood," Walt said.

"All right, then. You'd better make sure your son stays as far away from Mrs. Tolliver as possible. Court is adjourned."

During breakfast at the Cooper wagon, Solomon noticed that Hannah wasn't her usual cheerful self. "Sweetheart, you look awfully tired. Didn't you get to sleep after the storm let up last night?"

The entire family had bedded down inside the wagon, and though it was crowded and uncomfortable, Solomon had thought everyone slept well.

Hannah rubbed weary eyes. "No, I didn't. It was the wee hours before I fell asleep."

"But the storm was over."

"The one outside…it's the one inside that kept me from sleeping."

"Your parents?"

"I can't get them out of my mind…the look on their faces when they knew for sure we were moving to Wyoming."

Mary Beth took her mother's hand. The small loving gesture brought tears to Hannah's eyes. "Sol, I may never see them again on this earth. It's tearing me up to know how they feel toward you, and toward me. They're still blaming you the most, you know, and it bothers me deeply."

Solomon pushed his plate away and reached to enfold her in his arms. "Sweetheart, it bothered me, too, to see the hurt and the anger in their eyes. But we didn't leave Independence on a whim."

"I know."

"Remember the peace we both had when Colonel Bateman explained the need for the store at Fort Bridger...and how sure we were it was God's will for us to pack up and move?"

"Yes."

"And how the Lord had the Wilsons ready to buy the store, and the Donaldsons ready to buy the farm—both at very good prices?"

"Yes."

"And we looked into the church situation by talking to Reverend Kelly?"

"Yes."

"Then we're doing God's will in making this move, aren't we?"

"Yes, darling. Yes, we are. If it weren't for Mother and Daddy, I wouldn't be having such a hard time."

Solomon kissed her soft cheek. "The Lord knows all about this. And in time, maybe Ben and Esther will miss you and their grandchildren so much that Ben will swallow his pride and make the move to Fort Bridger."

"Oh, boy!" Patty Ruth said. "Maybe Grandma and Grandpa will come to Fort Bridger, too!"

Hannah managed a smile and caressed the little redhead's cheek as she said, "Once we get to Fort Bridger, I'll keep letters going to Grandma and Grandpa, telling them how much we love them and miss them. Maybe the Lord will work in their hearts, and they'll come to live near us, in spite of Grandpa's stubbornness. We'll pray for that very thing."

❦   ❦   ❦

The sky remained clear all morning as Solomon and Mary Beth walked beside the Cooper wagon. Solomon was used to looking at the lead wagon and seeing either Chris riding beside it or Buster tied to the rear of it. Today neither Chris nor Buster were at the lead wagon.

Solomon turned around and looked along the line of wagons. There was Chris, riding beside the Chuck Lander wagon.

Thinking aloud he said, "I wonder what Chris is doing at the Lander wagon."

Mary Beth giggled. "He discovered Joy Lynn Lander a couple of days ago, Papa. You haven't noticed it, but he's been back there quite often the last two days. It's just that he's stayed there all morning today."

Solomon grinned. "Joy Lynn, eh? I've noticed that both of the Lander girls are pretty. What's her sister's name?"

"Trina Lee. She's sixteen. From what I could tell, Chris was attracted to Trina Lee first, but lost interest when he found out she was an older woman."

Solomon laughed. "That boy. It sure didn't take him long to forget Lula Mae Springer."

"That doesn't surprise me. I heard Chris telling Micah that Joy Lynn likes the way he rides Buster."

"Oh-oh. Don't let your little sister hear about that. She'll be teasing him about Joy Lynn till we get to Fort Bridger."

Mary Beth giggled again. "Well, I won't be the one to tell her, you can count on that!"

It was almost noon when the wagon train reached the stream Ezra had promised would be there. The heavy rain of the night before had muddied it some, but they were able to get some clean water by using heavy towels to strain it. As the train moved on, the water barrels were blessedly full once more.

Later in the afternoon there was a short rainstorm, but nothing like what they had experienced the night before.

The next morning, the sky was clear again. Everyone had slept well, and the train pulled out less than an hour after sunrise.

By early afternoon, what was a clear sky began to take on a cloud cover. Soon the wind was growing strong, and overhead the sky became dark with swirling black clouds. Lightning flashed to the north and the west, and everyone who was walking began climbing into the wagons.

At the Lander wagon, Chris Cooper trailed at the rear, talking to Joy Lynn and her sister. Both sisters had jet-black hair and creamy complexions. Every time Joy Lynn set her eyes on Chris, his heart felt like it was going to leap through his chest.

As the storm took on a fierce look, Chuck Lander leaned from the seat and called back, "Chris!"

"Yes, sir?"

"It's going to rain pretty soon, son. Why don't you tie Buster on the back and climb inside?"

"Yes, sir!"

Chris was about to swing his leg over the saddle when Ezra Comstock came trotting along and shouted, "We're makin' a circle, Chuck! Storm's gonna be a bad one! Form a circle!" With that, the wagon master was gone.

The wagons ahead were already beginning to form a curve.

When Comstock pulled up to the Walt Cuzak wagon and repeated the message, Walt frowned. "Whatta you talkin' about, Ezra? That storm ain't gonna hurt us none. We gotta keep goin'."

"No we don't!" Ezra said. "I know about storms on these plains...I'm callin' for a circle because it's the safe thing to do."

Cuzak hawked and spat. "Look Ezra, if we stop now, we're losin' valuable time..."

"We could lose a lot more than time! We've got a dozen saddle horses in this train, plus yours. I'm tellin' you, we gotta secure 'em before that storm reaches us!"

Cuzak ejected a string of profanity, eyes blazing. "Look, man, every day me and my sons ain't in California is a day we won't be diggin' for gold! Delay will cost us money! We'll lose time if we stop. I say we keep goin'!"

"Your say don't count! Make the circle!"

"I ain't gonna do it, and neither are my boys!"

"Make the circle, and don't argue!"

"I ain't doin' it!"

Ezra shouted above the wind, trying to control his mount, who was dancing nervously. "You're free to go ahead on your own, if you please, but keep in mind that there are lots of hostile Indians between here and where you're goin'! Only four wagons in a train would be real temptin' for 'em!"

Walt cursed and shook his head. "Okay, okay, okay! We'll get in the circle."

Ezra guided his wagon train to a spot where several tall cottonwoods stood in a row and heavy bushes grew between them. The trees and bushes would serve as a windbreak.

When the animals were secured and the cords that held the wagon covers had been checked, everyone climbed inside their wagons to wait out the storm.

Solomon paused for a moment to look at the black, rolling clouds, and then climbed inside. When he had secured the canvas covers at both ends and eased onto one of the benches, he said, "This one's going to be bad. Let's ask the Lord to keep us safe."

When the "Amen" came, great streaks of lightning ripped

across the black sky, lighting the inside of the wagon. Thunder came rumbling almost immediately like the chest-deep growl of a monstrous, attacking beast.

CHAPTER FIFTEEN

T he rain came in torrents, driven by the violent, howling
wind. The lightning struck more frequently now, sometimes hitting the ground. The horses neighed in terror,
pacing in half-circles on their hind legs, pulling at the ropes
that held them.

In the Lander wagon, Elsie and her husband were sitting
near the front of the wagon, and sisters Trina Lee and Joy Lynn
were side by side at the rear.

Trina Lee wrapped her arms around her knees and put
her head down as lightning illuminated the interior of the
wagon. "I wish Bob was with us," she said.

Elsie smiled. "Funny how you and your brother pick on
each other and act like you're enemies, but at a time like this,
you want him with you."

Trina Lee grinned. "It's an act, all right. Bob is the greatest
brother any sister ever had."

"That's for sure," Joy Lynn said. "Right now I wish he was
riding our wagon instead of driving Mr. Cooper's."

Trina Lee giggled and elbowed her sister. "I have an idea,
little sis, that if you could choose between having Bob sitting
here with you or Chris Cooper, you'd choose Chris."

Joy Lynn blushed. "Well…"

Suddenly they jerked in surprise as a giant bolt of lightning struck a cottonwood tree next to the wagon, splitting off a huge section of the tree. With a powerful jolt, the limb crashed through the wooden ribs and canvas covering, landing in the rear of the wagon.

Chuck and Elsie sprang from their seats as Trina Lee's screams filled the air. Chuck strained to lift the tree but couldn't budge it.

"I'll get help!" he said, and leaped from the wagon.

Elsie peered through the leaves and clawed at the smaller limbs as rain poured through the torn canvas. "Hold on, Trina!" she cried. "Daddy's gone for help! We'll get you out in a few minutes! Is Joy Lynn all right?"

"I don't know, Mother!" Trina Lee wailed. "She's behind me, and I can't move! I can't turn to look at her!"

"Joy Lynn, honey…are you all right?"

When no answer came, Elsie cried, "Joy Lynn! Talk to me, honey! Are you all right?"

Elsie could hear voices above the sound of the storm. She wheeled around and looked past the ripped canvas to see her husband and son, along with Solomon Cooper, Curtis Holden, Tony Cuzak, and others.

Elsie fought to keep her fear at bay as she shouted, "Chuck, I can't get a sound out of Joy Lynn! And Trina Lee can't move!"

Chuck lifted Elsie out of the wagon and then went to help the other men. While the tree was slowly raised, Elsie looked up to see Hannah Cooper. Conversation was a lost effort against the noise of the storm, so Hannah just threw her arms around the worried mother and held her tight.

Finally the massive section of cottonwood dropped to the ground with a thud, and father and brother climbed inside the wagon.

Trina Lee moaned as Bob lifted her carefully into his arms. "Here, Bob. I'll take her," Solomon said.

Bob eased his sister into Solomon's arms and turned back to see about Joy Lynn, just as his father ejected a loud cry and wailed, "She's dead! Elsie, our baby is dead!"

Elsie tried to climb into the wagon. "No-o-o!"

"You don't want to see her, Elsie!" Chuck shouted, preventing his wife from coming over the tailgate.

"She's my baby! I want to see my baby!"

Hannah and the men stood by, their wet faces solemn, as Elsie pressed herself against the wagon and released a wild, almost demented scream. Chuck jumped down and folded her into his embrace, and together they wept for their inconsolable loss.

The violent storm raged on. Chris Cooper had been left to watch over his brother and sisters in the family wagon. Outside, Nipper and Buster were wild-eyed, pulling at their tethers. All the children pressed together closely, and Mary Beth held a terrified Biggie on her lap.

When B. J. began to tremble uncontrollably, Chris put an arm around him and said, "It's going to be all right, B. J. The storm will be over in a while."

"Why are Mama and Papa stayin' gone so long?" Patty Ruth asked, clutching Ulysses.

"It must be taking a while for the men to lift the tree off the Lander wagon, honey," Mary Beth said. "They'll be back soon."

Chris felt antsy at mention of the Landers and stuck his head out the back of the wagon to check on the horses.

Chris cared about Nipper, of course, but he had a special love for the horse that belonged to him. Three years ago he had watched Buster's birth and had raised him from a colt. The two of them were special buddies.

Suddenly a bolt of lightning struck nearby and Buster

pulled hard at his rope, loosening it. Chris gasped as his horse gave a shrill scream and bolted.

"No, Buster! Come back!"

In a flash, Chris leaped out of the wagon, running after Buster, who galloped across the open circle. The horse dashed about, pivoting and wheeling in fear. There was an opening in the circle where an equally frightened team of horses were giving Gordon Cuzak a real battle as he held tightly to the reins.

In his terror, Buster headed straight for the opening and plunged past the rearing, pawing horses. Chris was right behind him, yelling at the top of his voice.

Mary Beth leaned outside the wagon and shouted as loud as she could for Chris to come back, but the wind carried her voice into the rumbling thunder.

While the savage storm continued to lash the Nebraska prairie, Joy Lynn's body was wrapped in blankets and placed in the rear of Ezra Comstock's wagon.

The remaining Landers were invited into Stuart and Tracie Armstrong's wagon. Since they had no children, there was room for all. Bob joined them, and the family wept together, venting their grief.

The wind had torn another canvas top off a wagon, and Solomon went to help with it while Hannah hurried back to her children. When she arrived at the wagon and heard about Buster and Chris, she told Mary Beth, B. J., and Patty Ruth to stay in the wagon. She was going to try to find Chris.

At the Norwood wagon, Hank's saddle horse, eyes bulging, fought to free himself. Hank was watching him from inside, with an arm around Lisa.

"Is the rope strong enough to hold him?" Lisa asked.

"Should be," Hank said. "It's practically a new rope."

There were five wagons separating the Norwoods from Walt Cuzak. At the same time the Norwood saddle horse was fighting to free himself, Walt's team was rearing and pawing the air, neighing in terror. Lightning struck all around the outside of the circle, and thunder sent its deafening shock waves upon the prairie.

Walt sat on the wagon seat, pulling hard on the reins while Edmund was on the ground, gripping the bridles of the lead pair of horses. Their movement had worked the wagon to the side, leaving space between it and the next wagon.

Suddenly the bridle snapped on the Norwood horse. From his position on the Cooper supply wagon, Perry Norwood saw the family saddle horse break loose and charge through the opening left by the Cuzak wagon. Instantly, Hank Norwood was out of the wagon, following on foot. When Perry saw his mother running after Hank, he left his ox team and charged after her. By the time he caught his mother, she was outside the circle. Hank was already on the open prairie.

"Come on, Mom," Perry said. "There's nothing you can do. Dad will come back when he realizes he can't catch the gelding. Let's get you back inside the wagon."

Even though the rain had soaked them to the skin, Lisa hesitated. "Perry, I've got to bring back your father. He'll chase that horse till he drops!"

"You can't catch him, Mom. I couldn't either. Not with the head start he's got."

Both of them watched Hank as he continued to run after the horse who was no longer in sight. They saw him stumble and fall and get up again. And then a dagger of blue-white fire stabbed the black sky and struck Hank, turning him into a human torch. He stiffened and fell to the ground, his clothes smoking.

Thunder roared as mother and son stood in paralyzed disbelief. Perry's throat locked up, but his mother opened her mouth and screamed.

Hannah Cooper was returning from the prairie after losing sight of Chris. She was close to the wagons as she saw Hank dash from the circle. When the lightning bolt hit him, Hannah jerked in horror and glanced back to see Lisa and Perry, standing like statues.

Now Perry was holding his mother in an attempt to get her to the wagon, but Lisa wailed hysterically and struggled to free herself of his grasp. Hannah hurried toward them.

"Twister!" Jock Weathers, who was standing between his wagon and a team of mules, pointed north and repeated his cry. "Twister!"

Someone else picked up on it, and Ezra Comstock splashed toward Jock from across the circle, looking north. What he saw turned his blood to ice. Quickly, he wheeled and shouted, "Everybody under the wagons!"

The black funnel was no more than three or four miles away, and was headed due south, straight toward the circle of wagons.

"Perry!" Hannah cried. "Get your mother under the wagon! Fast!"

Even as she spoke, Hannah dashed for her own wagon. Solomon had just arrived, and Mary Beth was telling him about Chris and Buster. As he lifted Mary Beth from the wagon, Solomon said, "I want all three of you—and Biggie—to lie down flat under the wagon! I'm going to go find your mother and—"

"Sol!" Hannah cried, running toward him through the driving rain.

Solomon's head whipped around as he stood Mary Beth on the muddy ground and reached for Patty Ruth. "Where's Chris?"

B. J. slid out of the wagon with Biggie in his arms, and

Hannah told everyone that she couldn't find Chris and had turned back.

Solomon nodded toward the wagon. "All we can do now is pray he'll be all right! Hurry! That tornado is bearing down on us! Get under the wagon!"

"You're going to get under, too, aren't you?"

"Of course!"

"Sol, Hank Norwood was just killed by lightning…Perry and Lisa saw it happen. So did I. His horse got loose and he was chasing it. Lisa's in hysterics…I've got to go to her! I wish I could stay here with you and the children, but Perry's got his hands full. They both need help right now, and I think I can help Lisa."

"All right…but you lie down flat!"

"I will!"

Solomon hugged her. "I love you, Hannah!"

Solomon stayed on his feet until he saw Hannah and Perry drag the struggling Lisa under the wagon. He flattened himself beneath his own wagon and lay between his girls and reached a hand toward B. J., who had Biggie in his grasp.

Curtis Holden made sure that his grandparents got beneath their wagon before he ran toward the Marlins to see about Deborah. Lloyd Marlin was just bending down to hand baby James to Suzanne.

"Where's Deborah?" Curtis shouted.

"I don't know! She was running around the circle a minute ago, helping families with children to get under the wagons! She must be under one herself by now!"

"Lloyd, we've got to make sure she is!" Suzanne said.

"I'll find her!" Curtis said, then wheeled about and was gone.

Walt Cuzak's horses were out of their minds with terror. Walt was still on the wagon seat, tugging at the reins, and all of his sons were gripping the horses' bridles.

A lightning bolt crackled out of the roiling clouds, momentarily turning the air a silver-white. The bolt popped directly above the circle and was all the horses needed to spook. They bolted, throwing off the Cuzak brothers as if they were weightless, and charged insanely onto the storm-lashed prairie.

The brothers scrambled to their feet and watched as the wagon fishtailed across the rough land. They could hear their father's voice, shouting for the horses to stop. But the fear-maddened animals were in control now. The wagon hit a high spot, vaulted into the air, and landed hard. Walt sailed off the seat and did a full flip in the air before he struck the ground.

The crazed horses headed straight for the dangling inky tail of the twister. There was a deep rumble as team and wagon were caught up in the swirling black mass. The wagon shattered to smithereens and the horses were seen whirling in circles, pawing the air wildly as the powerful tornado whipped them into its pitch-black vortex, and they vanished from sight.

Word spread among the wagons that the black funnel had skewed to a westerly course. The men admonished their families to stay put while they crawled out to get a look. They began to shout for joy when they saw the twister maintain its westerly course.

When Hannah returned to her family, Solomon said he would take Nipper and find Chris. As he swung into the saddle and headed onto the prairie, word was spreading about Hank Norwood's death, and the Cuzak brothers were carrying their dazed father back to the circle.

Curtis Holden stood at the Croft wagon where he had found Deborah. She had been helping the Crofts when Ezra's high-pitched voice ordered everybody under their wagons.

Curtis had stayed with Deborah, holding her in his arms until the danger had passed. Now she thanked him in a shaky voice for caring what happened to her.

He pulled her away from the Croft wagon, and when they were out of earshot, he turned to face her. "I more than care what happens to you, Deborah. I'm so in love with you that I wonder why my heart stays inside my chest."

Tears welled up in her eyes. "Oh, Curtis, I've prayed that what I've seen in your eyes and heard in your voice is the same thing I feel for you. I'm in love with you, too."

People couldn't help but notice the two as they shared a tender kiss, totally oblivious to their surroundings.

Elmer and Maudie saw it, too, and smiled at each other.

Families all over the circle were weeping and clinging to each other, thankful that God had spared them, especially in light of the loss of Joy Lynn Lander and Hank Norwood. Several of the women now gathered at the Norwood wagon to comfort Lisa.

Some of the men went out onto the rain-soaked prairie and picked up Hank Norwood's charred remains. Hannah kept Lisa occupied so she wouldn't see her husband's blackened body as the men carried it to the Comstock wagon and placed it next to Joy Lynn.

Chris Cooper's last glimpse of Buster came when the galloping horse disappeared over a rise. He ran in that direction with all his might, praying the Lord would make Buster stop.

When he reached the top of the rise, his beloved horse was nowhere in sight. At the same time, he saw the huge funnel cloud bearing down no more than a few hundred yards away. He hurried to the small gully at the bottom of the rise and lay face-down, covering his head. The black mass roared above him, stinging his back with sheets of rain.

Chris stayed where he was for a long time, clenching his teeth and praying. He was still in the same position when the tornado passed and the wind and rain let up. Suddenly he felt warm breath on the back of his neck and heard a soft nicker.

"Buster!"

The horse nickered again, as if to say, "The storm's over now. We can go back to the wagons."

Chris jumped to his feet and wrapped his arms around Buster's neck. "Oh, Buster, I prayed so hard you wouldn't run away and never come back!"

Chris swung aboard his horse and said, "Let's go. Mama and Papa will be worried about us."

When they topped the rise, Chris looked toward the circle of wagons in the distance and told himself he had come at least two miles in his pursuit. He was about to put Buster to a gallop when he noticed movement on the prairie to the east.

It took only seconds to recognize Nipper. Though he couldn't make out the features of the tall man in the saddle, Chris Cooper knew it was Papa.

CHAPTER SIXTEEN

Hannah Cooper stood with her daughters and youngest son, watching the two riders come in.

As they trotted up and pulled rein, Hannah ran toward her oldest son. "Oh, Chris, I'm so glad you're all right! I—"

It was then she noticed his red-rimmed eyes.

"I told him, honey," Solomon said. "Had to. He asked me if Joy Lynn was all right."

Hannah patted her son's arm, wanting to comfort him as she had when he was little. Instead she said, "Oh Chris…I'm so sorry, son. We all loved Joy Lynn."

Chris slid from Buster's back and wrapped his arms around his mother. "Why, Mama? Why did she have to die?"

Hannah's tender mother's heart was at a loss to find an answer to such pain. She held him, smoothing his hair, and looked at Solomon.

Chris asked if he could tell the Landers how sorry he was about Joy Lynn. Solomon nodded but told him it was best that he wait until later. Right now, the family needed to be alone with their grief.

At that moment, Elsie Lander's high-pitched voice filled the air. "I want to turn back right now! Now, Chuck! Do you hear me? Let's bury Joy Lynn, take our broken wagon, and go home!"

"Elsie, listen to me," Chuck said, gripping her arms. "I understand how you feel. Joy Lynn was my daughter, too. But if we turn around and head back, it will put us on the prairie alone. We must go on. Joy Lynn would want us to."

Trina Lee, her own face stained with tears, moved close and put her arms around both parents. "Mother, I think Daddy's right. Joy Lynn would want us to go on."

"Yes, Mom," Bob said, "Our future lies in California. And I agree with Dad and Trina Lee. This is what Joy Lynn would tell us to do."

Hannah could hold back no longer. Her heart ached for Elsie. She hurried toward the Landers with Solomon and the children at her heels.

She moved in close and cupped Elsie's tear-stained cheeks in her hands. "Honey," she said, "you and your family drove onto these plains to follow your dream. Don't turn back now. Go on. Fulfill that dream."

"Why, Hannah?" Elsie said on a sob. "Joy Lynn was part of that dream. She's gone now."

"But you still have Chuck, Bob, and Trina Lee. The four of you must go on and build your new life in California."

"Listen to Hannah, darlin'," Chuck said. "She's talking good sense."

"But maybe more of us will die before we get there. We've got a long way to go!"

While Hannah was doing her best to reason with Elsie, a similar scenario was repeated across the circle at the Armstrong wagon.

Tracie stood with her back to Stuart, weeping against the rear of the wagon. Her whole body shook as she sobbed, "I can't stand any more of this, Stu! I want to go back to Toledo!

Let's travel with the Landers. Elsie wants to go home. Please, Stu! Take me home!"

"Tracie, listen. I know this storm was terrible, but we would be asking for real disaster if we turned around and went back—even if we went with the Landers. We would be easy prey for robbers and Indians. We must go on to California. Please. Get a grip on yourself. There's no other sensible choice."

"There has to be a way, Stu! I'm tired of all these storms. I—"

"Pardon me…" Hannah Cooper's voice came from behind Stuart. "I couldn't help hear what you were saying, Tracie. I know about the fears you have, and I'm tired of these storms, too. But you and Stuart left your home and joined this wagon train to follow your dreams just like the rest of us did. You have a fine husband and a wonderful future out there ahead of you. Don't rob yourself of it."

Stuart looked at Hannah gratefully and turned to watch Tracie's face.

"Hannah," Tracie said, "I appreciate your concern, and what you've just said. I…I'll think on it."

Hannah embraced her friend and whispered, "Follow your husband's dream, honey," then turned and walked away.

"Thank you, ma'am," Stuart called after Hannah. "We appreciate your concern."

Hannah waved and moved on.

Soon all the clouds had drifted away, and the sun was shining brightly out of an azure sky.

Ezra Comstock had been moving about the circle, speaking encouraging words as he assessed wagon damage. Only a few wagons needed repair—mostly wind-torn canvas tops. When he walked toward the Landers' wagon, he could see that Elsie was still determined to turn around and go home.

Ezra moved up to Chuck and told him that with a little work they could patch up his wagon. Since the bed had suffered only minor damage, all they would have to do was rig up a way to suspend the canvas top over the bed and stitch up the canvas.

Chuck said he was ready to go to work on it, and Ezra promised to bring several men to help.

As Ezra turned to go, Walt Cuzak and his four oldest sons hailed him. Walt limped and held a hand to the small of his back.

"Need to talk to you, Ezra," Walt said, clearing his throat nervously.

The nearest people stopped what they were doing to listen. Others, having seen the Cuzaks heading toward their wagon master, moved closer to hear what Walt and his sons had to say.

"What is it, Walt?"

"The twister destroyed my wagon and took my team. All our food was in my wagon. The other three wagons only have mining tools and supplies. My boys and I...well, we're gonna need food."

Before Ezra could reply, Solomon Cooper stepped up and said, "Hannah and I will share food with you and your sons."

"Vanessa and I will, too," Lafe Tolliver said.

For the first time on this journey, the Cuzaks were speechless.

The rest of the day was spent cleaning up after the storm and repairing wagon damage.

Perry Norwood, Bob Lander, Buck Mylan, and Tony Cuzak dug two graves in the shade of a cottonwood and constructed crude wooden crosses to serve as markers.

As the setting sun turned the spacious canopy of the sky a brilliant pink that faded to lavender on the horizon, the bodies of Joy Lynn Lander and Hank Norwood were committed to their graves. Solomon Cooper had been asked to conduct the service. While he stood between the graves with an open Bible in his hands, Hannah and her children grouped themselves around Lisa and Perry Norwood.

The Lander family stood huddled together, supporting Elsie, whose gaze never left the ground.

Everyone was at the service, even Walt Cuzak and his four oldest sons, though they stayed on the fringe.

Solomon read words of comfort from Scripture, then talked about repentance toward God and faith in the Lord Jesus Christ for salvation.

While he turned the pages of his Bible, he said, "There is only one Person in all existence who can save us from the wrath of God by forgiving our sins. That Person is the crucified, buried, and risen Son of God, the Lord Jesus Christ. We must put our faith in Jesus, and only Jesus, to save us. When we have our faith in Him, all we have to do is ask Him to save us. He says in John 6:37, 'Him that cometh to me I will in no wise cast out.' The Lord never turns any repentant sinner away."

With that, Solomon offered to talk in private with anyone who wanted to know more about salvation. He then closed in prayer, asking God to comfort the bereaved as only He could do.

When everyone had returned to their wagons, Perry and Bob lowered the bodies of their family members into the earth.

That night, as the moon shed its silver light on the prairie, Tony Cuzak worked alongside his father and brothers to repair a torn canvas.

To Tony, the lack of conversation almost felt like a truce. Perhaps now he could tell them what had been foremost on his mind ever since he'd met the Coopers. Tony broke the silence by saying, "I'm glad all of you attended the funeral service today. You've stayed away from the Sunday services, but today you heard it plain and clear that Jesus Christ is the only way to go to heaven."

There was no reply.

Tony tried again. "Pa, when you took that spill off the wagon this morning, it was moving pretty fast. If you'd landed wrong, it could have killed you. You know that, don't you?"

"Yeah, I suppose it could've. And let me set the record straight. The only reason your brothers and I attended that service was so we wouldn't irritate nobody. We don't want to jeopardize our chances of gettin' more food from these people. And what's more, don't you be comin' on to me with this Jesus stuff. It's all bunk."

"Pa, it's not bunk. It's—"

"Shut up! You listen to me! When a man dies, that's the end of 'im. There ain't no heaven, and there ain't no hell. That Charles Darwin's right! We humans are only higher forms of animals. So when we die, that's all there is."

"Darwin's wrong, Pa. Dead wrong. It makes a lot more sense to me that God created this universe, and that He made man in His own image, as it says in the Bible. I read it myself. The animals weren't made in God's image, so when they die, that's the end of them. But not so with man. He exists beyond the grave, either in heaven or hell."

"That's enough, Tony!" Dwight spat out. "You're nothin' but a fanatical fool! We don't wanna hear no more of this junk!"

The other brothers nodded their agreement.

Suddenly Tony backed away from the wagon. "Excuse me," he said, "I've got something important to take care of."

When Tony approached the Cooper wagon, the moonlight revealed Solomon and Hannah sitting outside the wagon, talking to Stuart and Tracie Armstrong.

The conversation cut off as Tony drew up. "Excuse me, folks," he said softly. "I'm sorry to interrupt. I just need to say a word to Mr. Cooper."

Solomon rose to his feet. "Sure, Tony. What is it?"

"Sometime before you go to bed, sir, could I talk with you?"

"Of course. As soon as Hannah and I finish talking to the Armstrongs, I'll find you."

When Tony was gone, Solomon said, "Tracie, Hannah's advice is solid. I sure want to see you and Stu go on and build your new life as planned."

Tracie sighed. "It's just that I'm so tired of all these problems we've been facing, Solomon, and I don't know what's coming next. I'm scared."

Tracie said she and Stu would sleep on it and talk some more in the morning. Then she hugged Hannah and bid her and Solomon goodnight.

Solomon took out his Bible and said, "Well, sweetheart, I think this is going to be Tony's big moment."

"I'd say you're right, darling. I'll drop in on the children at Ezra's wagon and see how Patty Ruth and Mr. Rabbit are getting along."

Solomon rolled his eyes. "It's going to be a little rough when we have to release Mr. Rabbit. She's gotten pretty well attached to him."

"Mm-hmm. Well, it'll be a few more days. We'll cross that bridge when we come to it. See you in a little while."

Hannah was sitting near the fire when Solomon returned an hour later. The children were already in their bedrolls beneath the wagon.

One glance at his face and she said, "He did it!"

"He sure did!" Solomon picked her up by the waist and lifted her above his head with a hearty laugh.

Hannah giggled, telling Sol to put her down, and the four Cooper children laughed and applauded beneath the wagon, rejoicing that Tony Cuzak had become a Christian.

When Hannah and Solomon were settled by the fire, talking in low tones, B. J. said, "What were you clapping about, Patty Ruth? You're not saved."

"It's 'cause I'm not old enough yet," the little redhead replied. "But Mama and Papa said I'm *safe*. If I died, Jesus would take me to heaven 'cause He died for babies and little children who don' understan' all 'bout bein' saved."

"That's right," Chris said. "But you're understanding more about it all the time, aren't you?"

"Uh-huh."

Mary Beth squeezed her little sister's arm. "It won't be much longer, honey. As soon as you understand about sin, and the fact that *you* sin before God, you'll understand why you're a transgressor and have to ask Jesus to come into your heart to save you."

"Yeah, B. J.," Patty Ruth said, bringing out a hand from under the covers to punch him lightly. "I ain't a Christian yet, 'cause I ain't one of them—what did you call 'em, Mary Beth?"

"Transgressors."

"Yeah, that. I ain't one of them, B. J. But you are. That's why you had to get saved."

"Oh, yes you are," B. J. said. "You just don't know it yet."

"I ain't neither."

"Yes, you are—"

"That's enough, B. J.," Mary Beth said. "You two get to sleep."

When they had all settled down, B. J. whispered, "Yes, you are!"

A tiny fist clubbed him on the chest. "No, I ain't!"

At sunrise, Ezra Comstock was already walking among the wagons, checking to see if everybody would be ready to pull out within the hour. They had lost most of yesterday and needed to make up time. When he came to the Lander wagon, he had a brief conversation with Chuck and Elsie, then moved on. At the Armstrong wagon he talked with Stuart and Tracie.

As he walked, his ears picked up a third dissenting voice. Lisa Norwood was telling her son there was no reason to go on to California without his father. There was no future for her there. Hank had been her life.

"But, Mom," Perry said, "I want to build a new life in California. I'll make a home for you out there. I'll find a good woman to marry and raise a family, and I'll see to it that you're taken care of. I promise."

Suddenly Perry thought of Hannah Cooper. He knew she had talked to Elsie Lander and Tracie Armstrong, and he called out to her now. When Hannah came toward them, he said, "Mrs. Cooper, Mom's wanting to turn back. Would you talk to her?"

Lisa flicked a glance at Hannah. "No offense, Hannah, but nobody's going to talk me into going any farther. I want to go home."

"Lisa," Hannah said. "May I say something?"

Lisa kept her arms folded and her eyes straight ahead. "Go ahead. But it won't do any good."

Hannah glanced at Perry, then moved in front of Lisa to look into her eyes. "Lisa, I know I can't sympathize with your grief, since my husband's alive...but doesn't Perry deserve to have his dreams come true?"

"Well, of course he does, but I want to go home."

"Honey, who's at home for you to go to?"

There was a long pause. "Nobody."

"Then why don't you think of Perry and go on to California with him?"

Lisa blinked away the tears that surfaced and looked away.

Hannah squeezed Perry's arm. "I think everything will work out."

Perry smiled and put an arm around his mother. "Thank you, Mrs. Cooper."

As Hannah turned to go, she almost bumped into Ezra Comstock, who was coming to talk with the Norwoods. "Perry, if your mother wants to go home, there's a way she can do it without traveling in danger."

"And how would that be, Mr. Comstock?" Perry asked.

"Well, about the time we cross the Little Blue River due west of here, we should run into a large wagon train that hauls supplies out west. It returns east about this time, and I usually run into it a few miles west of the Little Blue. You and your mother could travel back with the supply train. They have a lot of wagons, and plenty of armed men. The Indians have never bothered 'em…comin' or goin'."

Perry looked down at his mother and said, "Thanks for telling us about it, Mr. Comstock. I think Mom's decided to go on, but if I'm wrong, we'll talk to you about it later."

"Fine."

"Just how long till we reach the Little Blue?"

"If we can stay on schedule, 'bout another eleven or twelve days."

"Okay. Thanks."

As Ezra and Hannah walked toward the Cooper wagon, Ezra said, "I've already talked to the Landers and the Armstrongs about the supply train. Elsie is pushin' Chuck to join it and go home."

"And what about the Armstrongs?"

"Tracie is undecided. Stu told her they'd do whatever she wants."

Hannah nodded, as Ezra veered off in another direction.

An hour later the wagons were ready to pull out. The Norwoods and the Landers hurried to the graves to say "good-bye" one last time. It was an incredibly lonely feeling to leave their loved ones to the wide open spaces and the wind, and to the knowledge that they would never pass this way again.

Rain fell on the Nebraska prairie for about an hour that day but wasn't heavy enough to slow down the train. Polly Winters and Patty Ruth "bummed" a ride with Micah Comstock so they could travel with Mr. Rabbit.

B. J. and Billy Perryman played alongside the Cooper wagon for most of the day, and Corrie Weathers rode on the wagon seat next to Mary Beth and Hannah. Solomon and Chris rode their saddle horses.

Late in the afternoon the train came to a winding creek that ran swift and full because of the recent rains. Ezra told everyone to fill their water barrels. At the end of the day, he was satisfied with the fourteen miles they had come.

After the Cooper children were in their bedrolls, Solomon took Hannah's hand and said, "Mrs. Cooper, may I have the pleasure of a walk in the moonlight?"

"You certainly may, Mr. Cooper."

They left the circle and strolled over the grassy fields. "Hannah," Solomon said, "I appreciate the way you've tried to strengthen the women who've said they want to turn back. You're the most wonderful woman God ever made. You have such a marvelous way about you. I love you for being such a strong person."

Hannah squeezed his hand. "Sweetheart, what strength I have comes from the Lord. I have none in myself."

"I'm aware of that, but the Lord can only give strength to those who let Him."

Solomon stopped and took Hannah in his arms. "I think all the stars left the sky and are nestling in those beautiful brown eyes of yours."

Hannah slid her arms around his neck and half-whispered, "If there are stars in my eyes, you handsome lug, it's because I'm looking at *you!*"

They kissed long and lingeringly, then headed back to the wagon.

As they walked, Hannah looked west and said, "Out there, darling, is Wyoming. Oh, I know we're going to be so happy there!"

CHAPTER SEVENTEEN

W hen the wagon train made camp at the close of the eighteenth day, Ezra Comstock announced that they had come one hundred and forty-four miles since leaving Independence. Because of the storms, they had averaged eight miles a day. They must do better from this point on or face the possibility of running into snow in the Sierras.

The nineteenth day was Sunday, June 12. They had a service just after breakfast, and Solomon Cooper brought the Bible message, as he had the previous two Sundays. When Solomon was finished, Tony Cuzak raised his hand and asked if he could say something to the group. He announced that he had become a Christian on the night after the tornado had swept through. The Christians in the group rejoiced with him, but there was no rejoicing on the fringe of the crowd where Walt Cuzak stood with his other sons.

While Ezra closed the service in prayer, Walt swung his fist through the air and softly ejected a string of profanity. To his sons, he said, "That rotten, no-good kid has made a fool of himself! He's embarrassed the rest of this family!"

"We oughtta disown 'im, Pa!" Frank said. "He don't deserve to be a part of this family!"

"Yeah," Edmund and Gordon said in unison. Edmund continued to speak. "It's bad enough havin' to live with knowin'

Ma was one of them crazy fanatics, but at least she's dead. I don't cotton to havin' no more of them fools in the family."

"Right!" Dwight said. "If we disown 'im, he won't be diggin' gold with us, and we won't have to share none with him!"

"Well spoken, boys," Walt said. "We'll just take care of that right now."

Ezra dismissed the people, telling them to be ready to pull out in half an hour.

Tony knew his father and brothers were going to be upset at hearing his testimony. He turned to watch their approach and steeled himself for a tongue-lashing. "Morning, Pa...brothers," he said.

"Don't call me 'Pa' no more, you religious fool! As of this minute, you are no longer part of this family!"

"That's right," Frank said. "Don't you be callin' us your brothers no more. You ain't! We've disowned you!"

"An' don't you go spoutin' any of those religious lies to us," Dwight said. "You're wrong if you believe that Jesus talk."

Tony's voice broke as he said in a loving tone, "You're the ones who are wrong. The day you die and wake up in a burning hell, you'll know just how wrong you were."

"Bah!" Walt said, and ejected another string of swear words. "Let's get away from this fool, boys. He's no kin to us."

Ezra had guided his horse to the lead spot when Lafe Tolliver came running up.

"Ezra! Indians! I just saw a band of them near that stand of trees!"

Ezra swung his gaze to the north. "Don't see 'em now, Lafe."

"They were there, Ezra. Believe me. Vanessa saw them, too."

"Don't doubt it for a minute, son."

"What do you make of it?"

"Well, no white man ever sees an Indian unless that Indian wants to be seen. They appeared just long enough to be spotted."

"Are they going to attack us?"

"I can't rule that out. How many would you say were in the band?"

"About twenty. Would that few take on a train this size?"

"Prob'ly not. But they might have more with 'em than they let you see. Might be just a ploy to make us uneasy. They don't like us trespassin' their country, you know. Or it could be their short appearance was a prelude to a visit. I guess we'll find out."

The people were on edge as wagon wheels began to roll. Every man who walked or rode a horse had his rifle in hand. Those who drove kept rifles in easy reach.

As the day wore on, the biggest threat was the merciless sun. A few days without rain, and the sun-baked earth was ready to engulf the travelers with dust.

At midmorning the next day, Ezra was riding with Dave Croft when he saw a band of Indians straight ahead, waiting for them.

"Dave," Ezra said, "ride back and tell everybody we've got company. Tell 'em to be ready for anything, but not to panic."

It didn't take long for Ezra to recognize Chief Big Cloud. The Indian band stopped some thirty yards from the lead wagon, but Big Cloud and four braves kept coming. Ezra raised his hand in a sign of peace, and Big Cloud did the same.

Several of the men collected beside the lead wagon, rifles in hand. Among them were Walt Cuzak and his sons.

"Mama," came a small voice from inside the Cooper wagon. "Are these In'ians gonna scalp us?"

"No, Patty Ruth. Those are nice Indians. They're the same ones we gave food to back on the trail."

Ezra and Big Cloud conversed for several minutes, then the wagon master turned in his saddle and called toward the men at the lead wagon. "Big Cloud wants more food. Everybody in favor of givin' it to 'im?"

"We really don't have any choice, do we, Ezra?" Bill Perryman asked.

"Not if we want to keep peace with these fellas."

"Then let's get them some food."

"He ain't gettin' none of ours, Ezra!" Walt Cuzak stepped closer and scowled at Big Cloud and his braves.

"And why not?"

"'Cause what food we've got was given to us by the people of this wagon train, and it ain't right to give away somethin' somebody presented to you as a gift. We ain't givin' 'em nothin'. Besides…can't you see what they're doin', Ezra? They been followin' us! Sooner or later they'll attack us! C'mon, Ezra, wake up!"

Ezra straightened in the saddle and noticed Big Cloud eyeing the Cuzaks with displeasure.

Over his shoulder, he said, "These Pawnees roam the whole territory, Walt. They ain't necessarily followin' us. If they were gonna attack, they'd have already done it. Now you listen to me. The way Big Cloud's lookin' at you tells me he remembers you from before. I'd say you oughtta smile at him and tell your sour-faced boys to do the same."

The sub-chief spoke a few words in a deep, agitated tone.

Ezra spoke over his shoulder again. "Walt, he just said he remembers you. He knows by your voice and the look on your face that you hate Indians. Now, I'm tellin' you, you'd better be friendly and donate some food so I can tell him you did."

"Not on your life, Ezra! We ain't scared of them savages, and we ain't givin' 'em no food!"

Ezra said no more. It took the people of the train about ten minutes to sack up the food and present it to the Pawnees. Big Cloud managed a slight smile for Ezra and asked him to convey his gratitude to the people of the train. Before turning his horse to ride away, Big Cloud gave Walt Cuzak and his four sons a look of pure hatred.

For the next four days, the train traveled in a spread-out formation to avoid the dust churned up by hooves and wagon wheels. On the fifth and sixth days, rain showers brought some relief and allowed them to travel in a single line once again.

On the seventh day since encountering the Pawnees, Ezra announced they were nearing the Little Blue River. They would be on its east bank by late afternoon the next day.

Since there had been no more Indian sightings, the children were once again allowed to walk and play alongside the wagons.

Patty Ruth and Polly rode in the lead wagon all morning with Mr. Rabbit, who was completely healed and getting frisky. Patty Ruth knew that any day now, Mr. Comstock and her father would want to send Mr. Rabbit back to the prairie.

That afternoon, Chris decided to walk beside his family wagon for a while, and Hannah noticed him glancing back to the Lander wagon.

"You miss her, don't you, Chris?" Hannah's question drew Solomon's attention as Chris nodded solemnly, and he joined the conversation.

"There's nothing wrong with how you're feeling, son," Solomon said. "You may not be old enough to be in love, but you did have a special love for Joy Lynn. Just let her memory be a sweet thing. You'll always have the memory of her."

Chris nodded and said he would go spend some time with Micah. As he trotted toward the lead wagon, Hannah said,

"You have such a wonderful way of putting things, Sol. 'Just let her memory be a sweet thing...' That's beautiful."

Solomon smiled.

As Ezra trotted along the line, he told the people they were now entering buffalo and antelope country. If they made it to the Little Blue before dark, as he anticipated, the men who had saddle horses could go hunting. It would be a nice change from the quail, pheasant, and jackrabbit they had been eating.

About an hour after Polly and Patty Ruth began their walk, Polly pointed to a large area pocked by holes and mounds of earth. Little furry creatures that looked like fat squirrels were darting in and out of the holes while others sat up on hind legs, watching the wagons.

"Look, Patty Ruth," Polly said. "Prairie dogs!"

Patty Ruth giggled. "Those ain't dogs...those is western squirrels!"

Solomon looked down from his high perch on Nipper's back, and chuckled. "No, Patty Ruth. Polly's right. Those are prairie dogs."

"But they don't look anything like Biggie, Papa!"

"No, they don't. But they *are* prairie dogs."

Patty Ruth shrugged her tiny shoulders. "Okay. You're the papa. You oughtta know."

"This whole area you see here with all the holes in the ground, Patty Ruth, is known as a prairie dog town."

"You really *are* kiddin' me now, aren't you, Papa?" Patty Ruth looked at Hannah. "Papa's kiddin' me, isn't he Mama? That ain't a town!"

Hannah's smile widened and she broke into a laugh. "Papa's not kidding you, honey. That really is a prairie dog town!"

Patty Ruth turned to Polly. "Did you know that?"

"Sure. I've heard of prairie dog towns since I was a kid!"

Hannah and Solomon laughed all the harder.

Patty Ruth looked at her best friend. "I s'pose you knew it, too, Ulysses!"

Soon they had passed the prairie dog town and entered fields dotted with flowers—wild bluebells, buttercups, purple and white lupine, and a scattering of sunflowers and daisies.

Patty Ruth whispered something to Polly, and the girls drifted toward the rear of the wagon, out of sight of Hannah. Solomon glanced back, and when he saw what the girls were doing, smiled to himself.

Soon the Little Blue River came into view, snaking its way southeastward toward Kansas. Ezra announced they had made good time and would camp on this side of the river at a natural ford. Since there was at least two hours of daylight left, the men with saddle horses could go hunting.

When the wagons began forming the familiar circle, Patty Ruth and Polly parted company, each with a gift for her mother.

Solomon was helping Hannah down from the wagon seat when their little redhead glided up with one hand behind her back.

"Oh," Hannah said with a sigh, giving Solomon a hug. "That wagon seat gets pretty hard about this time every day."

"I know, sweetheart. But look at it this way. We're almost a quarter of the way to Fort Bridger. Just a little more than three times what we've done, and no more Oregon Trail."

"Hallelujah!"

Solomon gave her a squeeze, then said, "Honey, there's...ah...someone behind you who wants to say something."

Hannah turned and looked at her youngest daughter. "Yes, honey?"

"I have somethin' for you, Mama." With that, the five-year-old extended the bouquet of mixed wild flowers.

"Oh! How beautiful!" Hannah clapped her hands, then bent down to Patty Ruth's height and said, "And you picked all these and made me a bouquet because...?"

"'Cause I love you very, very, very much. You're the bestest mama in *a-l-l* the world!"

Hannah hugged Patty Ruth fiercely and said, "You're the bestest five-year-old daughter in *a-l-l* the world!"

Patty Ruth wondered if Polly's mother was saying the same thing to *her* daughter about now.

When darkness was falling, a dozen men rode into camp, dragging a buffalo. Four antelope were draped over horses' backs, and some of the men rode double.

Everyone in camp would have fresh meat, and buffalo jerky for a week, once it dried out in the sun.

When morning came, and the wagons were preparing to cross the Little Blue, Ezra stood at the edge of the water and shouted, "Hey, everybody! Look! The supply train I told you about!"

Across the river they saw a long line of wagons moving their way.

Elsie Lander said to those around her how glad she was to see the supply train. Now they could go home. Her family remained silent. They knew there was nothing else they could say, for Elsie was in no frame of mind to go on to California.

As Hannah looked on, her heart went out to Chuck. Not only had he lost his youngest daughter, he had lost his dream.

Bob Lander, who had been driving one of Solomon Cooper's wagons, said he was sorry he couldn't finish driving for him, but he must stay with his family. Before another word was spoken, Jock Weathers suggested that since the Cuzaks were down to three wagons, one of them could fill in for Bob.

Everyone looked toward the Cuzaks but they didn't say a word.

Sweet Maudie Holden's temper flared. "You Cuzaks oughtta be ashamed of yourselves! When you needed food, it was Solomon who first offered to give it to you!"

Walt stared at her in cold silence.

Vanessa Tolliver spoke up. "Mr. Cooper, I'll drive the wagon for you. Lafe and I were just talking about it. He and I agreed that I could drive it, and he would drive ours."

Everyone knew the Tollivers took turns driving so Lafe could lighten the load by walking a good deal of the time.

Solomon smiled and said, "Thank you both, very much."

"I'd like to ride that wagon and help her drive," Dwight said in a low tone. Walt and the others chuckled evilly.

Ezra Comstock raised his voice and told everyone they would wait until the supply train crossed the river. Then Ezra would deal with the wagon master and get him to take the Landers with him.

When the entire supply train had crossed the Little Blue, the Landers said their good-byes. Elsie clung to Hannah, weeping, while Chuck turned their battered wagon around.

As the supply train pulled away, Solomon talked to Ezra for a moment, then went to his youngest daughter and knelt down. "Honey," he said, "we've waited longer than we really should have to do this, but it's time to let Mr. Rabbit go back to the wild. He's well, now. The Lord didn't intend for him to live his life in a box."

Patty Ruth dug her fingernails into Ulysses and swallowed hard. "I understand, Papa. But...but—"

"What, sweetheart?"

"Where will Mr. Rabbit live? I don't want him to be lonely."

"He won't be lonely, honey," Hannah said, laying a gentle hand on Patty Ruth's shoulder. "You've seen all those jackrabbits on the prairie?"

"Uh-huh."

"Those are his cousins, even though he has never met

them before. He'll live with them and be very happy."

Patty Ruth nodded. "All right. Can I say good-bye to him?"

"Of course," Solomon said. "Look...Mr. Comstock is bringing him now."

"Well, Patty Ruth," the wagon master said, "Mr. Rabbit has his tummy full and he's ready to find his new life on the prairie. He told me he wants to find a home with the other jackrabbits."

"That's 'cause they're his cousins," Patty Ruth said.

Solomon took the box from Ezra. "How about you and Mama and me taking Mr. Rabbit out here on the grass to let him go?"

They walked some thirty yards from the wagons. Patty Ruth tried not to cry as she reached into the box and stroked the rabbit's long ears for the last time. "I'll miss you a lot, Mr. Rabbit," she said, her voice quavering. "We've had lots of good times together in Mr. Comstock's wagon. Jesus let me save your life so you could find your cousins and live with them. I hope you will love your family as much as I love mine."

"Would you like to flip the box on its side so he can find his new family, honey?" Solomon asked.

"Yes, Papa. Good-bye, Mr. Rabbit. Don't forget me. I love you."

With that, Patty Ruth tipped the box. When the jackrabbit felt the familiar grass under his feet, he hopped away. When he had gone a ways, he stopped and looked back. The furry little animal held his position for a few seconds, wiggling his nose, then bounded away.

As Patty Ruth walked back to the wagons, she hugged her stuffed bear tight and said, "It's all right, Ulysses. You're my very best friend. As long as I have you, everything will be fine."

CHAPTER EIGHTEEN

Ever since crossing the Little Blue River, the Comstock wagon train had seen great herds of buffalo dotting the Nebraska plains. The land was different too—rough and undulating beneath the wagon wheels. No more rain had fallen, and the grass had changed from green to a tawny gold.

It was sobering to see grave after grave along the trail. The farther they traveled, the more graves they saw, most with no markers except wooden crosses.

Late in the afternoon on Sunday, June 26, the Platte River came into view. This was the thirty-third day since leaving Independence. Ezra said that as soon as they reached the Platte, they would be at the 301-mile point. Thus far, they had averaged just under ten miles per day.

As the train drew near the Platte, they came upon the buffalowallows that dotted the land on both sides of the river. The buffalo, with their young, milled about by the hundreds, paying no attention to the wagon train. The murky water holes were putrid with excrement, and emitted a vile odor.

With the first whiff, Patty Ruth, who delighted in teasing her older brother, said loud enough for Chris to hear, "O-o-o-o-o! Mama! Chris took off his shoes again!"

Chris set his jaw in a stern line, acting as if he were perturbed. "You better be good, little sister, or we'll leave you here with the buffalo and you can smell it all the time!"

Patty Ruth came back with, "Once you put your shoes back on, the smell will go away!"

They camped that evening on the south bank of the rolling Platte. After supper and long-awaited baths, Ezra Comstock gathered all the people to outline the rest of their journey and told them that in two days they would reach Fort Kearney, which was not only a military installation but a supply depot for wagon trains. He was glad to see smiles break out as he told them they could buy food and other things they were low on.

Their journey would follow the Platte westward on its south bank until it split in two in western Nebraska. At the junction of the North and South Platte Rivers, the train would cross and follow the North Platte into Wyoming. If they maintained an average of twelve miles a day, they would reach Fort Laramie the last week of July. Fort Laramie was also a supply station for wagon trains.

After that they would pass Fort Caspar, which had been abandoned, and follow the North Platte until it met the Sweetwater River thirty-five miles southwest of Fort Caspar.

They would then proceed past Devil's Gate, a narrow cleft through a ridge called the Sweetwater Rocks. The cleft was four hundred feet deep, fifteen hundred feet long, and some fifty feet wide. The narrow river passage caused the water to violently rush through the cleft, creating a roaring, boiling effect.

From there the train would climb South Pass, which topped out at seventy-five hundred feet above sea level at South Pass City, another wagon train supply station. At their present rate of travel, they would reach South Pass City by the second week of August.

On the west side of South Pass they would descend through a long sweeping valley of creeks, green grass, trees, foliage, rock-crested buttes, and towering cliffs. This valley would lead them to Fort Bridger, where the Coopers would be leaving the train.

Then on to California.

The train stopped at Fort Kearney on the thirty-fifth day and replenished their supplies.

Some of the oxen had sore shoulders, where the neck bows had rubbed against their hides. The men cleansed the sores and found ways to pad the bows to make the oxen more comfortable.

At the close of the thirty-sixth day, the wagon train camped on the south bank of the Platte. Its swift, wide current was dotted with small islands. Ezra warned that along this part of the Platte the river bottom was quicksand. Bathing and washing should be done at the edge of the bank only.

The topography of the land began to change. There were fewer trees now, and the fields were dotted with cactus and sagebrush. The men were able to bag antelope and buffalo that evening to provide fresh meat and replenish the buffalo jerky supply.

From time to time, the Coopers had invited different families to have supper with them. On that particular evening, they invited the Armstrongs and Tony Cuzak for buffalo steaks.

While they ate, a spiritually hungry Tony asked many questions about what the Bible taught. The Coopers were glad Tony was showing growth in his Christian life. It was an added bonus that he was asking the questions in front of the Armstrongs. Solomon and Hannah were burdened in their hearts for Stu and Tracie, praying that they would recognize their need for salvation.

When the meal was over and the dishes were washed, Chris asked if he could spend some time with Micah

Comstock. The other children had made plans to spend the evening with their various friends, and B. J. agreed to take Biggie with him.

When the children were gone, Hannah and Tracie decided to take advantage of the time and do some washing at the river bank. With the now familiar banjo and fiddle music playing near the main fire, Tony continued to ask questions about his newfound faith. Stuart Armstrong, who had been listening intently to Solomon's Sunday sermons, felt something stirring deep within, and he was eager to learn more.

At the river bank, several women were washing clothes. Hannah and Tracie picked a spot upstream. Hannah prayed for a chance to talk to Tracie about her need for salvation, and God gave her the perfect opening when Tracie said, "That Tony is really full of questions, isn't he?"

Hannah smiled to herself, marveling at God's timing. "That's what happens when a person comes to know the Lord, Tracie."

"I guess it's more dramatic for some people than others."

"What do you mean?"

"Well, I've never had a sudden change like Tony. I've just believed in God and tried to please Him ever since I was a little girl."

"Have you always pleased Him?"

Tracie smiled ruefully. "No. I've done a lot of things that I know displease Him. But...I'm hoping the good things I do will outweigh the bad, and He'll take me into heaven when I die."

"Tracie, if I understand you correctly, you believe that missing hell and going to heaven depends on how good you live?"

"Of course."

"Tell me, how good do you have to live to go to heaven?"

Tracie was silent for a moment, then said, "Well, I'm not sure. I guess that's something you can't know until you die and stand before God."

"Mmm. Be a little late by then if you fell short, wouldn't it?"

"Guess so."

"Tell me, Tracie. Do you believe that Jesus Christ came from heaven to die on the cross for the sins of the world...including yours?"

"Sure."

"Well, if you could go to heaven by how good you live, why did Jesus bother to come down here and die at Calvary?"

Tracie pondered the question for a long moment. "You know, I've never thought of it in that light."

"When Jesus went to the cross, Tracie, He met every demand of God the Father so there could be forgiveness for our sins. The Bible says the wages of sin is death. Jesus died to satisfy the debt that God's righteousness and holiness demanded. God the Father has decreed that only by the shedding of sinless blood can our sins be washed away and forgiven. So, Tracie, Jesus' death made it possible for sinners to be saved. But a dead Saviour can't save anyone. Do you believe that Jesus rose from the dead?"

"Of course."

Hannah quoted verse after verse from the Bible on salvation. When she quoted Ephesians 2:8–9, Tracie said, "I think I'm understanding it now, Hannah. Let me hear that again."

Hannah's heart began to pound. "Listen closely, Tracie. God says, 'For by grace are ye saved through faith; and that not of yourselves: it is the gift of God: not of works, lest any man should boast.'"

"Not of works..." Suddenly Tracie's face lit up. "I see it!

Salvation doesn't come through good deeds or living right. It comes through faith in Jesus Christ."

"That's it, Tracie! That's it!"

A little farther upstream—past the heavy brush where Hannah and Tracie were doing their wash—Vanessa Tolliver and Lisa Norwood scrubbed some clothes.

"Lisa," Vanessa said, "my heart is so heavy for you. I can't even imagine how horrible it must be to lose your mate."

"You have to experience it to really know," Lisa said quietly.

"I know your decision to go on to California wasn't an easy one, but you'll be glad you made it. Perry's a fine young man and will see to it that you have a good life."

"I have no doubt of that," Lisa said. "I know I made the right decision, thanks to some straight talking by sweet Hannah."

"She's that, all right."

Moments later, Lisa said, "Well, my washing's done. Can I help you with yours?"

"No need," Vanessa said. "You go on and get your clothes hung up. I'll be along shortly."

"No, I'll wait. I don't think I should leave you alone."

"I'm not alone. There are people close by. You go on, now."

"Isn't there something I can wash to speed it up for you?"

"No, Lisa. I'm on the last piece. Go on. I'll see you in a few minutes."

"All right, if you insist."

Lisa headed back to the wagons, and Vanessa finished scrubbing Lafe's Levi's. She wrung them out, then picked up the other clothes and rose to her feet. When she turned around, a dark form stepped toward her.

"Oh!" Vanessa said with a gasp. "I didn't know anyone was— What are *you* doing here?"

"Just wanted to see you alone for a minute," Dwight Cuzak said, as he pushed his hat back on his shaggy head.

Tension knotted Vanessa's stomach and she took a half-step back. "Get away from me or I'll scream!"

Dwight closed the space between them and looked at her menacingly. "You do that and it would bring Lafe. He'd really be mad. Like I told you before, if Lafe makes another move toward me, I'll kill 'im. You think I'm kiddin', go ahead and scream."

Vanessa's heart lurched and she took another step back. This time she felt water seeping into the edge of her shoes.

Dwight moved closer. "I watch you all the time, Vanessa. I wish I could ride on the wagon seat next to you."

Vanessa slowly began inching her way along the river's edge. Dwight followed. "I know the kiss I gave you that day in the rain is one you've never forgotten. You can have more."

Vanessa's skin crawled at his words. If only someone would come along!

"I know you have to act like you don't like me," Dwight said "but I know you do. I see it in your eyes whenever you look at me. You're attracted to me; you're just afraid to show it."

"You're dead wrong, Dwight. What you see when I look at you is revulsion. Do you understand? You are a repulsive, uncouth barbarian!"

Dwight chuckled and grabbed her. A scream started from her throat, but it died to a whine as he pressed his lips to her mouth. She felt as if she was suffocating.

She kept struggling while the kiss lasted. Finally he removed his lips. But before she could get out a sound, he clamped a palm over her mouth. "I told you what I'll do if Lafe comes!"

She caught the heel of his hand between her teeth and bit

down as hard as she could. Dwight let out a stifled cry and relaxed his grip.

Vanessa ducked under his arm and ran toward the wagons as fast as she could.

Solomon Cooper had just led Stuart Armstrong to the Lord, and Tony and Stuart were talking excitedly, when Vanessa rushed past. Solomon excused himself and followed the obviously distraught woman.

"What's wrong, Vanessa?"

At the sound of Solomon's voice, Vanessa burst into sobs.

"Dwight Cuzak?"

She whimpered and nodded.

Solomon's temper flared. "That dirty—I'll get Lafe."

"Wait a minute, Mr. Cooper!" Vanessa kept her trembling voice low as she said, "Dwight…found me alone on that night on the trail…when it rained so hard. He…he forced a kiss on me."

"Did you tell Lafe?"

"No. Dwight said if Lafe came after him, he'd kill him. I'm sure he's capable of it, Mr. Cooper." She took a shuddering breath. "Dwight just pushed himself on me again when I was at the river bank."

Solomon's cheeks were flaming red. "This has gone on long enough! Don't you worry, Vanessa. I'm going to take Lafe with me to talk to Ezra. This Cuzak stuff is going to end right now!"

As he headed for the Oakley wagon, where Lafe was helping Dave Oakley repair a wheel, Solomon came face to face with Dwight Cuzak. It was evident that Dwight had been eavesdropping.

"You've pushed it too far this time, Cuzak!" Solomon said. "When I tell Ezra what Vanessa just told me—"

"You ain't tellin' nobody nothin', Cooper!"

Vanessa darted away to find Ezra as people on both ends

of the Tolliver wagon moved closer. Stuart Armstrong and Tony Cuzak had followed Solomon when they realized there was trouble brewing.

Solomon saw Dwight ball his fists. "You can come swinging if you want, Dwight, but pounding on me isn't going to change a thing."

Dwight grinned wickedly. "You're scared to fight me, ain'cha? You're a lily-livered coward!"

Word was spreading throughout the camp, and people were starting to gather. Hannah and Tracie followed Ezra and the Tollivers through the crowd and noticed that the other Cuzaks had pushed their way to the front.

"I'm not afraid of your fists, Dwight!" Solomon said. "But fists won't settle anything here!"

"Yeah? Well, maybe *this* will!"

There were gasps and shrieks as Dwight pulled a .42 caliber Derringer from his pocket.

Solomon had been in hand-to-hand combat in the Civil War, and now his instincts took over. Despite his game leg, he moved swiftly and seized Dwight's wrist with surprising strength.

The two men stood face to face with the small pistol between them.

Suddenly a shot cracked the air.

Hannah's knees went watery and she held her breath as she saw Solomon's bad leg stiffen and buckle. Blue-white smoke drifted up from between the men's bodies, and Dwight's eyes were burning into Solomon's with pure hatred.

All at once Solomon released his hold on Dwight's upper arm, and Dwight slowly crumpled to the ground. Solomon took a step back, and Hannah rushed to him, sobbing.

Ezra began to move forward, but Walt pushed him aside and dashed forward to roll Dwight on his back. He released a wild cry, wailing, "He's dead! He's dead! My son is dead!"

Vanessa clung to her husband, weeping with emotional exhaustion, as he said, "It's okay, honey. He won't bother you ever again."

Ezra stepped up to Walt Cuzak and said, "No more chances, Walt. You and your sons are out of this train. Take Dwight's body with you and get out. Now!"

"You can't do this, Comstock! It ain't right! It ain't our fault what Dwight did!"

"I told you before that I was holdin' you responsible for your boys' actions. Arguin' ain't gonna get you nowhere but deeper in trouble. Get out!"

Walt bristled, letting his hand drop toward his sidearm. He froze at the sound of the dry clicking of hammers from every side. More than a dozen rifles and pistols were aimed at him.

Slowly, Walt moved his hand from the gun butt and took a deep breath, letting it out slowly. "All right, boys, let's go. Pick up your brother's body and put it in one of the wagons."

While Frank, Edmund, and Gordon hoisted Dwight's body, Walt glared at Solomon and said, "You haven't seen the last of us, Cooper. Somewhere along the trail, we'll get you."

Walt held Solomon's stare for a few more seconds, then turned and looked at Tony. He fixed his youngest son with dark, brooding eyes and said, "Well, traitor, you see what your pal the Bible-thumper did to your poor brother? Christians! Nothin' but pious hypocrites!"

"Pa, Mr. Cooper acted in self-defense, and you know it. Dwight brought it on himself. He's the one that pulled the gun. If he'd stayed away from Mrs. Tolliver like Ezra told him to, he'd still be alive."

Walt's face reddened. "Bah!" he said, and walked toward his wagons.

Everyone remained where they were as the three Cuzak wagons rolled onto the moonlit prairie and headed west.

The spell was broken when Tony moved close to Solomon and said, "My father's threat was no idle one, Mr. Cooper. He and my brothers will be lying in wait for you somewhere up ahead."

When the Coopers got back to their wagon, Hannah and Solomon made an effort to distract the children from what had just happened. The fact that both Stuart and Tracie Armstrong had been saved that evening lifted their spirits.

After the Coopers had prayed together, and after much persuasion from Solomon that the Lord was not going to let the Cuzaks kill him, the children finally settled into their bedrolls.

Ezra set up watchmen in shifts throughout the night, in case the Cuzaks decided to come under the cover of darkness. This preventive measure would remain in effect until the train reached Fort Bridger.

The rest of the camp had settled down as Solomon and Hannah sat by their fire, holding on to each other. Tears glistened on Hannah's cheeks as she said, "Darling, I thought for a moment there—when that gun went off—that it was you who took the bullet. I...I don't know how I could ever face life without you. I am bone of your bone and flesh of your flesh. Our lives are so entwined, I wouldn't want to live if you died."

"But, sweetheart, you would still have the children to live for if the Lord took me home."

"Yes, of course. And I love them with everything that's in me. I didn't mean—oh, it's hard to say what I mean."

"It's all right. I understand."

They stayed in each other's arms for a few more minutes, then kissed goodnight and climbed into their bedrolls beneath the wagon. Tonight the girls were sleeping inside, and the boys slept only inches from their parents.

It wasn't long until Solomon was breathing evenly, while Hannah still lay wide awake.

She asked the Lord to protect Solomon, then claimed Isaiah 26:3, fixing her mind on the Prince of Peace. Soon the Lord flooded her heart with His own peace, and Hannah Cooper fell asleep.

Chapter Nineteen

As the wagon train rolled westward along the Platte, the river widened and became more shallow. The buffalo herds were much more numerous along the river banks, and that worried Ezra.

He rode along the line and warned everyone about water contamination. They would have to conserve what water they had and use it only for drinking and cooking until the buffalo herds thinned out.

Solomon Cooper refused to let Walt Cuzak's threat affect the way he faced each day. He continued to walk beside the wagon Hannah drove, and on some days he rode Nipper. But Hannah found herself studying every clump of brush, every knoll, every stand of trees. Fear often crept into her mind, and then left again when she fixed her mind on the Lord and let Him fill her with His peace.

As each day passed, they could see that more and more buffalo herds had claimed the Platte River as their habitat. Sometimes the herds were a great distance to the west, but since the river's current flowed east, the wagon train couldn't risk the possibility of disease carried by the water.

A week after the Cuzak incident, water barrels were getting quite low, despite rationing. When they made camp at the close of the forty-third day since leaving Independence, there were no buffalo in sight. Ezra walked to the river's edge and examined the water. There was evidence of contamination, but it was clean enough to wash clothes and bathe.

Ezra called everyone to the central fire. "Now, folks, I know we're all gettin' edgy as the water supply drops. I've never come this long without bein' able to use the river water. I had hoped the big herds would be somewhere else by now.

"I'm sure at times you've noticed some farms and ranches in the distance…"

Everyone nodded.

"As I recall, there's a small farm about a mile south of the river a half day's drive from here. Like all the farms and ranches in these parts, they get their water from wells. When we reach that farm tomorrow, I'll ask the farmer if he'll let us fill our barrels. The underground rivers all come from the Rocky Mountains, so there's plenty of water in the wells—we're not gonna hurt the farmer by fillin' our barrels. Another four days after that, we'll arrive at O'Fallon's Bluff. There's a spring there. We'll be able to load up the barrels again."

George Winters raised a hand. "Ezra, do you think we'll have this problem all the way into Wyoming?"

"Don't think so. We're just a week from the fork of the North and South Platte. Since we'll be followin' the North Platte, I think we'll be fine. The buffalo ain't as thick in those parts."

While the watchmen did their duty throughout the night, the rest of the travelers slept. Solomon took his turn as watchman, staying away from the firelight in case the Cuzaks decided to creep up to the camp.

The wagon train rolled out by seven o'clock the next morning with Solomon riding out front with Ezra.

The Cooper children had asked to ride in other wagons.

Hannah took advantage of the empty wagon to invite Deborah Smith and Tracie Armstrong to ride with her. As a new Christian, Tracie loved to spend time with Hannah, and though Deborah was older in the Lord, she enjoyed being with Hannah, who seemed to have an unusual grasp of the Scriptures.

The two young women were intrigued with Hannah's explanation of the tranquillity she had in her heart, in spite of circumstances. Hannah expounded on Isaiah 26:3, telling them what a pillar of strength the verse had been to her, not only in the Cuzak situation, but in making the decision to leave Independence and move to Fort Bridger.

"Mrs. Cooper—" Deborah said.

"Hannah. You can call me Hannah."

"I was going to ask you, Hannah, exactly how is it that you stay your mind on Jesus?"

"What I do is list in my mind all the things I love about Him. That will occupy you for a long time, I assure you. Then I think about Calvary, picturing Him on the cross, dying for Hannah Marie Cooper. You can stay there a long time too. Sometimes I run through my mind everything I can remember from the gospels that came from His lips. Other times I call to mind the many names Jesus is given in Scripture…you know, Son of God, Son of man, Prince of Peace, Lamb of God.…

"When you think on Him this way, your mind is most definitely fixed on Him. And no matter what storms are beating against you, He will give you His perfect peace."

Up front, Ezra and Solomon were discussing the Cuzaks.

"I don't know if you should be riding Nipper for the next few days," Ezra said. "The Cuzaks could hide behind one of these hills around here and try to ambush you."

Before Solomon could reply, Ezra looked to the southwest and said, "Hey! We're gettin' near that farm I was tellin' the folks about. We can see it from the top of that mound yonder. Let's you and me go take a gander."

Ezra turned in the saddle and motioned to Micah that he and Solomon would ride ahead.

As the two men trotted toward the mound, Ezra pointed out some tracks. "Looks like somebody decided to leave the trail. Let's have a look-see."

The view from the top of the mound sickened them. Three wagons, just like those in the wagon train, lay on their sides. The bloody bodies of Walt Cuzak and his boys lay sprawled amongst their mining equipment and supplies. They had been scalped, and food from their own supply had been stuffed in their mouths.

"Big Cloud," Ezra said. "He was showin' his contempt for the men who wouldn't share food with him and his braves."

Solomon studied the bodies for a moment. "I'd say they've been dead about two days, Ezra."

"That's what I was thinkin'. It's a wonder the wild animals haven't eaten 'em by now."

Solomon nodded. "I'll ride back to the train and tell them what's happened. Tony may not want to see this. I'll leave it up to him."

"Okay. I'll wait here. We need to bury 'em quick and get on to that ranch." He pointed to the southwest. "There...see it?"

Solomon squinted against the sun's glare. In a low area about a mile away, he could see a barn, farmhouse, and small outbuildings nestled in a stand of cottonwood trees. "Sure enough. Be back shortly."

When Solomon reached the lead wagon, he reversed his direction to ride alongside Micah.

"What's goin' on up there?" Micah asked. "I saw you two charge up the mound, then disappear on the other side."

Chris and B. J. listened intently for their father's reply.

"Pawnees got the Cuzaks," Solomon said. "Took their scalps. Stole their horses."

Chris and B. J. eyed each other.

"I don't wish anybody to suffer like they must have, Papa," Chris said, "but at least we don't have to wonder anymore if the Cuzaks are going to ambush you."

Solomon smiled tightly. "That's right, son. Micah, when you reach the near side of the mound, haul up. I don't want the women and children to see the Cuzaks. We'll do a quick burial and be on our way."

"That farm's right down there to the south, isn't it?" Micah asked.

"Yes. I'll move on back and tell everybody what's happened, and explain that we're going to stop long enough to bury the bodies."

As Solomon drew up to his own wagon, he smiled at Hannah and the two young women who rode beside her. "It's okay, now, sweetheart," he said to Hannah.

"Pardon me?"

"The Cuzaks are dead…Pawnees killed 'em. Micah's going to stop the train long enough for us to bury the bodies, and then we'll head for that farm Ezra told us about. You can see it from the mound."

Tears filmed Hannah's eyes.

"I've got to let the rest of them know…especially Tony," Solomon said.

When Solomon had moved on, Tracie said, "The Lord knew the Cuzaks were dead, Hannah. Isn't it wonderful that He could give you peace like He did, even though you thought they were still a threat?"

Hannah adjusted her grip on the reins. "Yes, it is wonderful, Tracie…and it's wonderful to realize that the Lord *always* knows what's ahead of us in life and can prepare us for what comes our way. He's already in eternity, which means He's already in the future. So, He's already in our tomorrows."

"He certainly was in my tomorrows before I met Curtis," Deborah said. "He already had us made for each other."

Hannah reached over and patted Deborah's hand. "That's right, honey. And I'm so glad for both of you. For all of His goodness to us, our Lord deserves all of our love, service, and devotion."

Solomon and the men decided to dig a common grave for the Cuzaks. Tony had insisted on helping, even though he could hardly look at the bodies. When the men were ready to head back to the wagons, he asked for a minute alone.

Tony's heart was heavy as he looked down at the dirt mound. "Pa...Frank...Gordon...Edmund...now you know how wrong you were about all that 'Jesus stuff' and about hell. But it's too late." He thumbed the tears from his eyes and said, "Thank You, Lord, for Solomon Cooper. If he hadn't led me to You, I'd be in that grave, too."

When they were within five hundred yards of the farmhouse, Ezra halted the train and asked Solomon Cooper and Dave Croft to ride with him the rest of the way.

As they came within two hundred yards of the farm, Solomon noticed that it had a shabby look to it. "Ezra, looks like the place is abandoned. The roof of the house looks caved in on one corner, and the barn roof is in pretty bad shape, too. I'd say it hasn't been lived in for a while."

"I think you're right. All we can do now is hope the well's still functional."

"Wait a minute," Dave said, "there's wash hanging on the line at the rear of the house."

"And a cow and two horses in the corral," put in Solomon.

They could see two small children playing near the back porch, and a woman at the hog pen, trying to adjust a pole in the split rail fence.

When they rode through the gate, the woman spotted them and quickly picked up a double-barreled shotgun and cocked both hammers. "Hold it right there!" she commanded.

The woman was no older than twenty-five, and quite pretty. The afternoon breeze lifted her long black hair. Her dress was well-worn and patched, but clean.

Without moving her eyes from the strangers, she said, "Jason, take Caleb inside the house!"

The boys obeyed immediately, walking past a well pump at the back of the house. The men could see another pump at the small corral, and the stock tank was full of clean water.

"What do you want?" the woman demanded, fear in her eyes.

"Ma'am," Ezra said, touching the brim of his battered hat, "my name's Ezra Comstock. I'm wagon master of that wagon train back yonder." He arced a thumb over his shoulder in the direction of the train.

The woman's eyes flicked eastward and then back to the three men.

"These gentlemen with me, ma'am, are Solomon Cooper and Dave Croft. Their families are in the train. You won't need that scatter-gun. We mean you no harm. We've plumb run out of water. Buffalo have contaminated the Platte all along the trail. We came to ask if you would let us fill up our water barrels. I see you have a couple of wells."

The young woman lowered the shotgun and eased the triggers. "You can come closer," she said.

When they halted their horses a few feet from her, she smiled. "My name is Amanda Kline, gentlemen. The water in my wells is plentiful. You're welcome to fill your barrels. You can water all your animals at the stock tank, if you wish."

"Ma'am, we really appreciate your kindness," Ezra said. "I...ah...take it Mr. Kline isn't here at the moment."

Amanda's eyes filled with quick tears. "My...my husband, Barry, died two months ago. Fever. Came on him suddenly."

She turned her head and pointed with her chin. "That's his grave there near the bushes at the back of the house."

"Ma'am," Solomon said, "our hearts go out to you in your loss."

"Thank you. Right after Barry died, there were a series of rain and hail storms, along with some high winds. That's a sod roof on the house. The rain was so heavy it collapsed the roof on one corner. And the hail and wind damaged the barn roof, as you can see. Now I'm having trouble with some of the fences. I was working on the hog pen when you rode in."

"Yes, ma'am," Ezra said. "So you've got nobody to help you keep the place up?"

"No. I wrote to my brother in Billings, Montana, about a month ago. I wanted him to know about Barry, but I also told him I needed help. He said he would come as soon as possible, but he didn't say when that would be."

While Amanda was talking, Solomon noticed the lush vegetable garden near the barn, and the large field of corn alongside a larger field of alfalfa. Admiration welled up in him for this gallant young woman who had stayed here after her husband's death and was making a living off the farm.

Dave noticed the two small boys peeking out the back door. "Those are fine boys, you have there, Mrs. Kline."

Just then, they heard a baby's cry.

Amanda glanced toward the house. "I need to tend to my youngest, gentlemen. Please come in for a few minutes, then you can bring the wagon train down here."

From the side of his mouth, Ezra said, "There's no need to go in, Sol. Let's tell her we'll just go get the wagons."

"You've been out of civilization too long, old fella," Solomon whispered. "We must show the lady the courtesy of responding to her invitation. Don't have to stay long. Then we can go get the wagons."

Ezra raised bushy eyebrows. "Well, pardon me for bein' a backwoods hick."

The parlor was in a pitiful condition where the roof had caved in. Amanda had done what she could to cover the opening with several wide strips of canvas. Otherwise, the house was immaculate.

The baby stopped crying at the sight of his mother. As the men looked around, they noticed wall plaques with Scripture verses on them. And a large black Bible lay on the kitchen table.

"Mrs. Kline," Solomon said, "There's some pretty good indications that somebody who lives here knows the Lord."

Amanda smiled warmly. "Yes, Mr. Cooper. I've been a born-again child of God since I was ten years old. My husband was saved when he was fourteen. I have peace knowing he's in heaven with Jesus."

"Well, all three of us are born-again Christians, ma'am," Dave said. "And there are several just like us in the wagon train."

She smiled. "I'm glad to hear it. This is my youngest, Matthew. He's nineteen months old."

Solomon's heart was heavy for the young widow. "Ezra," he said, "this dear lady needs help. We can't just take the water we need from her wells and drive away."

Ezra's face showed his puzzlement. "What are you thinkin', Sol?"

"I know you've got to get over the Sierras before the snow

flies. So you go ahead and pull out after the barrels are full. I know when Hannah sees the situation here, she'll agree with me. We'll stay and fix up her place, then go on to Fort Bridger. A couple of weeks, and we can have this place looking good. Her brother will probably be here by then."

Ezra rubbed his bristly chin. "Ain't no need in you stayin' behind, Sol. If every able-bodied man in the train pitched in, we could fix everything for her in a couple of days. We can spare that much time."

Tears glistened in Amanda's dark eyes. "That...that's very kind of you, gentlemen, but I can't ask you to—"

"You didn't, ma'am," Solomon cut in. "We're volunteering."

"Oh, bless you! If the roofs of the house and barn were repaired...and the fence at the hogpen, the boys and I would be fine until my brother comes."

While some of the men were watering the animals and others were filling water barrels, others went to work on the roofs and fences. Chris and B. J. worked alongside their father.

Ezra and Dave rode out to find fresh meat.

After the women had introduced themselves to Amanda, some of them borrowed her wash tubs and began to wash clothes. Amanda was tending to little Matthew, with Jason and Caleb looking on, when Hannah, Mary Beth, and Patty Ruth stepped onto the back porch.

"Oh, please come in," Amanda said, hurrying to open the screen door.

"You just had a whole lot of names thrown at you out there," Hannah said. "I'm Hannah—"

"Cooper! I can't remember them all, but I remembered your name because of that very nice husband of yours."

Hannah smiled. "He is that, Mrs. Kline. These are our daughters, Mary Beth and Patty Ruth."

"Hello, girls," Amanda said. "I'm so glad to meet you."

The girls returned the greeting, then Amanda introduced her boys. "These are my sons, Jason, five, Caleb, three, and Matthew, nineteen months."

Amanda noticed Matthew eyeing the stuffed bear cradled in Patty Ruth's arm. "I see baby Matthew likes your bear, Patty Ruth. What's his name?"

"Ulysses Cooper, ma'am."

Amanda giggled. "I like that name!"

Patty Ruth gave her a thin smile.

"May I call you Amanda?" Hannah asked.

"Of course."

"Amanda, the girls and I came to invite you and the boys to eat supper at our wagon tonight. Would you do us the honor?"

"Oh, yes. Thank you!"

"My husband told me you're a Christian," Hannah said.

"I sure am. Let's sit down here in the kitchen so we don't bother the men in the parlor."

As they talked about the Lord, Hannah and Amanda felt the beginning of a strong kinship. Amanda shared how the Lord had given her strength to go on when Barry died. They had come to Nebraska from Kentucky with a big dream to build a new life. Amanda was carrying on the dream because it was so important to Barry.

Hannah told her about Hank Norwood's death, and how Lisa was going on to California with her son for the same reason.

Amanda nodded. "I can understand. Barry is in heaven, but somehow it's like part of him is still here—especially when I look at the children."

Hannah leaned against the table in a casual manner and put a hand over her midsection. She suspected she was carrying a child, but hadn't yet said anything to Solomon. She would give it a little more time. Solomon had always been so delighted when she told him there was a new life coming into their home, and she didn't want to disappoint him if it really wasn't so.

Just then Amanda started to cry. When Hannah left her chair and put her arms around her, the long-denied tenderness seemed to break a dam within the young widow. Hannah motioned for Mary Beth to take Matthew. Without hesitating, Mary Beth picked up the toddler and herded the other boys and Patty Ruth into the parlor to watch the men work on the roof.

"Go ahead, honey," Hannah said, softly. "Cry it out. God gave us tears to alleviate our emotions. Let it all out."

CHAPTER TWENTY

When Amanda's sobs finally subsided, she felt completely drained yet somehow peaceful. She and Hannah continued to sit at the kitchen table and talk.

In the parlor Mary Beth held Matthew on her lap. Jason and Caleb sat beside her on the worn-out old couch and watched Lloyd Marlin and Tony Cuzak work on the ceiling where the roof had collapsed. William Perryman and George Winters were approaching it from the roof side.

Patty Ruth, who sat on the floor at her sister's feet, making faces at baby Matthew, kept him giggling. Mary Beth smiled at her little sister's natural talent for entertainment.

At one point, Matthew stretched out a hand toward Ulysses. Patty Ruth's smile vanished and she turned her body away from the baby's reach. Matthew let out a high-pitched wail.

"Patty Ruth," Mary Beth said in a low tone, "let Matthew see Ulysses."

"No!"

"Mary Beth…" Hannah called from the kitchen, "what's the matter with the baby?"

"He wants to play with Ulysses, and Patty Ruth won't let him."

Scrape! went the chair, followed by rapid footsteps, as Hannah entered the room with Amanda on her heels.

"Patty Ruth, I thought we settled this selfishness thing. Now, let Matthew play with Ulysses for a while."

"Why can't he play with his own toys, Mama?"

Amanda looked down with a smile and said, "Honey, Matthew doesn't have any toys. His daddy and I were working hard so that one day we could buy our sons some playthings, but then his daddy died. I just don't have the money to buy toys right now. Jason and Caleb have some rocks and sticks they play with, and sometimes I let Matthew play with a wooden spoon I have in the kitchen. But there's another reason Matthew likes Ulysses."

Patty Ruth's eyebrows lifted. "What's that?"

"Matthew used to have a stuffed bear, something like Ulysses. But when the roof collapsed, the bear was over there in the corner where all the rain came through. It got wet and began to fall apart, and I had to throw it away."

Patty Ruth thought how bad she would feel if something like that happened to Ulysses. Reluctantly she said, "Matthew can play with Ulysses for a couple minutes."

Matthew giggled as he closed his fat little fingers around the bear. Immediately he stuck a stuffed paw in his mouth. This galled Patty Ruth, but she held her peace.

Tony Cuzak turned from the corner, where he and Lloyd Marlin were working, and headed for the door. He paused and smiled at Amanda. "We'll have this fixed for you shortly, ma'am."

"You'll never know how much I appreciate it," she said.

"Amanda," Hannah said, "this is Tony Cuzak. My husband led him to the Lord after we started this journey."

"Wonderful! I'm so glad for you, Tony. I've been a Christian since I was ten years old. It gets sweeter the longer you walk with Jesus. There are many heartaches and trials along the way, but nothing can compare with knowing Jesus and living for Him."

"I'm finding that out already, ma'am. I'm sorry about your husband's death. And I want you to know I admire your spunk. Not many women would have stuck it out like you have."

Amanda smiled warmly. "Thank you for the compliment, Mr. Cuzak. I don't recall meeting a Mrs. Cuzak out there. Are you not married?"

"No, ma'am. I realize most men my age already have a wife and two or three children, but I've just never found the right woman."

"You will. The Lord knew you would be saved on this journey, so He no doubt has a very special Christian lady picked out for you. He'll bring her into your life when He's ready."

A wide smile spread over Tony's mouth. "Thank you for the encouragement, ma'am. It's good to know the Lord has a plan for each of us. Mr. Cooper is teaching me about the way God works in the lives of His children."

"Yes…God's hand is on our lives," Hannah said. "We don't always understand everything that comes our way—like the Lord's taking Barry home—but we know He never makes mistakes."

Ezra Comstock and Dave Croft rode onto the Kline place in late afternoon, dragging two buck deer. Everybody would have venison that night.

While the hunters strung up their bucks on cottonwood limbs and dressed them out, the rest of the men continued their repairs on the Kline farm.

Back at the wagon, as Hannah did some cleaning and prepared food for supper, her mind went back to those few moments earlier in the day when Tony had stopped and talked to Amanda in the parlor. She knew the look in a man's eye when he was attracted to a woman, and that look was in Tony's eye. Of course it was too soon after Barry's death for Amanda to think about romance, but what would it hurt to let them get better acquainted? After all, Tony was footloose and fancy free. He could come back and see Amanda later if she agreed to it.

Hannah smiled to herself. *Why not?*

Hannah looked around and spotted Chris, who was helping his father and B. J. with the corral gate.

"Chris!"

"Yes, Mama?"

"Could your father spare you for a few minutes?"

Chris looked at Solomon, who nodded, then ran to the wagon. "What do you need, Mama?"

"Tony is working inside the house. Would you ask him if he'd like to eat supper with us tonight?"

"Sure. Be right back."

Hannah returned to the wagon and was dipping flour from a small barrel when her eldest stuck his head over the tailgate. "Tony said he'd be delighted to eat supper with us, Mama...and he said to thank you."

"Fine, honey. Thank you for your help. You can go back to your father now."

"Guess I'd better. Papa might mess it up if I'm not there to show him how to do it."

Hannah laughed. "You're a case, Christopher Cooper. I love you."

"I love you, too, Mama. See you later."

By the time the sun was setting, the aroma of roasting venison filled the air. The men continued to work, taking advantage of what daylight was left, and the women merrily prepared supper. Everyone in the wagon train was eager for this meal. It had been a while since they'd had fresh meat.

Amanda had joined Hannah at the Cooper wagon to help her with supper. Mary Beth and Patty Ruth were looking after the Kline boys inside the wagon.

Little Matthew learned that if he reached for Ulysses and Patty Ruth refused to let him have him, all he had to do was cry, and she would give in.

While the two mothers worked side by side, Amanda said, "Hannah, could I ask you about Tony Cuzak?"

"Certainly."

"Well, call it feminine intuition or womanly insight, but even though Tony shows genuine joy in his newfound salvation, there seems to be a shadow of sadness in his eyes. Do you know anything about it?"

"Yes. You see, he started out this journey with his father and four older brothers. They were bad, Amanda...all the way to the core. Even though Tony was not a Christian, he was nothing like them."

"You speak in the past tense. Are they dead?"

While they continued to work, Hannah told Amanda the whole story of the Cuzaks and their horrible end.

Amanda's heart went out to Tony, and she marveled aloud at the way God had preserved him out of such an evil family life. Twilight had settled when the Cooper boys showed up, looking famished. They greeted Amanda, calling her Mrs. Kline, and then turned to their mother, wanting to know how soon supper would be ready.

"In about twenty minutes. You boys need to go do what your father and Tony are doing right now. Wash your hands."

B. J. started to protest.

"No washee handsee, no eatee, Mr. Cooper. Understand?"

"Yes, ma'am," the eight-year-old said, and followed his brother toward the well at the stock tank.

Amanda chuckled. "I think all boys are alike."

"Well, my three are."

"Three? I thought you had two."

"The third one is thirty-six years old."

"Oh. I understand. Husbands *are* just little boys in large bodies, aren't they?" Amanda's smile faded at the thought of Barry. Quickly, she said, "Both of your sons strongly resemble their father. And I can see you in Mary Beth."

"Mm-hmm," Hannah said with a smile. "And Patty Ruth?"

"There's a slight resemblance to you, but she's pretty much her own little person."

"In more ways than one," Hannah said, and chuckled.

Tony arrived with Solomon and the boys. When they all sat down to eat, he looked at Amanda and smiled, an appreciative look in his eye. Amanda smiled back, and Solomon noticed the exchange.

"So, Tony," he said, "I think it's time you learned to pray aloud before a meal."

Tony's face blanched. "Well, I...ah...I..."

"First time's always the hardest."

"Yes, sir, but—"

"You've heard others pray before meals since you got saved, haven't you?"

"Well, yes, but—"

"Are you thankful for the food?"

"Sure am. The venison's got my mouth watering."

"Then just thank the Lord for it, and say it out loud."

Tony swallowed hard and bowed his head.

"Lord," he said, "I sure am thankful for this venison...and all the other things we're about to eat. Ah...and drink. Thank You for letting us meet Mrs. Kline. She's a nice lady. Ah...in Jesus' name, Amen."

"Why, Tony," Hannah said. "You did great."

"Thank you, ma'am."

"Everybody dig in!" Solomon said, and laughed.

That night, as Solomon and Hannah settled in their bedrolls beneath the wagon, Mary Beth and Patty Ruth slept in the farmhouse by special invitation from Amanda. The boys were asleep inside the wagon.

Solomon took Hannah in his arms. "Mrs. Cooper..."

"Yes, Mr. Cooper?"

"Did you observe something in Tony earlier today while you were inside the house?"

"Like what?" she asked innocently.

"That he has great admiration for Amanda?"

"Well, since you bring it up, I did."

"And I assume she was as nice to him as she was at the table tonight."

"Of course. Amanda's a very nice person."

Solomon gave her a squeeze and started to laugh.

"What's so funny?"

"You."

"What do you mean?"

"When we get to Fort Bridger, I'll file papers to have your name legally changed from Hannah Marie Cooper to *Cupid* Marie Cooper!"

The more they tried to muffle their laughter, the more hilarious they felt, until Solomon covered her mouth with his and they kissed long and sweetly.

When he released her, Hannah said, "I've gone as far as I can. I realize it's too early in her widowhood for falling in love, but I just wanted to do what I could to set things up. The Lord will have to take it from here."

By the end of the next day, the barn roof was completely repaired, and the only fences in need of attention were at the back of the property, where a few men continued to work. Most of the men were concentrating on completing the repairs to the sod roof.

Tony Cuzak went out of his way to hoe the weeds in the garden and clean out the barn, pig shed, and chicken coop. He also did some work on the screen door at the back of the house and found time to play with Jason and Caleb, who were on the back porch, watching him.

When Amanda carried little Matthew to the back door to observe the fun, she felt a strange elation as Tony tickled Matthew under the chin, making him giggle.

"These boys have really taken to you, Mr. Cuzak," she said. "You'll make a wonderful father someday."

"I sure hope so, Mrs. Kline. The Lord knows I certainly want that. I can hardly wait to meet that special young woman the Lord has picked out for me somewhere in California!"

Amanda smiled. "You can call me Amanda."

There was no relief from the heavy-hanging sun for the men working at the back of the property. They were tamping dirt around loose fence posts, and with each breath it felt like they'd taken fire into their lungs.

Ezra looked up as Solomon straightened and leaned the tamping bar against a post. Time for a breather. Solomon stepped back into the thick grass, and removed his hat to wipe his forehead. The sound of tamping filled the air.

Suddenly Ezra drew his revolver and swung it toward Solomon. No one noticed his action until a bullet plowed the dirt. Solomon jerked around and saw a wriggling, headless rattlesnake. The body continued to move from side to side, as though the snake had another set of eyes...another brain. A cold chill slithered down Solomon's spine when he realized how close the snake had come to biting him.

"He was coiled up and ready to strike," Ezra said, holstering the gun. "We didn't hear its rattles because of the tamping."

At sundown the repair work was all finished. The wagon train would pull out the next morning.

Hannah had invited Amanda and Tony for supper again. Later in the evening, when all the people gathered around the central fire to talk with Amanda, she wept as she expressed her thanks for what they had done.

When the conversation drifted to Solomon's close call with the rattlesnake, Amanda said she was aware they were in the vicinity, but she had never seen one on her place before.

Ezra warned everyone to be careful from now on, and to watch where they stepped.

Lafe Tolliver stood near the fire with an arm around Vanessa. "I take it you know a lot about rattlers, Ezra," he said.

"Enough."

"Have you ever seen anyone bitten?"

"Yes, and it's awful."

"Do victims of rattlesnake bites always die?" Lloyd Marlin asked.

"No, but there's no medical treatment for snakebite. The only thing to do is slit open the punctures and suck out as much of the venom as possible, and hope your body can recover."

Hannah squeezed Solomon's arm, telling him by the pressure how thankful she was that his life had been spared.

"If any of you ever get bit," Ezra said, "*don't panic.* You don't want to make the heart pump faster and push the venom through the body."

"How do you keep from panicking?" Maudie Holden asked.

Ezra laughed. "Well, it ain't easy!"

"If a person doesn't panic, and he gets the venom sucked out, can he still die?" Suzanne Marlin asked.

"Oh, yes. Even the smallest dosage can be fatal."

Tony Cuzak raised his voice. "We can all thank God our dear friend Solomon Cooper wasn't bitten."

"Amen," Ezra said. "Let's bow our heads and do that right now. Tony, you lead us."

Every person who looked at Tony found themselves staring into the face of panic. The new convert had been able to hurry through a prayer at supper last night, but this time the whole crowd was looking on.

There was no way out of it. Tony could tell that by the look in Ezra's eyes. He bowed his head and said, "Let's pray."

Though many of the people in the wagon train were not Christians, Tony's simple and heartfelt prayer for Solomon Cooper moved them profoundly.

The next morning, at 8:45, Ezra called for every wagon to get in place.

Amanda Kline wrapped her arms around Hannah while Mary Beth held little Matthew, and Jason and Caleb looked on.

"Rider coming!" someone shouted.

Amanda eased her hold on Hannah to look toward the road. "Oh! It's Todd! It's my brother!"

She lifted her skirts and started running. Before she got very far, her brother slid from his horse and lifted her off the ground in a bear hug.

Amanda clung to him tearfully and explained that these wonderful people had stopped to get water two days earlier and stayed to help her until everything was repaired.

"Well, Sis, I came to stay a week. So even though the

work is done, I'll be here with you that long."

Amanda turned toward the crowd with a radiant smile and said, "Everybody...I want you to meet my brother, Todd Webley."

A chorus of voices greeted him and he smiled broadly, thanking them for what they had done for his sister.

"Well, folks, we gotta move out!" Ezra shouted.

Patty Ruth kissed little Matthew. As he reached for Ulysses, she said, "We have to go, Matthew, but I'll let you kiss Ulysses good-bye."

When Matthew took hold of the bear, he hung on for dear life, and Amanda had to step in. "Matthew, you have to let go of Ulysses. Patty Ruth has to leave." As she broke the baby's hold, he let out a wild cry.

The others made their way to the wagons as Tony rushed up to Amanda and spoke above Matthew's wailing. "Amanda, I know it's too soon after Barry's death for anything to develop in your heart for another man. But after I see the Coopers to Fort Bridger, could I come back and see you and the boys?"

"Why yes...of course. California's out?"

"California's out."

"You're welcome back any time, Tony. I'll be watching for you."

"Wagons ho-o-o!" came Ezra's cry, as he flung his arm forward. The wagon train creaked into motion.

Tony hugged Jason and Caleb and kissed the unhappy Matthew on the forehead, then dashed to his wagon, his heart banging against his ribs.

From her place on the wagon seat next to her mother, Patty Ruth watched Matthew, crying as if his little heart would break. She licked her lips and felt a constriction in her throat. Suddenly she tugged at Hannah's sleeve. "Mama..."

"Yes, honey?"

"We have to stop. Please? Can we stop? It's very important."

"What is it, honey?"

"Please. Can we stop?"

Hannah turned to Solomon, who was on Nipper, and said, "Darling, we have to stop. Will you tell Ezra?"

Solomon looked puzzled but trotted ahead to do as she asked.

"What is it, Sol?" Ezra asked.

"I'm not sure, but would you hold on?"

Ezra raised a hand to halt the train.

The whole wagon train watched Hannah and Patty Ruth walk quickly back toward Amanda and her family. Matthew had stopped wailing, but his cheeks and eyelashes were wet with tears.

"Did you forget something, Hannah?" Amanda asked.

"No, but Patty Ruth said she just had to come back and see Matthew. She said it was important, and by the look in her eyes, I have no doubt it is. Patty Ruth…"

"Mrs. Kline…" Patty Ruth said, her voice quavering with emotion.

"Yes, honey?"

"Mrs. Kline, I am very sorry that Matthew's bear died…an'…an'—" Patty Ruth's heart felt as if it was being squashed inside her chest. "An' I would like to give him Ulysses so he'll have a good frien' to play with."

Amanda glanced at Hannah, who closed her eyes and nodded.

Amanda turned Matthew around in her arms and knelt down to Patty Ruth's level. Matthew's eyes lit up like midnight stars as Patty Ruth extended her best friend to the little boy who had no toys. "Here, Matthew," she said, "Ulysses is yours now."

Matthew grasped the bear, smiling from ear to ear, and stuck a paw in his mouth.

"Thank you, Patty Ruth," Amanda said. "Thank you very, very much."

Patty Ruth's heart ached as she took a step back. "Good-bye, Ulysses. You'll always be my very best friend. Please don't forget me."

"He won't sweetheart," Amanda said. "I promise."

Patty Ruth looked up at Hannah and took her hand. "We can go now, Mama."

Hannah had never been more proud of her little daughter.

Solomon felt the same heart-swell of pride as he watched his youngest walk back to the wagon train. Suddenly children were running from other wagons, carrying toys to Jason and Caleb, and there was a loud cheer along the whole line.

Solomon got off his horse as Hannah and Patty Ruth walked up, and he took his little daughter in his arms and said, "You're the bravest, most generous little pigtailed girl in all the world."

CHAPTER TWENTY-ONE

L ate in the afternoon, on the second day after leaving the
Kline farm, Fort Kearney came into view. Ezra rode
along the line, telling everyone they would make a circle
just outside the fort and spend the night. They could purchase
supplies at the fort's trading post, and fill their water barrels at
the well.

Chris Cooper pointed toward a column of riders in blue,
approaching from the south.

Micah nodded. "Yep. That's one of the regular patrols
returning to the fort."

Chris sat up straight, saluted, and said, "That's what I
want to be, Micah! A soldier on horseback!"

"Let's see," Micah said with a chuckle. "Is this the millionth
time you've told me that, or the billionth?"

Chris laughed. "Probably the *zillionth!* I hope I can be as
good a soldier as my papa was in the Civil War."

"I have no doubt you will be." Micah paused, then said,
"You really admire your father, don't you?"

Chris grinned. "More than any man in the world. He's the
best, Micah. He'd do anything for his family."

"I don't doubt it for a minute," Micah said.

At the Cooper wagon, Hannah watched her husband trot Nipper to the head of the line where Ezra was riding. Mary Beth and Corrie were talking together.

"Does Patty Ruth talk much about Ulysses, Mary Beth?"

"She hasn't mentioned him to me since we left the Kline place. Has she said anything to you, Mama?"

"No," Hannah said, "but I see a touch of sadness in her eyes. I know she misses Ulysses. He was her constant companion for almost as long as she can remember. I'm sure she'll get over it in time."

"Mama," Mary Beth said, "I haven't said anything, but Patty Ruth has cried herself to sleep each night since she gave Ulysses to little Matthew. I've tried to talk to her, but she just clams up. I just hurt for her."

"I know. Me, too. But the choice was hers. Down in her heart, she knows she did the right thing. I'm sure she knew she would miss Ulysses terribly, but bless her heart, she chose Matthew's happiness above her own."

There was a silent moment, then Mary Beth said, "Mama, you and Papa told Patty Ruth the Lord would bless her for what she did. What do you think the Lord will do? I mean…in what way will He bless her?"

"I don't really know, and neither does your papa. We just know that the Lord smiles on that kind of sacrifice. Sooner or later He will bring something into her life to let her know just how she pleased Him by giving her most prized possession to Matthew."

Mary Beth nodded. "I hope its sooner than later."

"We'll leave that to Jesus, honey."

They had a pleasant overnight stay at Fort Kearney and pulled out early the next morning with the water barrels full and plenty of food and supplies.

The weather stayed hot. The sky was nearly cloudless and the land remained parched and dry.

On Thursday, July 21, they arrived at the fork of the North and South Platte Rivers. The fork was a quarter-mile wide where the rivers parted, and was only about two feet deep.

There were no signs of buffalo on the banks or anywhere near the area. Ezra checked the water and told the people he could see no indication of contamination. It was as he had said—the buffalo had thinned out in this part of the territory.

A strong, hot wind blew as some of the men filled their water barrels in the river, while others watered their animals downstream.

It was while he was leading his horse to the stream that Ezra's nose detected the acrid odor of smoke. He looked toward the west, where the wind was coming from. The land gently sloped to a high point in that direction, and at first Ezra thought he was looking at a long bank of low-lying clouds. But the smell of smoke met him again.

Prairie fire!

Most of the people were busy with their water barrels and watering their animals, but a few had noticed the smoke.

Quickly, Ezra called everyone to gather round. "Listen up!" he shouted. "The water's shallow out there, so we're gonna pull all the wagons to the middle of the fork. Right now, the fire's about four miles from us, but the wind is powerful, and it's comin' fast. It'll be here in less than half an hour.

"Thank God the fork is as wide as it is! We'll get plenty of smoke, but just stay in the middle of the fork till the fire has burned past us. Keep your canvas tops doused with water."

Ezra pointed to the best place to drive the wagons into the fork. "We'll go in single file. It'll take longer that way, but we don't need to be breakin' any axles by pullin' 'em in where the bank's humped. Everybody follow Micah and line up like he does. Okay, let's move!"

As Hannah gently nudged the oxen to keep them close behind the wagon in front of her, Mary Beth's attention was drawn to a mother prairie hen and five little chicks making their way toward the river. "Mama..."

"Yes, Mary Beth?" Hannah replied, keeping her eyes on the fire and holding the reins tight.

"There's a mother hen and her little chicks running toward the river. Do you suppose they know the fire's coming?"

"The mother does. If nothing else, she can smell the smoke. That's why she's taking them to the water."

"Can they swim?"

"No."

"Couldn't we stop and pick them up?"

Solomon was listening to the conversation. "Sweetie, if we tried to pick them up, they'd scatter, and the mother would fight us. Besides, there isn't even time to try. That fire's getting awfully close."

"But, Papa, they'll burn to death!"

"Honey," Hannah said, "Papa says there isn't time. We've got to get into the river. Maybe the mother hen can find a wet place close to the water where she can—"

"I'll try," Solomon said, and was quickly out of the saddle, limping toward the prairie chickens. As soon as the mother hen saw him coming toward them, she squawked and flapped her wings and hurried her chicks away.

"Sol!" Ezra shouted. "You're wagon's almost ready to enter

the river! Hannah needs you to stay close in case anything happens!"

Sol nodded, took another look at the fleeing chickens, and mounted his horse.

"Thank you for trying, Papa," Mary Beth said, then stood up to follow the hen's progress. Her last glimpse before the wagon eased into the water was the hen guiding her chicks to the water's edge.

Great billows of smoke threatened as the last three wagons moved down the river bank. Though the wind carried the smoke to the middle of the river, it wasn't as thick as it had been on the south bank.

The wagon train waited in the river fork for about an hour. When the wall of flame and smoke was a good mile beyond them, Ezra announced that they could resume their journey. In spite of the sparks that had flown to the north side of the fork, the grass had not caught fire. They would go ahead and cross, then follow the Oregon Trail along the south bank of the North Platte.

While they were waiting for Ezra to lead them out of the river, Mary Beth stood up in the wagon box and looked back toward the bank.

"Looking for the chickens, honey?" Hannah asked.

"Yes. I hope they didn't burn to death."

"Do you want me to see if I can find them, Mary Beth?" Chris asked.

"Oh, would you?"

Solomon smiled and said, "Let's both go, Chris."

The Cooper women watched as Solomon and Chris rode to the south bank and looked around then focused on one spot. Solomon motioned to Hannah. "Bring the wagon over here, honey! I want the rest of you to see this!"

When Hannah urged the oxen in a turn, Ezra rode up and said, "Where you goin', girl? We're gonna pull outta here in a few minutes."

"Solomon wants to show us something," Hannah said. "Come with us."

Father and son were off their horses, looking at something by their feet.

When the wagon hauled up, Ezra was beside it, eyeing Solomon. "What's goin' on?"

Solomon looked up with wonder in his eyes. "Hear that?" he said.

"I do, Papa!" Mary Beth said. "It's the little chickens cheeping! Where are they?"

Solomon put his toe underneath the charred body of the mother hen and flipped it over. Five little chicks cheeped loudly.

Ezra gasped. "Why, that little hen used her body to take the fire so she could save her chicks!"

Mary Beth started to cry. "Oh, bless her little heart! What courage…and what wisdom!"

Hannah put an arm around her daughter.

Solomon cleared his throat and blinked at the moisture gathering in his eyes. "I want all of you to think about what you've seen here. This is a perfect example of what Jesus did when He was on the cross. He put himself between us and the fiery wrath of God. He sacrificed Himself so that we could be saved."

On August 12, the eightieth day, the wagon train pulled into Fort Laramie, Wyoming.

While the women and children were inside the large trading post, the men were filling the water barrels before they took their turn in the store.

By the time Tony Cuzak had entered the store, most of the people were back at the wagons. After purchasing a new straight-edge razor and some shaving soap, Tony was about to leave when he heard one of the clerks say something about unpacking the toys and getting them on display.

"Excuse me, gentlemen," he said, "but did you say you have toys?"

"Yes, sir," the younger clerk replied. "The boss decided that since so many wagon trains come through here, we would carry them. Our latest shipment of goods had three crates of toys."

"I see," Tony said, rubbing his chin. "There wouldn't happen to be any stuffed bears among those toys, would there?"

"There certainly are. I made the order myself."

Hannah had invited Tony to eat supper with them that night. During the meal, he talked about Amanda Kline and left no question that he intended to go back and marry her.

"Mr. Tony," Patty Ruth said, "when you go back to see Mrs. Kline and her children, will you do somethin' for me?"

"Of course, sweetie. What is it?"

"Would you tell Ulysses that I miss him and love him?"

Tony smiled. "I sure will. And I'll tell him something else, too."

"What's that?"

Tony rose to his feet. "Be right back."

When Tony returned, he had one hand behind his back. "Patty Ruth," he said, "I'll tell Ulysses that you have a new friend." As he spoke, he handed her a brown stuffed bear. It was factory made but had black shoe-button eyes, and was nearly twice the size of Ulysses.

It took Patty Ruth a moment to find her voice. "Is...is he really for *me*?"

"He sure is, sweetie. The Lord Jesus wanted you to be rewarded for giving Ulysses to Matthew, so when I was in the trading post, He let me learn that a shipment of toys had just came in. And guess what? They had this bear just waiting for you!"

As Tony placed the bear in Patty Ruth's hands, she hugged him to her chest and said, "I know what I'm gonna name him! *Tony!*"

The Cooper family applauded the name, and Patty Ruth's parents thanked Tony for his generosity.

That night, Patty Ruth went to sleep without crying.

On August 23, the train passed Fort Caspar, which had been closed and abandoned in 1867.

Two days later, they rolled along the southern edge of Rattlesnake Hills. During the next two days, the men of the train killed five rattlers. Everyone was glad when Ezra announced that they had passed the dangerous area.

Soon they left the North Platte to follow the Sweetwater River. They made camp about a mile west of Devil's Gate. They could still hear the roar of the water.

After supper, Ezra met with the weary travelers and explained that they were now only two hundred miles from Fort Bridger. They would be there in about twenty days.

There was no moon that night, and when bedtime came, the night was thick and black. It was an especially warm night, and the Coopers decided they would all sleep on the ground next to the wagon to take advantage of any breeze that might come up.

Solomon read Scripture to his family by firelight, then led them in prayer. Soon the children lay asleep in their bedrolls. Patty Ruth slept soundly with her new stuffed bear wrapped in her arms.

Solomon and Hannah settled down side by side with the children around them. When he took her hand, he noticed she was trembling. He raised up and said, "Sweetheart...something wrong?"

"No. Not wrong. Just exciting."

"Because we're only twenty days from our new home?"

"No, that's not it."

"Well, out with it. What are you so excited about?"

"Sh-h-h! Not so loud. It's a secret."

"Okay," he said in a low tone, "what's the secret?"

"Well," she said, her voice quavering, "I've waited to tell you until I was sure. We're going to have another child."

Solomon breathed in sharply. "Really? Really, Hannah?"

"Mm-hmm. Come spring there'll be a new little Cooper in our home!"

"Oh, I want to shout!"

"Not till we let it be known."

"Well, I'm shouting *inside!*" he said, and folded her in his arms. "I love you, sweetheart. That's the best news I've had since you told me the last time."

"And didn't we get a sweet one?"

"That she is, darlin'. That she is."

Solomon kissed his wife soundly and settled back, taking her hand again. They prayed together, thanking the Lord for the new little life growing beneath Hannah's heart.

In the deep of the night, Solomon awakened, wondering what had snatched him from a sound sleep. Hannah was on her side now, facing the other way. He could hear her steady breathing, and that of the children.

Suddenly there was a sensation of movement against his bare left arm, and he realized it was the same sensation that had awakened him. Then he heard a slight rattling sound.

The snake slowly slithered between him and Mary Beth, who lay no more than a foot to his left.

Solomon's skin crawled and it seemed as if a lump of ice had congealed in his chest, sending cold chills through his entire body. Though the snake had stopped moving, he could feel its scaly skin touching his arm.

If he could only see! The night around him was like the inside of a tomb. Horrid images of the rattler striking out at Mary Beth's arm or Patty Ruth's chubby cheek flooded Solomon's mind.

One movement from any of his family and the snake might strike.

Solomon knew there was only one thing to do. In one smooth move, he rose to his knees and swung his left arm wildly toward the snake's head to draw its attention. Instantly he felt a sharp stab in his forearm. He tried to grab the rattler's head but missed. Pain, like the sting of a thousand wasps, exploded in his arm and shot up his shoulder.

In spite of the pain, Solomon swung the arm again. This time when the fangs struck flesh, he found the scaly body with his right hand and gripped it tight. He was trying to find the head when the third strike caught him in the side of the neck.

His family was beginning to stir when he finally gripped the snake behind the head and scrambled to his feet.

"Sol," Hannah's sleepy voice called, "what's going on?"

"I've got a rattler in my hands," he said, breathing hard. "I've been bitten." Even as he spoke, he stumbled away from his family, carrying the hissing diamondback.

He remembered there was a large rock a few feet to the south. He found it and smashed the snake's head against it. When he dropped the dead snake, he saw the flare of a match as Hannah lit a lantern.

She ran to her husband, her breath coming in ragged spurts, and held the light to capture Solomon in its glow. He was down on his knees now.

A tiny cry escaped Hannah's lips. Solomon was breathing hard, and she knew that with every beat of his pounding heart, the venom was driving through his bloodstream. She grabbed hold of his good arm.

"Lie down and try to calm yourself," she said.

A few people were coming with lanterns, asking what had happened.

"Sol's been bitten by a rattler!" she cried. "Somebody bring a knife, quick!"

Ezra Comstock dashed in, wielding his hunting knife. "Let me do this, Hannah," he said, his leathered old face a pale mask. "I've done it before. How many bites?"

"Three," Solomon said. "One on my neck and two on my arm."

Hannah saw her children stumbling sleepily toward her. "Mama, what's wrong with Papa?" Mary Beth asked. "Did a snake bite him?"

"Yes, honey," she said, trying to gather all four children in her arms.

Tony Cuzak knelt beside Ezra, who was cutting the neck wound open first. "I'll suck the venom from that one, Ezra," he said. "You get the ones on his arm."

Soon the entire camp was gathered in a circle, watching the frantic scene. Solomon's temperature rose rapidly, and he was growing weak. He looked up at Hannah and the children with languid eyes.

"Sol, darling, what—how—?"

"I woke up and felt the snake by my arm. I...I couldn't see it. You...the children. I couldn't let it happen—"

"O, please, dear God!" she cried. "Please, Lord, don't let him die!"

Solomon's tongue was swelling now, and he tried to focus on his family. "Hannah, I want you to go on. Take the...children to Fort Bridger. Build the new life we planned."

"No-o-o! Sol, my precious husband...I can't do it without you!"

Solomon was fading fast. He reached toward his family. "You children...take care of your mother."

Hannah and the children bent over him, tears flooding their cheeks.

"Jesus...is calling, Hannah. I love you with all...my h—"

Solomon's body relaxed and a soft rush of air left his lips.

CHAPTER TWENTY-TWO

S olomon Cooper was buried at midmorning, under a bright blue sky.

Tony Cuzak had asked Hannah if he could read Scripture and say a few words before Solomon's body was lowered into the ground. Hannah was pleased to give her permission.

Tony ran his gaze over the faces of his friends and fellow travelers, and said, "I want to read some verses in Second Corinthians 5 that drew my attention when I first started reading the Bible on this trip. Mr. Cooper and I discussed them not long ago.

"'Therefore we are always confident, knowing that, whilst we are at home in the body, we are absent from the Lord: (for we walk by faith, not by sight:) We are confident, I say, and willing rather to be absent from the body, and to be present with the Lord.'

"Solomon Cooper is not in this body. Because he died as a born-again child of God, he is with the Lord in heaven."

Tracie Armstrong and Deborah had their arms around Hannah, letting their strength flow to her as she held her children close in front of her.

"In Psalm 116:15," Tony said, "it says, 'Precious in the sight of the LORD is the death of his saints.'

"Mr. Cooper was one of God's saints. When he died before dawn this morning, his death was precious in the sight of Almighty God because Mr. Cooper is now in His presence."

Through her tears Hannah nodded at Tony's words, though her heart ached with a dreadful grief.

"Just one more verse," Tony said. "Revelation 14:13. 'And I heard a voice from heaven saying unto me, Write, Blessed are the dead which die in the Lord from henceforth: Yea, saith the Spirit, that they may rest from their labours; and their works do follow them.'"

Tony's voice broke as he said, "I am one of Solomon Cooper's works. He cared enough about me and my eternal destiny to lead me to Jesus Christ. One day—only God knows when—I will follow him into heaven."

Tracie squeezed Hannah's arm and whispered, "And I'm one of *your* works, sweet Hannah. We'll be in heaven together forever because you cared enough to lead me to Jesus."

Tony took a deep, shuddering breath. "Solomon Cooper was a very brave man. Not only did he show valor on the battlefield in the War, but he demonstrated unparalleled courage and heroism by dying to protect his family.

"He loved his dear wife, Hannah; his dear daughters, Mary Beth and Patty Ruth; and his dear sons, Christopher and Brett Jonathan more than he loved his own life. God bless the memory of this gallant man in each of our hearts."

When Ezra Comstock had closed in prayer, the people gathered around Hannah and her children, speaking words of comfort and love.

Ezra was the last person to speak to Hannah as the others lingered around her. "Hannah," he said, "I know you probably feel like you want to turn around and go back. I'd like to see you go on to Fort Bridger…but not too far along the trail we'll come upon another supply train headin' back east. If you wish to join it, I'll make arrangements for you."

"Mrs. Cooper," Stuart Anderson said, "if you choose to go on, I'll drive your wagon for you until you feel up to it. Tracie can handle ours."

Martha Perryman stepped close. "Hannah, if you decide to go on to Fort Bridger, William and I will do whatever we can to help."

"The rest of us, too, Hannah," came the voice of Mary Croft.

There was a jumble of voices offering their support.

Ezra touched Hannah's arms. "I know you'd probably like to spend a little time here at the grave, once the body's been covered. I want you to know that we'll wait as long as you want. It will be Hannah Cooper who says when we go. Understand?"

"Yes," she said, and nodded.

Hannah took her children to the wagon so they would not see the men lowering their father into the grave and filling it in. She embraced each child, telling them how much she loved them.

"Mama," Mary Beth asked, "are we going on to Fort Bridger as Papa said he wanted us to?"

Hannah patted Mary Beth's tear-stained cheek. "I...I can't answer that question right now, honey. I need to talk to the Lord. You understand."

Mary Beth nodded.

"We'll be praying the Lord will show you, Mama," Chris said.

Hannah thanked him and said, "You stay here while I go to the grave. I'll be back shortly."

The Cooper children had no lack of friends who pressed close to comfort them.

As Hannah stepped up to Solomon's grave, she broke down and sobbed. It took several minutes to bring her emotions under control. Finally she spoke out loud. "I know you're not in this grave, Sol. Only your earthly shell is there. You're in the presence of our Jesus."

She faltered for a moment, then swallowed hard. "Lord Jesus, You saw fit to take my husband to be with You. I do not pretend to understand. I—" The brokenhearted widow dropped to her knees and sobbed again. "Why, God? Why? Why would You take my husband when we had a new life ahead of us out here? I don't understand…I don't understand…I don't understand! O dear God, I know You don't make mistakes. Help me to trust You in this."

A few more minutes passed before she said, "Lord, I can't go on. I can't! I must take the children and go back to my parents. I can't do it without you, Sol! I can't do it! I'll swallow my pride and go back to Mother and Daddy.

"Lord, I'm going back. I know Sol said he wanted us to go on to Fort Bridger, but I just can't do it. I—"

Hannah, child, came the still small voice, *remember your own words to Lisa Norwood about going on with her husband's dream?*

"Yes, but I—"

And it was your words to Tracie Armstrong that caused her to go on. Now, Hannah, what kind of a testimony will you be to Lisa and Tracie if you turn back? Especially since they heard Solomon tell you and the children to go on and build your new life at Fort Bridger.

"But, Lord, I keep thinking if we had never left Independence, Solomon would still be alive."

His time of departure from this earth was already appointed.

Hannah bit down hard on her lower lip. "Yes. Yes, Lord. But this poor earthly mind cannot grasp that. It seems that if we'd stayed in Independence—"

Hannah, if you had stayed in Independence, what about Tracie and Stuart and Tony?

Suddenly it came over Hannah Cooper like a warm wave of water: None of those three would be Christians now if the

Coopers had not been in the wagon train!

Hannah's thoughts went to Isaiah 26:3. As she fixed her mind on Jesus, she bent over and put her face against her knees. She thought of God's love for her...His death at Calvary...His compassion for her as a lost sinner, and how He had drawn her to Himself through His Word and by the power of the Holy Spirit.

A sweet, perfect peace flooded her heart and soul.

Yes! Hannah Cooper would go on to Fort Bridger with her precious children and build the new life she and Solomon had planned!

The new baby!

Hannah sat up, looked toward the sky and whispered, "O Lord Jesus! The baby! I almost forgot! Oh, thank You that I have this part of my darling Sol to carry with me to our new home...this part of him that will add to the joy of all our lives!"

Hannah rose to her feet, her eyes bright, as she looked down at the grave with the peace that passes all understanding. "All right, darling, the children and I will do as you said. We'll go with God's strength and build our new life!"

When Hannah returned to her four children, she smiled and gathered them in her arms. They looked into her eyes, waiting eagerly to hear her decision.

"My wonderful sons and daughters," she said, "the Lord has worked in my heart. I know that He wants us to go on to Fort Bridger, even as your papa said. And that's what we're going to do!"

"O Mama," Mary Beth said, "we'll all miss Papa terribly, but we'll know he's smiling down from heaven at us when he sees that we're going on to Fort Bridger!"

Suddenly Hannah was aware that people were applauding her decision. She wept again and smiled at them through her tears.

Hannah looked at Ezra and said, "Mr. Comstock, I need a

few minutes to talk to my children, then we can pull out."

"You say the word when you're ready."

Hannah took her children to a private spot beside their wagon. "I'm glad we all agree that we're doing the right thing to go on, but your mama's going to have to lean a lot on all four of you."

Patty Ruth held Tony the Bear in one arm. "We'll do whatever you tell us, Mama."

The others spoke their agreement.

"When we open our store, we'll all have to work together. It will be very hard at first. Can I count on you?"

Again the children nodded their heads.

Hannah smiled down at her children and caressed their faces.

Stuart Armstrong helped Hannah into the wagon, then climbed up and sat beside her, taking the reins.

Chris was on Buster, and Nipper was tied to the rear of the wagon.

Mary Beth and B. J. were in the back of the wagon, and Patty Ruth sat between her mother and Stuart, holding Tony the Bear.

Hannah smiled at Stuart. "Thank you for offering to drive. I should be feeling up to it in a couple of days."

"My privilege, ma'am," he said.

Up front, Ezra stood in the stirrups, pointed westward, and shouted, "Wagons ho-o-o!"

As the wheels began to turn, Hannah glanced back at the grave and remembered Solomon's words to Chris when he was grieving over Joy Lynn's death. In her heart, she said, Solomon, your memory will always be a sweet thing. And I'll always have the memory of you. Yes, and five children who are part of you.

She brought herself around and looked forward. Twenty days to Fort Bridger…and many tomorrows. Abruptly her own words to Tracie and Deborah reverberated through her mind: *The Lord always knows what's ahead of us and can prepare us for the trials and heartaches that come our way, even before they happen. He's already in eternity, which means He's already in the future. So, He's already in our tomorrows.*

"Thank You, Lord," she said under her breath. "Thank You for that wonderful truth."

The wagon rocked and swayed as Hannah lifted her gaze to the magnificent canopy of the sky. As she studied the blue horizon, Solomon's words, three months ago in Independence, filled her with hope.

"Out there, Hannah, under the distant sky, is our new home and our new life."

OTHER COMPELLING STORIES BY
AL LACY

Books in the Battles of Destiny series:

☞ *A Promise Unbroken*

Two couples battle jealousy and racial hatred amidst a war that would cripple America. From a prosperous Virginia plantation to a grim jail cell outside Lynchburg, follow the dramatic story of a love that could not be destroyed.

☞ *A Heart Divided*

Ryan McGraw—leader of the Confederate Sharpshooters—is nursed back to health by beautiful army nurse Dixie Quade. Their romance would survive the perils of war, but can it withstand the reappearance of a past love?

☞ *Beloved Enemy*

Young Jenny Jordan covers for her father's Confederate spy missions. But as she grows closer to Union soldier Buck Brownell, Jenny finds herself torn between devotion to the South and her feelings for the man she is forbidden to love.

☞ *Shadowed Memories*

Critically wounded on the field of battle and haunted by amnesia, one man struggles to regain his strength and the memories that have slipped away from him.

☞ *Joy from Ashes*

Major Layne Dalton made it through the horrors of the battle of Fredericksburg, but can he rise above his hatred toward the Heglund brothers who brutalized his wife and killed his unborn son?

☞ *Season of Valor*

Captain Shane Donovan was heroic in battle. Can he summon the courage to face the dark tragedy unfolding back home in Maine?

Books in the Battles of Destiny series (cont.):

☞ *Wings of the Wind*

God brings a young doctor and a nursing student together in this story of the Battle of Antietam.

Books in the Journeys of the Stranger series:

☞ *Legacy*

Can John Stranger bring Clay Austin back to the right side of the law...and restore the code of honor shared by the woman he loves?

☞ *Silent Abduction*

The mysterious man in black fights to defend a small town targeted by cattle rustlers and to rescue a young woman and child held captive by a local Indian tribe.

☞ *Blizzard*

When three murderers slated for hanging escape from the Colorado Territorial Prison, young U.S. Marshal Ridge Holloway and the mysterious John Stranger join together to track down the infamous convicts.

☞ *Tears of the Sun*

When John Stranger arrives in Apache Junction, Arizona, he finds himself caught up in a bitter war between sworn enemies: the Tonto Apaches and the Arizona Zunis.

☞ *Circle of Fire*

John Stranger must clear his name of the crimes committed by another mysterious—and murderous—"stranger" who has adopted his identity.

☞ *Quiet Thunder*

A Sioux warrior and a white army captain have been blood brothers since childhood. But when the two meet on the battlefield, which will win out—love or duty?

Books in the Angel of Mercy series:

☞ *A Promise for Breanna*

The man who broke Breanna's heart is back. But this time, he's after her life.

☞ *Faithful Heart*

Breanna and her sister Dottie find themselves in a desperate struggle to save a man they love, but can no longer trust.

☞ *Captive Set Free*

No one leaves Morgan's labor camp alive. Not even Breanna Baylor.

☞ *A Dream Fulfilled*

A tender story about one woman's healing from heartbreak and the fulfillment of her dreams.

Available at your local Christian bookstore